Return to Madison River

ALLEN ANDREW COOPER

Return to Madison River

V1.1

Cover art by KGee Designs.

ISBN: 978-0-615-99044-6

PRINTED IN THE UNITED STATES OF AMERICA

To Wally and all those with Huntington's Disease

The author appreciates and acknowledges the following:

L, you are the queen of my soul and
my inspiration to finish this book.

Thank you to my editor; Kathleen Marusak for your hard work.

Thanks to author Linda Rae Sande of Cody, Wyoming
for providing much needed marketing advice.

I am grateful for the special places I have visited and extraordinary
people I have met that are the backdrop for this book. The true
beauty of your scenery and depth of your character reminds me
that my writing is only black and white.

And…Special thanks for coffee and red wine, much of
which was consumed in the writing of this novel.

Chapter 1
On Fishing

Rowan sat behind the wheel of the Chevy, pistol in one hand, bottle of Jim Beam in the other, of which only a swig remained. His knuckle bled just above his class ring. In frustration, he'd punched the pickup radio that now made a static-driven crackling sound.

He was tired of seeing her face, fighting with his demons night after night, the guilt of his still living keeping him awake. She had been dead for months and he had not slept in as much time. He was angry at himself for not going to the memorial service, he had been too drunk. Too drunk to shave, too drunk to drive to the church or stand up at the cemetery.

Now, stars filled the sky and without a blanket of clouds, the air of the Montana night was crisp and cool. He took another pull from the bottle, the vaporous sting of bourbon overcome by his sadness. He tasted the polished steel, cold at first then taking on the temperature of his breath. The bourbon mixed with the residue of gunpowder, sulfuric and metallic tasting. The faint smell of leather lingered on the gun barrel as it had long been stored in a brown cowhide holster speckled with mildew stains. He wasn't even sure if his grandpa's pistol would fire, but he intended to find out. He had checked the cylinder, still marked black from the last time the gun had been fired, probably at a beer can or midnight alley cat decades ago.

The gun was loaded. He could not remember it never being so. He set the barrel on his tongue, the pointed blade of the front sight touching the roof of his dry mouth.

The hammer was pitted with rust and he peeled it back until it clicked and set, ready to slam shut on the cartridge waiting in the chamber. His forefinger caressed the smooth steel of the guard until it touched the grooved trigger. Never would he have memory of what occurred next.

When he awoke, the gun lay cradled in his lap like a puppy and the bourbon and sulfur residual was replaced by the taste of stale vomit. His mouth was dry as the river bed he lay on. The sun rising over the Absaroka Mountains was a sight that Rowan Sojourner had not intended to see today. In his blackout drunk, he had managed to park the Chevy off the county road and he lay on the ground only a few yards from the Madison River, one cheek against the cool rocks and the other warmed from the early summer sun peeking over the mountains. With one bloodshot eye, he watched the ripples of the Madison pour over the shallow riverbed as his mind drifted back to Mississippi.

With his sights set on Montana, he had spent the first summer and fall after high school working at a saw mill, making money for college. On a Saturday night, after an overtime shift, he had stopped to visit friends hanging out on Main Street, and went for a joy ride with a classmate that had stolen some whiskey from a neighbor's garage. When the car stopped, it was at the Piggly Wiggly Supermarket parking lot, a popular hangout for teenagers at night. The Pig, as the kids called it, sat on the edge of town. Surrounded by a mini mall and a soybean field, they could be reasonably loud without a noise complaint and a resultant visit by the police officer on duty.

It was there in that grocery store parking lot that Bailey had pulled him away from his friends. She always had a subtle way of removing him from his circle and often they went for a drive past the lights of the small town to the dark woods at the end of some gravel road.

"Want me to drive?" he asked.

"No," was all she said. No smile, no playfull look. Unusual.

She'd been unusually quiet while the others talked high school gossip and plans for the future.

"Parker's Pond?" He touched her knee.

Bailey just stared ahead over the steering wheel. A tear ran down her cheek.

"I'm pregnant."

She waited for his reaction, which was delayed as a montage of his life as a father flashed before him as if he were sitting in front of a movie screen. The two had only dated that summer. Bailey was a beauty, and fun and exciting, but like with any boy, the thought of getting her pregnant had been the last thing on his mind. Rowan saw a big world out there and it had nothing to do with Crystal Springs, Mississippi or a pregnant girl, not even Bailey.

Bailey, already upset, sensed his apprehension and became defensive. She wanted to leave. She wondered how he could just sit there, silent at the news.

The sound of a beer bottle shattering on the asphalt outside the car brought him back to reality. The heat of the deep southern night caused the teenagers to grow restless. Their rowdy adolescent hoots and wails along with the sound of breaking glass would eventually attract the attention of the town cop.

"We'll make it work, babe, it's all right." He didn't know what else to say.

His words seemed to fuel her fury.

"Get out."

Rowan opened the door and was halfway out of the car. He turned to face her, searching for words yet unable to speak.

"Get out!"

He did.

She left the Piggly Wiggly in a blue cloud of loose gravel and burnt Goodyear rubber, scattering rocks all over the

3

teens in the parking lot. She drove hard and fast out of sight of Crystal Springs, Mississippi, around a curve and through a guardrail.

He owed Bailey and his unborn child something; her death was his fault. He made her so mad that she had driven too fast on her way home. If he hadn't got her pregnant, if he had only found comforting words to say to her, if he had only reacted with more excitement, she would still be alive and perhaps she would be with him now. Or maybe he would have stayed in Mississippi, happy to be working at the mill. Nobody knew about the pregnancy but him. That bothered him the most. As guilty as he felt about her being dead, he left town sooner than expected, running from his demons, hoping to lose them somewhere between the hardwoods of Mississippi and the east slope of the Rockies. But stronger than ever, they came with him, as if their travels strengthened the unwanted bond with him and here he was, piss drunk on a riverbank in Montana.

He lay there reliving those moments and watching a mayfly nymph crawl across a rock, slow and deliberate as if the bug was as hung-over as he. Rowan figured that as drunk and hideous as his appearance may be, he was a step ahead of the nymph, which looked part cockroach, part crawfish, absolutely unappetizing, unless of course you were a trout.

He pushed himself up on his elbows and looked around. The sun was growing intense, illuminating the Gallatin Range. His head pounded mercilessly. He dusted himself off. A swarm of mosquitoes swirled, their tiny bodies reflecting the morning light. They looked as if they were dancing to greet the sun, which was quickly warming the crisp morning air.

The hammer on the Smith & Wesson was still poised for action. The gun lay there on the rocks. He picked it up with the realization that he lacked the courage to kill himself. He carefully unloaded it and put the pistol under the front seat of the truck. He took the final pull from the bottle of Jim Beam. He swished the last of the bourbon like mouthwash and spit on the gravel shore. Rowan grabbed his fishing gear and fly rod out of the toolbox of the truck and pulled his waders on. He felt like fishing. He felt like living.

The Pale Morning Dunn lit on the water's surface. Rowan had crafted it to mimic the Mayfly, whose annual spring hatch was recently underway on the Madison River. All that signaled its arrival on the surface of the stream were a few rings of tiny ripples. When Rowan pulled the line through the rod guides with his left hand, the dry fly responded. The subtle movement created the behavior of a wounded bug, enough to lure the keen eyes of a trout. Sure enough, with a thrashing of color and water, the tiny fly disappeared, and Rowan set the hook. The rainbow's tail fin danced across the water as it struggled to free itself from the hook, showing off its vibrant colors in the process. Rowan kept the rod tip up and the line tight. Judging by the smile on his face, it was a toss-up as to who was hooked more, Rowan or the fish.

The water was high and rising fast from the late spring runoff, too cloudy to be considered perfect fishing conditions, as the mountain snow continued to melt in the high country, staining the water cloudy with mud. Still, there was some good fishing to be had before the river became muddy and fast moving.

Since he had filed the barbs off the hooks, Rowan easily unhooked the skillet-sized Rainbow Trout without damaging the fish. He admired its colors, a green back dotted with black circles that faded to a pink hue, giving way to a silver belly. The fish mouth gaped open, the creature starving for its gills to work in the dry air. He gently set the fish back in the water, allowing the oxygen-rich water to flow over its gills, the shock of certain death releasing its grip on the fish. The trout swished its spotted tail and wriggled loose from Rowan's gentle hand.

Rowan watched the flash of colors fade and blend with the

water and river bedrock as he wiped the slime from his hands onto his waders. Where he stood, the water was shallow and rushed over the riverbed. He looked a few yards upstream at a pool that formed as the river cut underneath a willow tree, the water claiming the exposed roots from the soil. He wondered how much longer the tree would be able to cling to the riverbank. Surely, one last spring runoff was all that was required for the river to claim the tree and send it floating downstream. That was the story of the river; giving life and taking life. Rowan smirked at the thought that the tree, hanging from the bank by no more than a thin root, had almost outlived him.

He waded towards the willow and the deep pool underneath it, the water up to his thighs. He had enough time to make a few casts before the pin-sized hole in the right leg of his wader allowed enough water to fill up the leg, making it difficult to wade back to shore. His foot was already wet to the ankle, reminding him that he'd been too lazy to patch the leak.

There was something about landing a hand-tied fly on the water's surface that had lured Rowan since he was a little boy. He saw it as the perfect blend of art and adventure. The anticipation of the fish swallowing the fly and emerging from his world into the world of the fisherman was pure excitement. Only a thin membrane separated those two worlds and it could be broken at any moment with a good cast and faith that there was a fish below it.

He continued working the fly rod, mending the line with the rod tip to prevent the line being pulled by the current and dragging the fly unnaturally across the water. He could feel the rhythm of the river in the rod, through the fly line, his fingertips and into his soul.

In spring, the river was like a teenager, a destructive force, a wild rampage of torn timber and eroded river banks. However, in the summer the river was like an old man playing with grandchildren, easy and gentle. Rowan was fishing the stream in its annual adolescence as drops of melting snow dripped off the frozen banks and pools of water emerged from the ice swirling around boulders and cutting underneath banks. By late summer, those banks would be left muddy and heavy with the sweet stench of decaying microorganisms as the water receded, the smell of life and death on the river.

He gazed into the water, endlessly surprised at how he was able to see the natural fish habitat, the rocks, sandy shallows and tree stumps. It was a far cry from fishing for catfish in sunken barrels and old tires in the black water of Mississippi where he had learned to fish. There, the fishing was superb, but water visibility was nonexistent. Besides, the scenery was no match for the Gallatin Valley, a place where the Jefferson, Madison and Gallatin rivers all converge to form the Missouri River just outside Bozeman. There was always a view for miles, unlike the hardwood forests of the south that held their own beauty, although devoid of vast open spaces.

He split his concentration between the fly line and the snow-capped Bridger Mountains before him. It was hard to focus surrounded by all the beauty. His mind drifted from the river to the mountains, to Bailey and to the realization that hours before he had intended to pull the trigger on a .357 that would send a lead bullet and explosive gases through the top of his head. He heard the massive beating of wings and glanced up to see a pelican fly low overhead. The irony was that he had been too drunk to kill himself. Who says drinking will kill you? he thought, his eyes still on the bird.

He worked the tiny fly low over the water. After several casts without a strike, he cut the fly off the line with fingernail clippers and tied on a Royal Wulff. The fly's tiny body was comprised of a dragon-like collar of white and brown feathers with a bright red band of tightly wound string separating its black tail from the hook eye. The entire imitation was no bigger than his smallest fingernail and often hard to spot on the water, unless you were a fish looking up at it. Then, every detail of the imitation came under the scrutinizing eyes of the trout.

The bigger, older and wiser the fish, the more scrutiny came into play. There was a great sense of accomplishment catching fish on hand-tied flies he himself had made.

Rowan enjoyed the sensation of the absolute weightlessness at the end of his line. He had grown up casting huge plastic poppers for large-mouth bass in Mississippi. One of those three-inch-long bugs with a body the size of a quarter and bold fluorescent colors would scare the living hell out of a finicky trout. At times it seemed the trout was the restaurant and food critic of the fish world. One day the fish would sip the water like fine wine, sucking the fly inside its mouth. Other days the fish would attack the fly in a frenzy of splashing and thrashing. It could take several changes in fly patterns to find the right one, while other times the trout would hit anything that set on the water. Either way, casting the line in anticipation of the strike was always magical.

Rowan stopped wading short of reaching the deep pool then pulled some line from the reel and began casting. Each forward and back stroke brought more line until he estimated the distance and lowered the rod. The line, heavier than the fly, straightened and uncurled as the Royal Wulff set on the water.

He deemed his presentation acceptable, the fly landing in the ripple made by the current and drifting towards the undercut bank. There, the water was dark with depth and Rowan guessed it to be a perfect hiding place for a much bigger rainbow.

Rowan had recently moved to Montana from Mississippi in search of adventure, exploring the big sky country despite talk from the southern literary culture that he had a promising future as a southern writer. They'd speculated that perhaps he would be the next great one, his namesake being William Faulkner's home in Oxford, Mississippi.

His mother had been a Faulkner fan and thought the name strong for a boy. It was indeed a strong name. The Rowan Oak was a sign of strength in Scottish folklore. Rowan had studied facts of Rowan Oak and Faulkner and knew the legendary writer to be more of an imaginative creator than an adventurer, a hero nonetheless. But Rowan craved adventure and the mountain streams seemed to invite it at every turn.

Even though he was born and raised in the south, he felt boxed in by the dense population, thick as the trees that made him feel claustrophobic. Here, the dry mountain air was good for his asthmatic lungs, with less pollen and molds than the thick damp air of the south. He could breathe better and he had room to breathe. In the wide open space surrounded by mountains, he found a new lease on life. He felt free. Though his head was foggy and throbbing from a hangover, he was viewing the world around him clearer than ever before.

Rowan had grappled with remorse when Bailey died, for what he said and for what he didn't say in their final moments together, and hearing that he had almost been a father had broken his heart and fueled his guilt. Other than this heartbreak, he was happy making a new life for himself in the college town of Bozeman. It didn't hurt that his college of preference just happened to be smack dab in the middle of the best trout streams in the west. These joys had been forgotten in his young life in a time of desperation. The life crisis of the moment overshadowed all he had to be thankful for.

He had forgone the offer of a partial scholarship at Ole Miss. He was sure that his writing would be well received there, but he wanted to go to school in Montana. Writing could wait, he sought adventure now. He could never explain his fascination with the mountains; in his soul, this was where he had wanted to be as long as he could ever remember. As soon as he had moved to Bozeman, he found the Madison and spent most of his time fishing. The wide-open spaces and fresh mountain air took possession of his blood and coursed through his veins, a stronghold that never let go.

He peeled some line off the reel so he could gain enough distance to cast underneath the eroded riverbank. There was no action from several casts and he silently promised himself just one more try before heading back to the truck. His persistence was rewarded. The Royal Wulff had not even hit the water when the splash came. The line tightened and began to un-spool from the reel before he could set the hook and gain control of the line. He cursed himself for daydreaming and set the hook. This time it was a bigger rainbow and it danced across the surface, putting on an acrobatic display of tail dances before breaking the leader. The fish escaped and left Rowan with a broken line, leaky waders and a strengthened addiction to fly fishing, as well as life itself.

Spring was in the air, but winter had yet to release its grip completely. There was a light frost on the yard as she had walked the kids out to greet the school bus. Sadie gave each of them a hug and a kiss knowing that it would not be long before such acts of motherly love were forbidden, at least in public. She waved at Bree who sat looking out the back window scornfully at her mother. No doubt, Toby was happy in his seat behind the driver, eager to do anything, including go to school. Sadie waved until the bus rounded the corner at the end of the block and disappeared from view.

Toby was excited to ride the bus. The overweight cranky driver and smell of sweat and vinyl was a new adventure for the six-year-old. The world was one big round ball seen through the eyes of her son and those eyes didn't belong to her. He was his father's son, with his curiosity and most of all, his impatient eyes.

On the other hand, Bree had been picked on by older girls the year before while riding the bus, thus she was less than impressed with the occupants, especially the curmudgeon driver. She hated the bus and was quick to remind Sadie that she would much rather her mother take her to school than be reduced to riding bus number twenty-two. Bree missed being home with her mother all day.

Not long ago, Sadie had stayed at home with the kids. They were home schooled and she had protected them from the unjust social and academic inadequacies of public education. She was proud to be a mother, a teacher and a wife. It was all she had ever wanted since the day she had met him in junior high. A life lived so perfectly simple was theirs; kids, work and play. It was the kind of happy marriage that most men and women could only wish for. They grew up together, fell in love, graduated and got married. They were not so simple in their views of the world, however. Immediately following high school, they traveled Europe and considered themselves students of the world. After their travels, they returned to Montana to raise kids, something that both of them wanted more than anything.

On the day he died, she was at home with the children. Bree had finished her lessons and Sadie was setting the table for dinner. Her happiness ended with a phone call that briefly explained the accident. In the fraction of a second when two cars collided on a narrow Montana highway, Sadie's world and the world of her children were changed forever.

She stood on the riverbank among the willows and bear grass to spread her husband's ashes on the ripple made by the Yellowstone River Current at the place where they had been married, while her children clung to their mother's dress. The next morning, she sat on the bank of the river crying, alone. She sat there all day thinking of drowning herself, of making a new start, and of what she would do next.

That day on the riverbank, Sadie vowed to overcome her loss and raise her children in a happy home. Her family was changed forever, but it was not ruined. Every hardship was met with a smile and a tenacious zest for life. That was what she wanted to pass onto her children.

It wasn't until her husband died that she had ever considered attending classes. She loved college. What she hated was being away from her children. Between classes and bartending there was too much lost time. She knew she was being somewhat neglectful leaving them at night to work, but she had no choice. Her family lived far away and her in-laws had cut all ties to her and their grandchildren.

So, as Sadie waved goodbye to her kids on the bus, she thought of him again, as she often did this time of day. But not for long, she didn't have time. Class started in twenty minutes. She was always sad after watching the kids go off to school. It reminded her of how little time she had with them now that she was a single parent. A degree would allow her to be a better provider. It wasn't easy, though, and she wished she could just stay home with them all day.

She dressed hastily and wore her favorite sweater. There was a cute boy in class and it had been a long time since she looked forward to seeing someone. She was concerned by how much she thought about this one. As a matter of fact, she had thought of him the night before and it had been over two years since that had happened.

She longed to hold a man, to sleep next to him, to make love with him, but her needs were overshadowed by her concern for her children, her hectic schedule and memories of her husband. The thought of any other man had been alien to her. She had not wanted to contend with the psychological consequences of any pleasure she may seek with another man.

For a long time after her husband died, she had felt a devotion to him as if he were just gone for a while and would walk back into her life at any moment. Only lately had her desires and wants become needs and now, she may be ready to satisfy them.

A non-traditional student, Sadie was older than most of the girls in her classes. Seasoned, but still in her prime, she had the look and walk of a woman who has lived and lost her dreams. Her beauty, her smile and her outgoing personality lit up every room, and when out of doors, made stiff competition for the sun.

A beautiful woman more mature than the coeds, Sadie was mysterious to the twenty-something young men. She carried herself with more awareness than a sophomore, and she had a certain look of confidence lacking in freshmen girls, flashy, headstrong, and she had legs. As she walked the hallway of the social sciences building in her skirt and heels, she parted the crowd that scrambled for classes like a sandbar parts the river current.

In part due to personality and in part to life experience, Sadie was different. All the men knew who she was, but very few knew anything about her. All they knew was that she went to school full-time and would give any man the time of day, but not her phone number. They also knew that she bartended and she dressed for tips. For her that was all they needed to know.

As she walked into the classroom, her presence was felt by every man in the room, including Professor Henry. Her tardy arrival interrupted his thoughts every time she came through the door and he joined every other man in the room in a hard swallow of nerves and lust. The professor would stutter as he spoke of whatever social theory on which he was lecturing. As he stood in front of the class, you could hear him gulp from the very last row, beads of sweat forming on his brow. You can put a bow tie on a man, but he's still a man.

Rowan cradled his coffee mug in the back row of the class-room. The coffee smelled good, with an extra hint of sweet-ness courtesy of Maker's Mark Whiskey. He had to keep an impending hangover at bay. The silver flask hugged the inside of his leg, safely tucked in his cowboy boot. The class was a sleeper, the scenery was good though, worth waking up for, and that was the only reason he had not dropped the class. He needed the elective, and why not have scenery with your bor-ing lecture?

Rowan's writing assignments helped his grades, but there was too much drinking and fishing to excel at school. Besides, he didn't give a damn about the Dean's List. He was waiting for the writing assignment that would carry his grade for the class. This class was becoming his favorite but it had little to do with the subject matter.

He always tried to make it early so he could watch the best part of class enter the room. It could be distracting sitting in the back row, looking at the backs of heads, but Rowan enjoyed seeing the tall blonde walk in notoriously late.

Rowan had many talks with himself about his shyness and how he should strategically plan his arrival hot on her heels and sit beside her, but he had not worked up the courage to do so; besides, he couldn't drink whiskey if he sat up front. Someone would take notice, and he would face being thrown out of school for violating the campus alcohol policy.

Rowan had thought of approaching her, but was waiting to think of something intelligent to spark the conversation.

He had remained tongue-tied all semester.

So, as had become his custom, his palms began to sweat when she walked into the room, only on this day, she sat right next to him in the last row. His heart pounded unmercifully in his throat and he began to feel empathy for Professor Henry, who stood now in front of the class sweating and stuttering. Rowan understood the professor's plight.

She situated her lovely thin frame in the student desk next to him and smiled as he politely glanced in her direction and shyly smiled back. As the professor mumbled something about the steps to bereavement, Sadie leaned toward Rowan. Her tight black sweater hugged her thin arms and busty chest. Rowan tried to think of something clever to say and took a drink of his high octane coffee, just praying the professor didn't call on him while his mind drifted to the prize that was encased underneath her tight sweater. Turned out, he didn't have to think of something clever to say for an icebreaker.

"Could I borrow your notes sometime?" she asked, looking right into his eyes, still smiling.

This was a new one for him. Rowan usually overcame his shyness by asking girls for their notes. Daydreaming and sleeping through eight o' clock classes made his note-taking a bit sketchy. It was a good way to talk to girls and maintain a bad boy image. It had worked well on several occasions. Now, though, she was asking him.

He panicked. Rowan's notes consisted mostly of doodle marks and fourth grade-quality sketches of female body parts. He was unsure if her reaction to the elementary remarks and drawings in the margins of his notebook would work in his favor. What the hell, he still hadn't thought of anything clever to say.

"Absolutely," said Rowan as he handed his spiral bound notebook to her.

"After class," she laughed, handing the notebook back.

Sadie grabbed Rowan's mug lightly with one hand and he was amazed at how her fingers melted his grip. She smiled at him as she took full control. Rowan felt his erection would bust out the zipper of his Wranglers. She held the mug under her nose a moment, inhaling the bourbon fumes. Bourbon itself, when mixed with coffee, emits a noxious sweet scent. It was a wonder that in a room full of hung-over college students, nobody seemed to notice. If they did, nobody said anything, perhaps fearing it was their own breath.

His lips trembled as his Phillips 66 mug touched the lips of the most intriguing woman he had ever met in his life. The coffee-stained mug had never been washed, and as Rowan watched Sadie drink from it, he decided that it never would be. After a healthy sip, she grinned at him.

"Mmm. Good coffee. We should have a cup after class," she whispered.

Rowan never remembered what he said in response, but nevertheless they got a coffee after class and sat in the sun on campus emptying the flask and joking about professors, classmates and life. Somehow, that morning class led to a friendly game of pool at the Crystal Bar, which led to a day of missed afternoon classes and a kiss in her driveway.

A couple of days later, they went out to dinner. Rowan dropped his month's budget on a steak dinner at a little place west of town. He was able to make her laugh and they enjoyed the usual questions associated with first dates; with Sadie, he thought it was fun being interrogated. Being older, Sadie had more of an intriguing history than he and he was consumed by her story. He hung on her every word.

It was still light when they finished dinner. Rowan didn't want the date to end. His mind churned for ways to extend their evening together and the best he could think of was one of his favorite places, so they drove down the road to the Madison River, one of Rowan's best fishing spots and the very place where he had almost ended his own life just days ago. It had become his outdoor cathedral. Sadie's eyes lit up when Rowan turned down the gravel access road that led to the river.

"I bring my kids here, we love it," she said.

"I like it too, easy access to fishin', minutes from class."

Rowan parked the truck. They walked and talked their way along the riverbank until it was dark and the night chill drove them back to the warmth of the pickup truck. It was as perfect as a date could be with clothes on and both were left eager for more time together. They were at ease with each other and the conversation was void of awkward silences. Rowan found it interesting that just like casting a fly, he had broken the thin membrane that separated Sadie's world from his. It seemed they excited one another; left the other feeling exhilarated, drawn to one another like trout to flies.

Chapter 2

The One That Got Away

Summertime in Montana's Gallatin Valley was inviting, invigorating and welcomed by the locals, for one never knew how long summer would last in the northern Rockies. In between late spring snows and early fall frosts, the weeks of summer passed quickly. Sadie and Rowan took full advantage, spending most days on the river soaking up each day of the summer sun like it would never appear again. They often floated the Madison River on inner tubes. Their tubes and beer cooler floated past die-hard fly fishermen cloaked in thousands of dollars' worth of Orvis gear. Rowan could always make her laugh and as they drifted, her laugh echoed off the canyon walls.

Rowan felt like an early explorer. Other than an occasional irrigation dam or a cow, there was little sign of man or industrialization along that stretch of water. The limestone cliffs reflected off the water where it was calm and the rush of Rowan's heart, beating like deer skin drums, competed with the sound of the rapids. Rowan thought that if he could go back to the turn of the twentieth century with his modern fishing rods and hunting rifle, his life would be perfect. He loved being on the river and now he loved sharing it with the woman he had fallen in love with.

They stopped here and there to explore the banks of the

river or lay on the sand to dry and feel the warmth of a kiss. When kissing Sadie, sometimes Rowan tasted the cold metal barrel of the pistol and a chill ran up his spine, reminding him that he had almost killed himself. Now, he was on top of the world. Bailey still haunted him, but the sharp pang of guilt was now a dull heartache. Rowan wasn't sure how long he was supposed to grieve, what he did know was that Sadie made him feel good and he never wanted to taste the barrel of a gun again. He felt more alive than ever.

The days by the Madison River continued as did the late nights in the Chevy. On a calendar, that summer was a brief ninety days, but for Rowan, it never ended. There was the swimming hole where a rope hung from a huge cottonwood, there was "the beach," a large sand bar where they would swim and lay on the sand, and Rowan's favorite, a place they referred to as "the picnic spot."

The picnic spot was a shady stretch of river near a public fishing area. The banks were wild with overgrown willows, and for the two lovers it was as if nobody had been there before them. A large spread, the Baker Angus Ranch, owned both sides of the river, pristine in its beauty. Rowan would park the truck at the public access in the gravel lot and they would walk along the Madison a few hundred yards upstream to an inviting flat piece of sand shaded by aspens and cottonwoods. Often, Sadie would bring a sketch pad and draw pictures of birds, trees or Rowan as he fished. It was quiet and serene, and seemed to be created just for them. Maybe it was.

One late afternoon, Rowan parked the truck and he and Sadie strolled down to the river holding hands. Sadie commented several times that she should have been allowed to bring a bottle of wine and sack lunch. It was a calm afternoon with an inviting coolness in the air as the sun sank low in the sky.

"Would have been a perfect day for a picnic," she remarked with a pouty lip.

Rowan just smiled and held her hand. As they went across the river rock and through the thick wall of willows, they emerged at the picnic spot and saw a blanket on the ground, a picnic basket with dinner for two that he had picked up from the caterer and a bottle of wine. A dozen red roses lay on the blanket wrapped in green paper. He'd thought of everything.

A pair of Magpies was squawking over the closed picnic basket. Rowan waved his arms at them.

"Looks like we got here just in time," he said, inspecting the basket for damage.

Sadie was more than surprised. She was breathless. For a moment, Rowan wondered if she was all right until her lips curved up. She clasped her hands together and brought them to her face. It made Rowan laugh.

"It ain't many times you're speechless, guess I should enjoy it," he joked.

She slapped his shoulder at the smart remark and gave him a kiss. She held his face in her hands and stared at him. There was that smile again. He loved to bring her joy. Rowan, proud of his secret mission, was certain he'd truly surprised her.

"No one has ever done anything so nice, so sweet and thoughtful for me, ever. I love you, Rowan."

"That's all I want."

Rowan picked up the wine, a bottle of white zinfandel, and with great effort wrestled with the cork, some of which broke off and floated in the bottle. With both their glasses full, they sat down on the blanket. He had packed real plates and linen, a great meal and huckleberry cheesecake.

She leaned back on her elbows, beaming at him, and he knew she was wondering if he was going to propose. This beautiful woman he loved was here with him on the river smiling. He thought it the most successful thing he had ever done, a very fulfilling moment, one he would relive many times throughout his life.

Rowan lay down beside her, touching her face gently. He kissed her lightly and she relaxed on the blanket, wrapping her arms around him, pulling him on top of her.

On his knees and elbows he then ran his fingers through her hair as he kissed her neck. She responded by wrapping her legs around him and squeezing him with her inner thighs. Her hands ran underneath his shirt, touching his back with her fingertips.

They kissed playfully, taking turns teasing one another. Sadie would kiss his bottom lip as he relaxed his mouth. Then she would suck on his bottom lip and run her tongue all around his lips, ending with a hard kiss of passion.

They gazed into each other's eyes for a moment, and then kissed one another so deep that both were breathing heavy. Sadie pulled his shirt over his head and tossed it aside.

Rowan unbuttoned the top of her blouse, massaging her breasts and kissing her nipples. Sadie arched her back in response. He helped pull her blouse over her head and he slipped his hands behind her back to unbutton her bra. Her naked breasts and flat tummy invited a frenzy of kissing and touching. When she'd had enough, she grabbed the back of his head and pulled his lips to hers, kissing him forcefully. Then she let go.

She bit her lower lip. "Make love to me."

They quickly pulled off their jeans as they lay beside one another. When Rowan lay on top of her, the heat from her body forced him to take a deep breath. He entered her and she gripped his shoulders, digging her fingernails into his back. He kissed her neck and her earlobes as her mouth opened and her eyes closed.

As he thrust himself into her, he could not imagine anything else that had given him so much pleasure. She felt so good that he tried to think of baseball in a feeble effort to prolong his climax. He could not help himself and was relieved to hear her moan in ecstasy with him, her body quivering and her legs pinching him.

That night on a blanket by the river touching her, with her breath on his face and his finding rhythm with her body, Rowan felt something he'd yet to experience, making love to Sadie.

Rowan and Sadie spent the dwindling light of dusk wrapped in the blanket on the sandy bank of the Madison. They left when the well-packed basket of food was reduced to crumbs and dirty linen and the stars were bleached by the moonlight. Sadie kissed Rowan in the truck.

"This is now my favorite special place. I will love you forever."

He smiled. Who knew what lay ahead for the two of them? Whatever their future held, he knew one thing was certain and he said it, "I will always love you."

Many times that summer, they took her kids with them to the river to swim and play. Rowan had never spent much time around kids and was surprised at how much he enjoyed being with them. Having the love of such a gorgeous woman made him feel good, while being included in her life, with her kids, made him feel wanted. The young man's fear of commitment he'd once had was squelched by her willingness to share all of her life with him. He thought about their future together, as a family, and it didn't scare him.

Rowan taught her son, Toby, how to thread a worm on a hook and helped him catch his first fish, a small rainbow trout. Rowan had been more excited than Toby, who abandoned the fishing pole and was feeding marshmallows to a Mallard as Rowan was still taking pictures of the prize fish.

Rowan climbed the tree at the swimming hole and secured the rope swing for Bree. He was now a part of something. It wasn't his family, but at the time he could not imagine a more perfect one. Rowan fell in love with everything about Sadie, especially her kids.

The four of them spent their days fishing and playing,

enjoying the freedom and reward of living near the river. When there was a babysitter, Rowan and Sadie went out, often just going for a drive down one of the many country roads that connected the valley to the mountains. They would find a place to park and make love in the truck, on a blanket or anywhere else that suited them. The world was theirs and their world was the river. They were in love. Rowan fell hard and fast for her and was pleased to experience the warm sting of love's hook in his mouth. Sometimes you are the fisherman. Other times, you are the fish.

The wind rattled through the cottonwood leaves as they dried and turned yellow. The summer gave way to fall and Rowan saw Sadie growing restless. He could feel it just as he felt the wind on his skin days before she ever said a word.

They sat on her deck smoking cigars and drinking merlot. The sun was setting and taking the warm air with it. They were reliving the sex they had just moments ago.

"So, I have been thinking of going to graduate school." Sadie blew a ring of smoke and they each watched the blue halo extend over her head. "I have only been out of school for the summer and miss it already."

"With no professors to debate, you must be miserable."

"I am miserable. I mean, except when I'm with you or the kids. I know that I will be working a job I hate until I get a master's degree."

Rowan flicked his ashes over the railing. "Do it then, go back."

"Thing is, I've been thinking about it a lot and I am going back. I want to go to school in Madison, Wisconsin."

She said this with raised eyebrows and a half smile to gauge his reaction, inviting his response. Rowan forced his closed lips to form a smile to show her his support.

"Wisconsin?"

"I know," she said, cringing at his reaction.

"Gotta go so far away?" he asked with a forced voice.

"It's the best program for me. Part of me wants you to go with me."

Rowan could see she was struggling to bleed all the words she wanted to say, as he asked, "And the other, the other part of ya?"

"You know…maybe we should take a break."

Rowan leaned forward and tossed the remainder of the Macanudo in the coffee can that sat on the deck for just such purposes. He scooted his chair so that he turned to face her.

"I'm in love with you. I don't need a break. Tell me what you wanna do."

"Rowan, I love you too. I really do. I heard a friend once say that it's funny who you fall in love with, and I think it is true. I never expected to fall in love with you. I also believe you deserve a family of your own, not a ready-made family. I am depriving you of that. And, let's face it; I am almost a decade older than you. Maybe you should fall in love with someone your own age."

She gave him a nervous smile.

Rowan's eyes started to tear. His voice quivered.

"You said it. It's funny who ya fall for. The age difference don't bother me. I love you, I love your kids, I'm happy."

"I am too, I just want more, and I want more for you."

"Me?"

"Yes, I want you to be a fishing guide or whatever it is you want to do. A family, we, will distract you from your dreams. You should go off and make your dreams come true, not take on mine or sacrifice your own aspirations for mine. If it's meant to be, one day we'll meet again."

"Sadie, we can make this work."

"It's too soon for me. I feel guilty. Here I am, a widow, a mother. I just can't keep going on this way. I need more time."

"You know I understand that. Who's pressuring you?"

"Nobody. It's just bad timing."

Sadie didn't invite him to move with her to Wisconsin and

even if she had, Rowan wasn't sure he would have followed her. Rowan was certain he could have her and his dreams. She felt differently.

So, Rowan saw Sadie in every ripple on the water of every trout stream in the Northwest. With every day that passed, he struggled with the break-up. It had been civil; they had even made love after deciding to give things a rest, and had parted ways as if they would see each other the next day.

He had told her that he loved her. He told her that he wanted her, but no matter what he said, it wasn't convincing enough. Sometimes Rowan thought that he should have fought for her. On the other hand, he had made his love for her clear and if she wanted him, he should never have to convince her to stay.

Sadie sold everything and drove the kids and a trunk full of clothes to Wisconsin. She rented a furnished apartment and everything else seemed to fall in place. She excelled in the graduate program. The kids liked their school and the two years that it took her to complete her Master's degree passed quickly. Although she thought of Rowan often, she did not have time to think about a relationship and she had enjoyed narrowing her focus to her and her children's education. A job offer kept her in Wisconsin. She and her children were happy, but she dreamed of moving back to Montana.

As the years passed, Rowan's heartache lessened and his fondness grew.

Chapter 3
Be My Guide

Carl Peterson never knew how close he came to drowning. There was no accident, no mishap to suggest that he almost died that day. Still, it was close. Thankfully for him, his river guide was patient and calm. Guiding and babysitting some of the world's most finicky clients, Rowan had learned to draw in deep slow breaths and count to ten in order to avoid killing them. But Carl Peterson was a special case, surely no one would miss him.

Carl was a proud man. In his world of concrete and glass, he was a well-respected legal counsel. But on the river, he was nothing more than a pain-in-the-ass incompetent client who had more money than good sense. His nasal New England accent only fortified Rowan's initial summary that the man was flaky as breakfast cereal. The complaints that emanated from the mouth with the accent grated on Rowan's nerves like fingernails on a chalkboard.

"I'm accustomed to a rod with a faster action. This new one is rather slow," said Carl.

The rod was a custom Simms, having just cost Carl several hundred dollars, the only thing wrong with it was that the wrist holding it was connected to a genuine asshole. The fishing conditions were perfect. Cool air, clear water and a sun that was slow to dry the dew off the grass. Rowan had set Carl up for success on several occasions before nine a.m., only to have him blunder a cast, get snagged on a tree or be so self-absorbed in his own storytelling that he missed the strike.

Rowan oared the drift boat within novice casting distance of a downed spruce. The slow current collided with the branches that fingered the water and swirled in lazy circles before reuniting with faster moving current downstream. There was sure to be a big boss trout lurking there. As a matter of fact, Rowan could not have made more guarantee of catching a fish there unless he tied its fins to the tree.

Carl locked his beady eyes on the tree that had fallen in the river to his left and pointed with a wiry finger that Rowan daydreamed of ripping off and tossing in the current.

"There, right there, that tree, get me in closer."

Rowan choked back a "shut up" and instead replied, "That's where we're headed, Carl. Get ready."

Rowan watched Carl fumble with his reel, oblivious to how fast they were approaching the treasured trout hole despite Rowan's coaching. Rowan had put many a fisherman on a trout here all summer. Rowan amused himself with the thought of standing in the river and holding Carl's head under water.

He grinned when he thought of the disgusting sexual act known as "The Hot Carl," which involved Saran wrap and defecation. As puzzling as that behavior was, Rowan entertained the thought of wrapping Carl's head in plastic wrap, possibly until he could not breathe. Hot Carl was a good name for his troubling client. The pet name made Rowan smile as he wondered: If it took twelve muscles to smile; it must take hundreds of muscle movements to whack Hot Carl with an oar repeatedly until his nasally voice could no longer speak.

Hot Carl began casting furiously and promptly hung his grasshopper in the middle of the downed spruce on the second cast. For the most part Rowan loved his job, just not that day.

"God damn it!" cried Carl.

Rowan shared the same thought as he pushed the boat into the tree to retrieve the hung up line as a big trout splashed a goodbye at the boat's intrusion of its hiding hole. Carl had yet to catch a fish and they were more than halfway to the boat ramp. He should be weary from pulling in fish, but the only weary one in the boat was Rowan, having survived the excruciating narcissistic stories and incessant complaining.

"Water temp is too hot," or "I believe the PH levels are too high," or "This river is highly overfished." Rowan had heard every excuse before and most of them he'd heard again in a single morning from Hot Carl.

Rowan reached into the spruce and unhooked the hopper and line from the branches. He tossed the bird's nest of fly line in the boat at Hot Carl's feet. Silently, he backed the drift boat out of the downed tree and let it glide downstream. Pulling his rod out, he made one cast on a water-smoothed rock that jutted out of the water. He let the fly effortlessly roll off the rock and as soon as it hit the water, the line straightened and the rod doubled over. He handed the rod to Carl like a frustrated father instructing his young son on the art of fishing.

"Here Carl, reel it in," said Rowan, as he leaned forward and handed the rod to a now quiet Carl in a tone that offered no recourse for argument.

For the first time all day, Carl was speechless. He pulled the fish towards the boat and Rowan reached overboard to scoop the rainbow up in the net. As Rowan leaned over to catch the fish, Carl tried to do the same and the side of the boat dipped dangerously into the water. Hot Carl almost fell in the river.

"Fuckin' sit down!" Rowan commanded as he brought up the fish.

Carl's bottom lip quivered for fear of being left on a sandbar. He was silent the remainder of the trip, which was less than a half hour. Carl didn't leave a tip and Rowan was neither surprised nor upset about it. He was just glad that bludgeoning Carl to death with an oar was a mere daydream. He was a free man, having not committed murder. Fortunately, there was no penalty for considering it.

Despite a few clients like Carl, the Madison, Jefferson and the Gallatin kept Rowan happy during the summer seasons. Though he traveled, the Gallatin Valley provided good fishing and with the college, there was never a shortage of young beautiful women. His confidence grew as a guide and playboy so that his presence filled a room much more than his five-foot nine-inch frame. He fished for trout, trolled for women and headed south during the winter months to practice his skill sets in a warmer climate.

Rowan's knowledge as a guide and the likability he possessed to be able to instantly bond with high-dollar clients won him respect and advance bookings. He had repeat clients that invited him to fish with them on other rivers. Four years after graduating college and earning his degree in biology, he was guiding trout fishermen on every major tributary in the northwest, and salmon fishermen in Alaska and British Columbia.

In the winters, he lived in the Caribbean working as a fishing guide or on a commercial ship, only to return to the trout and salmon streams in the spring through late fall. He worked on a charter boat in Prince William Sound and obtained his captain's license there. He worked on boats from the icy waters of Cook Inlet to the crystal-blue waters of the Exumas.

A future of financial stability and dreams of owning a home seemed a world away to Rowan. He was certain there had to be more to life and when the time was right, he would find it; for now, he was living an adventure.

Rowan's classmates entered the job market while he put on his waders. They pursued careers with major corporations and promising startups as he guided clients through blue ribbon trout waters. His friends found girlfriends who turned into wives and they traded their motorcycles for mini-vans.

When those friends called to catch up, they talked about

their kids and asked him, "Rowan, when are you going to get married?"

His usual response to the question was, "When the fish stop bitin."

Rowan had a bare bones existence. If it didn't fit in his backpack, it was left behind. He was young. Employer benefits and retirement programs did not interest him. He managed to live out of that backpack for several years, saving his money except for expenditures on travel expenses, booze and women. Everything else was a waste of money. Through the years, he also kept a journal.

One winter in Grand Bahama Island, he was working as a crew member on a private yacht. A friend of a friend in British Columbia got him the job, which was to fill in for a couple months while another crewmember had surgery. The crew of seven sailed at the mercy of the boat's owners, an overbearing and overweight couple from New Jersey who traveled with their three Shih tzus. A January storm pushed freezing temperatures and high winds past Miami and deep into the islands. The weather was unfit for sailing so the boat was moored for a week. The owners went farther south to Nassau in order to avoid the cool temperatures, so the ship was quiet. With all the work aboard completed, Rowan started writing a story.

Writing soon became a daily addiction, a need that he filled morning and night. At a clip of only a thousand words a day, he had time to fulfill his obligation with the ship and holed up in Grand Bahama for a while. A year later, he was in New York knocking on the doors of publishers. Within two years of finishing his first book, he had a publishing contract.

His publisher loved his book, an adventure story. Rowan pitched it as excerpts from his life, embellishing it in order to make it interesting. But, of course, his life was interesting and his writing was edgy and fresh. The publisher and the readers loved Rowan and he adapted easily to traveling to book signings and book promotional duties. Before long, he was wearing Dockers more often than waders.

The second book came easily and landed him another spot at the top of the best seller list. Rowan loved writing and the benefits of being a successful author. He still fished, but he didn't have to guide. He traveled, but no longer had to bum rides.

His new life as a best-selling author brought money into his "para expatriate" lifestyle. Now, when he traveled, he could spend the night wherever he wanted and he began opting for quick and expensive plane tickets over working on a ship for weeks or months in exchange for a ride. Every now and then, he would disappear for a while, washing ashore thousands of miles from his last locale of choice. He still traveled light. Living out of a pack kept him fresh and his book ideas sharp.

Rowan had long admired the life of Earnest Hemingway and was able to recreate a modest version of Hemingway-esque adventure in his own schedule. He fished from Alaska to New Zealand chronicling his adventures in articles, novels, and a series of guidebooks about Belize, the Virgin Islands, Montana trout streams and British Columbia. He became an expert on international fishing, and an advocate for sport-fishing and conservation. He used his time in the Caribbean to attain his dive master certification, which he used when leading tours of endangered marine habitat. He was proud to say he was finally utilizing his college degree.

There were women, lots of beautiful women, and in every one of their faces, he saw Sadie's eyes. Rowan could not travel far enough, drink in excess enough or have enough sex to satisfy his longing for Sadie. They had not spoken in several years. He wanted to find her and learn what her life was like now, and he continued to ponder what his life could have been like with her.

Chapter 4

Take Me to the River

When Sadie returned to Bozeman, she was able to purchase a small home in town not far from where she had lived six years earlier. She wasted no time in opening her own office. Since she was an environmental engineer, the rapidly expanding Gallatin Valley would prove to be a sound location for her consulting business. Aside from local development, the area was becoming a popular place for green businesses and those who considered themselves environmentally aware.

It was a quiet weekday afternoon and she had looked forward to drawing the river on her easel while enjoying the summer breeze. She loved her work, which had proven to be lucrative. Even more than the money it provided, Sadie loved the freedom it extended to her kids. She was finally able to set her own schedule and spend more time with them, although for her it was never enough. On this day, the kids were with friends. They had rekindled old friendships from when they lived here before and so today, she had some time to herself.

Someone else had free time that day. Jack Gibbons had left his insurance office early to take his dog to the river for some exercise, which they both needed. The sight, smell and sound of the river was beginning to calm his nerves, frazzled by a lime green Volkswagen micro bus he'd been forced to follow for twelve miles on the two-lane highway from town at the speed of thirty-five miles per hour. A steady stream of oncoming traffic had prevented him from passing the slow-moving vehicle. He finally reached his destination and turned onto a gravel road that led to the river.

"Goddamned gorp-eating hippies," he yelled through the open window of his car. He knew the occupants of the van could not hear him, yet he felt better after venting his frustration at them.

Jack was pleased to see only one other car parked in the public access lot, a red Saab. On a day as beautiful as this, everyone was either at the river or wishing they were, he thought as he lit a Cohiba.

He carried a fly rod and used his free hand to toss a stick for the dog, Maitai, a four-year-old black Labrador retriever who shared her name with Jack's favorite vacation cocktail.

As he pushed through the willows and emerged at the dry late summer river bed, he was pleased to see a woman sitting at her easel, facing the river with her back to him. Maitai headed straight for her and at first Jack feared the dog would knock over the easel with her tail, which wagged spastically as she inspected the lady with her wet nose.

The woman patted Maitai on the head and turned to look around for the dog's owner and when their eyes met, she waved. Jack walked over to her, hardly noticing the painting she was creating.

"Beautiful," he said.

She looked up at him and smiled, making his pulse pound in his throat. She was gorgeous. In her blue-and-white sundress, she pierced his heart with sky-blue eyes and golden hair that danced in the soft summer breeze.

"Thanks, it's getting there," she said as she looked back at her work.

"The painting is beautiful as well," replied Jack. He was proud of himself for being so quick on his feet with a comment.

She laughed at his boldness. She looked back up at him

and Jack almost fell over backwards. "I'll bet you say that to all the girls you meet at the river."

Jack also laughed. "You've got me. After all, this is a popular pickup joint for me and Maitai."

Maitai sat obediently on the rocks enjoying a good ear scratching from the lady.

"Maitai? That's a great name," she said in a sweet voice that the dog responded to with several licks to her hand. "So, what is your name?"

Jack could not believe his luck. She looked at him over her shoulder, smiling. The wind blew her hair over one eye and he thought she must have been satisfied with the way it enhanced her profile because she didn't brush it away. Jack's voice cracked as he replied, a bit weaker than he would have liked.

"Jack." He cleared his throat. "Jack, and you are?"

"Sadie."

They visited for about an hour until Sadie packed her easel. Then they stood by the river, taking turns throwing a stick for Maitai.

Jack felt a little silly talking to such a good-looking woman while he stood there in the sun dressed in waders and fishing vest with flies and hooks dangling off him like he was a dirty pincushion. He sweated profusely from the lack of ventilation his waders offered and the nervous energy he fought as he searched for what to say next. When they stopped visiting, it was almost dark, leaving Jack only minutes to do some late day fishing, but he didn't care. They agreed to meet in the same spot the very next day.

Less than a year later, they were engaged.

Chapter 5
The Retreat

"Thanks for remembering how much I wanted the Baker place," said Rowan, holding his shot glass high.

"It's about time you owned something more than a fly rod," Storm replied.

They toasted with a drop of Pendleton splashing on the bar at Fred's Saloon. Rowan felt the whiskey singe his gullet as he and Storm watched the bartender's blue jeans disappear around the center island of the bar.

They were faded blue jeans. Not faded from wear and washing, but made to look worn and washed. Sequin designs on each back pocket were accented with white-and-black mock cowhide for a slightly trashy but very inviting pair of jeans.

"Designs on girls' jeans," said Storm.

Rowan sipped his porter. "How come we didn't have that in college? No designs on girls' asses, words on panties like 'juicy,' or pink, either. Why didn't we think of that?"

The bartender and jean model returned with two plates each laden with a kitchen sink burger, a mammoth artery-clogger mannishly formed with one half pound of buffalo burger, fried egg, cheese and chili with some pickles, and lettuce for a fraction of one's daily veggies. The burgers were buried in a mound of sweet potato fries.

She smiled as she set the plates down in front of them, having overheard bits of their conversation, noting they liked her ass. She was enjoying their attention and imagined they were good tippers, especially the cute one with a two-day stubble. He was probably several years older than her, but there was a distinct air of confidence about him. Besides, his face was familiar, although she couldn't place him.

She set the plates down and leaned on the bar, saying, "Getcha anything else, guys?"

"Yeah," answered Rowan. "Let's do something cheap and superficial."

Her crescent-shaped smiled turned to an open circle and her eyebrows shot up.

Rowan grinned even bigger.

"How crass," she said but smiled back with a wink.

"We'll have a shot. Have one with us, your choice."

"Jameson," she said, accepting the invitation and immediately upping the ante with a real shot.

Her back straightened as she said it, which pushed her breasts even closer to him across the bar. Her tight powder-blue tee revealed her cleavage like melting spring snows reveal the Tetons.

"Jameson it is," returned Rowan.

She nodded and walked away to grab a bottle. Rowan and Storm worked on their burgers in silence.

"Nice to see that you haven't lost your touch," said Storm as he chewed on a potato fry, his eyes glued to the designer jeans.

The girl returned, filling the glasses again and setting the bottle on the counter before them.

"What's yer name?"

"Casey."

"Casey, I'm Rowan. This here is my friend Storm. Here's

to you, Casey."

They clinked their glasses and downed the shots.

Casey set her empty shot glass on the bar with a thud. "I'd better go check on the others. Next one's on me," she promised.

Rowan and Storm again returned to their burgers in silence as it was foolish to have shots on empty stomachs, or to have shots of anything, for that matter, at their age.

As they ate, they watched the television, but mostly Casey. She was at the end of the bar pouring liquor into glasses, mixing them like a science experiment gone mad, performing with the grace of a ballerina.

She poured the Kahlua, and returned with three shots of what appeared to be chocolate milk.

"We are grown men, sweetie, we don't drink chocolate milk," said a grinning Storm. "What is that?"

"Have the shot, then I'll tell ya."

Rowan raised his glass. "Here's to the bull that roams the woods, who does the cows and heifers good. If it weren't for him and his big red rod, we wouldn't have any burgers, by god."

They downed the shots.

The sweet taste was familiar to Rowan, as most alcoholic beverages were. Storm nodded his head in approval. Casey just kept smiling.

"So, what is it?" asked Storm.

"Cowboy cocksucker," replied Rowan and Casey in unison.

Storm shook his head. "Good stuff. Call it something else and make me another!"

Casey winked at Rowan and left to wait on another patron.

"She reminds me of someone," said Storm.

"Me too," replied Rowan, "Jesus, me too."

"Saw her last week. She asked about you. She was surprised to hear you'd be in town."

"What do you know about her?"

"She lives up the canyon, works in town; wears a big-ass engagement ring, and she looks good too."

Rowan took a sip of beer and pushed his plate away. The food was too much and the whiskey probably wasn't the best idea he'd ever had. At least he'd reached the age where he could recognize the warning signs of upcoming sickness and prevent himself from further self-inflicted damage.

He looked in the mirror across the bar at himself. He had to tell her that he came to see her. He cared too much not to see her again. But, engaged? He couldn't possibly have expected her to wait on him. He just didn't think she had moved on. He wanted to see Sadie again.

Storm continued to attack his kitchen sink burger. Rowan's monolithic gaze in the mirror was interrupted by Casey's arrival. "I'm closing out. Can I get you anything else?"

Rowan pushed a credit card across the bar towards her. "That's all. When you're all done, have another one with us."

She cocked her head with shy crooked grin. "Okay, Just as long as I'm not interrupting man time."

Storm swallowed a slurry of burger and beer and announced, "No way. I've had all of this guy's bullshit I can stand. I have church in the morning."

Casey left to close the tab. They watched her ass make its wondrous way to the register.

Storm stood and patted Rowan on the back, saying, "Remember those of us less fortunate souls who must settle for women our own age. Call me in the morning when you figure out where you are, and we'll do breakfast. I'll show you the property."

"Thanks, amigo." Rowan watched his good friend leave.

Without turning, Storm waved, adding, "Manana."

Rowan turned to Casey who now sat on the barstool next to him. Her bright white smile reached from one high cheekbone to the other. Her posture had changed from a bartender's to that of an interested woman. Rowan knew he was only trying to fill the holes inside him with this much younger girl, but she was so cute, he was so lonely and besides, what if Sadie had no interest in seeing him? As he studied her young inviting body, he decided this was an opportunity not to be missed.

"So, how come I haven't seen you in here before?" she asked as she perched on the bar stool like a cat. If she had a tail, it would have been flicking from side to side.

He smiled at her. "I haven't been around for a while. I travel a lot." Rowan skipped the details to turn the conversation back to her; he would rather learn something about this Cheshire cat than tell her something about himself.

He put his hand on the back of her chair. "What about you?"

"I'm from Minneapolis, worked here while going to college, elementary education, made good money. Teaching doesn't pay this good, but I still get to use my degree here. Drunks are like dealing with little kids."

They both laughed and as they did so, Rowan felt the energy between them, a primal, instinctive attraction.

He was sure Casey felt it too.

He interlaced his fingers in hers, lifted her arms above her head and pinned the back of her hands against the wall in the narrow hallway of her apartment. He kissed her neck gently at first and then harder as she pushed herself into him. His hands came down her long thin arms, touched her soft face and he grabbed the bottom of her shirt. The powder-blue tee fell to the floor.

She fumbled with his button down shirt as Rowan unbuttoned her pants. Casey grabbed two fists of shirt and pulled them apart, ripping off the buttons. They stumbled and kissed their way down the hall, locked in an embrace. A trail of clothing led to her bedroom.

He made love to her twice, a feat he was proud of. She was so young and gorgeous and the way she touched him was what every thirty-year-old man needs. He didn't remember falling asleep. He didn't wake up in the middle of the night to piss or even look at the clock. A hard orgasm, alcohol and the satisfaction of sex with a much younger woman made for a good night's sleep.

U2's "Beautiful Day" blared from the nightstand. Sunlight poured into the room, penetrating his eyelids. One or the other would have been gentle enough, but the combination of sunlight and a wailing Bono sent Rowan up on his elbows to gain his bearings and looking for the time of day.

Jesus Christ, he thought. I'm getting too old to sleep around because I actually fell asleep.

He was almost disappointed in himself. A few years ago, he would never have allowed this to happen; waking up in a stranger's bedroom? If he was truly on top of his game, he would have gathered his clothes from the floor in the middle of the night and dressed his way to the door. He had fallen asleep beside her. He felt comfortable next to her, even now as he pondered this, and that made him even more uncomfortable.

From under the covers, a delicate arm fumbled for the radio alarm clock and with a touch, Bono was silenced. Then, without as much as a good morning, she moved between his legs and held him in her mouth. Rowan threw back the comforter to watch her and she looked up at him and smiled.

"I read your books, you're my favorite writer."

Rowan moaned, eyes closed as he ran his fingers through her tangled morning hair.

"You're my favorite reader."

The waitress at The Western Café poured their coffee, smacked on her bubble gum and mumbled a "good morning."

The special was two eggs, meat and hash browns with white gravy and a biscuit, hangover food. Rowan usually ate fruit and coffee in the mornings, but the special sounded like an appropriate morning-after meal.

Storm leaned forward across the table and lowered his voice to a whisper, asking, "Can she fuck like I imagined?"

Rowan leaned towards his friend and sipped his coffee and grinned. "Whatever your deviant little mind imagined about her; well, she is capable of fulfilling all your twisted fantasies."

Storm shook his head. "Damn. I should have taken that creative writing class in college."

"Tell me about the property."

"Before they even shoveled dirt on old man Baker's bones, the family chopped the ranch up into parcels. I purchased four tracts, each with river frontage. I'll give you first pick. I'm glad you're here. Saves me from having to track you down in Maui or Alaska or wherever the hell you've disappeared to."

The waitress set a mound of food in front of each of them, temporarily interrupting Storm.

"Greasy food is best enjoyed after a night of drinking and fornicating. You, my friend, have earned the right to pig out, but you are a bastard." said Storm as he shook out Tabasco over his biscuits.

Rowan looked up from his plate to ask, "Why's that?"

"Because, jackass, now every time I go in there to salivate over her impeccably stunning ass, I'll immediately think of you defiling her."

"Sounds like you got issues," Rowan replied with a laugh.

"You are an asshole," returned Storm nonchalantly.

"Consider it my contribution to your much-needed sex addiction treatment."

"I don't think I'm the one with a sex addiction."

"Touche."

Storm took a sip from his coffee. "Seriously, you pursue women the same way you fish."

Rowan acknowledged the remark by staring at his friend quizzically. "How's that?"

"Catch and release, my friend. Catch and release."

The pickup tires crunched the gravel county road as Storm slowed and pointed to metal posts marking the property from the road down to the river. Realtors had salivated over the ranch for years, waiting for Ben Baker to die and when he finally did, they swarmed like vultures for a piece of the prime real estate. The Madison River cut the ranch in half. The Gallatin Range sloped down to flat fields crisscrossed with aspen groves and stands of willows that clutched the fence lines. Prime hay ground and elk winter refuge, yes, but better, development property.

As Storm proudly recounted how he had been fortunate enough to get one hundred and sixty acres to subdivide and develop, Rowan's thoughts drifted across the weed-ridden hayfield, through the trees to the river. He was gazing at where he and Sadie spent so many summer days laughing and loving at the water's edge.

"There. I want that spot."

Storm stopped the truck and put on his reading glasses as he unfolded a map. He looked back and forth from the map to the river. "How much acreage you want?"

"It ain't acreage I'm after," he said as he got out of the truck.

Rowan slipped through the barbed wire fence, its top strand loose from being pummeled by the hooves of elk migrating to the hay field in winter. He walked across the dry alfalfa stubble that crunched loudly with each step from lack of irrigation. The vigor of the land had died with old man Baker.

Storm lengthened his stride to keep pace with Rowan, who was hell bent to reach the river. The dry aspen and cottonwood leaves crunched under their feet before the soles of their shoes traversed the large round river rocks sticking out of the sand like dented and distorted army helmets.

Rowan stood at the water's edge. "How much?"

"This is the best lot on this side of the river. It's ten acres." Even Storm gulped before telling his friend the price. It was best to give a per-acre price and let the client do the math.

"I'm giving you a deal at twenty thousand per acre."

"Two hundred-thousand?" He took off his shades and

looked back across the field, past the pickup, squinting at the Spanish Peaks in the distance.

"You still pissed I fucked Cheryl Newman first?"

Storm's jaw dropped. "I didn't know you fucked Cheryl."

"Oh. Whoops."

"You are a whore. Look, they're not making any more, my friend."

"Not making any more whores?"

Rowan never took his eyes off the sand under the big cottonwood where he and Sadie had a picnic so many years ago. It remained unchanged. He looked through the trees and across the river.

"No, not whores, land. Especially land like this."

The place was just as lovely as he remembered. He had to have it.

"Guess I'll write more books, get a movie option, and drink cheap wine." Rowan turned from the river to face his friend and stuck out his hand. "It's a deal."

She was in the phone book. He hovered over the hotel phone, sweating over what to say until he grew so clammy he needed another shower.

"Hello?"

He had hoped she would pick up the phone. Still, he hadn't prepared himself for the sound of her voice, her flawless enunciation of the English language, yet spoken in a tone that sounded as if she would break out in laughter at any moment. It was unmistakably her. Her voice sent shock waves through his body. Rowan was embarrassed that his palms got sweaty and his voice cracked as he heard her strong pronounced greeting.

"Hey, old friend, I went to the river today." He felt proud to form a complete sentence without speaking nervous gibberish.

"Oh. My. God. Rowan?"

"How've you been?"

"Great! Are you in town? Where are you?"

Rowan arrived at The Bacchus Pub twenty minutes early. Nervous with palms still sweating, he ordered a Bombay gin and tonic. He sat in a lounge chair in the lobby admiring the place that had remained the same through the years.

A lot of liquor had spilled on the marble floors. No doubt a few marriages, divorces and conceptions had found their inception within these cherry-wainscoted walls. The enormous marble columns rose to the intricately tiled tin ceiling. A wide stone stairway led to a cozy balcony. The place was quiet this time of day, but would soon be loud with live music and the noise of a crowd.

Rowan sipped his gin and started to relax when he saw her walking through the wood-and-glass door. She was as striking as ever. Her hair, her gait and infectious smile, it was all still there. She walked towards him and he met her halfway across the marble floor. She put both her arms around him in a hug from one old lover to another, not the one arm half-hearted hug among friends who are too afraid to say I love you, but rather a long lost hug that had waited a long lost time.

She gazed up at him and asked, "So, come here often?"

They laughed together at her nonchalant use of the cheesy pickup line.

"Not often enough."

They took a booth and she ordered a gin. Rowan ordered another. They talked and laughed about her kids and work. She mentioned something about her fiancé as Rowan struggled to listen. She was as beautiful as ever. Everything about her drew him in. The laugh lines in her face and the makings of crow's feet around her eyes only added to the depth of her beauty; she was as exquisite as he remembered.

She asked about his travels, his books and his plans for the future. They reminisced about their time spent together. The conversation came easy and Rowan stopped sweating. He fell right back into the familiar rhythm of their comfortable dialogue.

"Remember the time I taught you to fly fish on the Madison?" he asked.

Sadie folded her hands up under her chin. "I remember it well, one of my favorite memories, as a matter of fact."

"I bought that piece of property yesterday. The cottonwood where we used to picnic, the sandbar, the aspen grove that lined the banks of the river, it's all still there and now it is mine."

She covered her mouth in excitement. "That is so great! It was so beautiful. I think about that place now and then. I haven't been there in a long time. How long has it been?"

"Probably six years," he said, realizing he knew exactly how long it had been.

He wanted to get her alone for a moment. As she talked, he'd been driving himself out of his mind searching for a way to tell her that he still wanted her. Perhaps she felt the same way about him.

"Say, why don't you just ride out there with me, for old times' sake."

Sadie shifted in her seat, feeling overwhelmed. It was great to see her old lover and the attraction was still there, but she was getting married. She wanted so many things at once and she could only choose one. Surely she could spend more time with Rowan while remaining faithful to her fiancé, and in the end continue a friendship with Rowan. She'd always had power over men; surely she could be in control of this situation.

"I would like that," she returned.

The washboard gravel road rattled the antique1954 five-window Chevy pickup and sent the rear end fishtailing so that Rowan had to gear down the stick transmission to slow while avoiding spilling the beers Sadie had opened for them. The open windows let in the warm afternoon air and dust filled the cab. The beer and the country roads brought back memories. He had convinced her to go with him, see their old stomping grounds and extend their visit. His intentions were mostly good, but being a man, he was not always responsible for his intentions when in the presence of a beautiful woman. And she was the most beautiful woman he'd ever seen.

A log had fallen so close to the water that it was difficult to imagine someone had not set it there just for them, like an invitation from nature to relive the past. The top had broken off at the edge of the river and the base was still attached to the stump by thick splintered strands of cottonwood, so Rowan and Sadie could sit and dangle their feet over the sand.

The beer bottles were sweating in the paper carton so Rowan set the remainder of the six-pack in the river, wedging it between rocks so it would not topple over. He sat down with her straddling the log beside him, her posture warm and inviting like the sun that beamed down on them.

"I remember the surprise picnic right here. I swear I thought you were going to propose that day."

Rowan grinned. "I know. I just wanted to do something nice for you."

She reached out and touched his arm. "To this day, it was the nicest thing anyone has ever done for me."

A flood of memories came roaring back, most of which were made right there almost a decade earlier. He reached for her hand. Sadie pushed herself closer to him. Together, they closed the distance between them and met each other with a kiss, a kiss that took them back in time, a kiss that stopped time.

Sadie straddled Rowan, her fingers in his hair, his face on her breasts. His hands cradled her and he thought her body was just as firm and lovely as in his dreams.

Sadie smiled as Rowan's hands ran up and down her arms, over her hips. His hands cradled her face and tousled her hair.

She closed her eyes as he kissed her neck.

She grabbed the hair on the back of his head, ran her fingers through it and turned his face to hers and kissed him hard, as if by doing so they could turn the clock back. His grip on her tightened and soon the waves of passion flooded him.

Rowan was thinking that sex outdoors could be tricky. Too quick and it seemed a waste of time taking off clothes and trying to find a comfortable position. Nobody wanted the 'did I shave my legs for this?' feeling. On the other hand, if it took too long, someone was bound to tire of the lack of creature comforts like a bed or a couch. An arm or leg would fall asleep and take away from the pleasure of it all, especially when sitting on the hard bark of a cottonwood.

Rowan wanted it to last forever, but his attraction to her was so intense, he knew it couldn't. As soon as he felt her body quiver, he climaxed with her. They held each other tight, breathing hard.

"I'll get us a beer," she said.

Sadie lifted herself up from him and walked to the water naked and proud. She gripped two bottles, feeling like a reckless young lover again, having sex in the afternoon and drinking beer. Over the years, Sadie had thought of making love with Rowan. What she remembered was exhilarating and rejuvenating. Today, it was better than she remembered. She wondered what in the hell she was doing, but it felt good.

Rowan watched her and admired her beauty and her confidence, as while many women would scramble for some clothing to hide under, this woman couldn't care less if a canoe full of cub scouts had passed by. She looked great and she knew it. He shifted his butt on the tree and slid his blue jeans under him. The tree bark was making his ass fall asleep.

She held the beers out for Rowan to open. He popped the tops off with his belt buckle. She took a swig of a beer and handed the bottle back to him. Still excited, she knelt on the sand before him. She liked the feeling of the cool sand on her knees. She loved the power she had when she held a man in her mouth. She could ask for anything and she could take anything she wanted when she gave head, but she didn't want anything from Rowan except one last time.

The warm spring sun on his naked body felt good. He thought of the Old Milwaukee commercials where the guys are sitting around the campfire with no women present, remarking that it "doesn't get any better than this." Rowan thought that at the moment with the beer by the river and the warm sun, sitting there with Sadie between his legs, it in fact did get better than that, much better indeed.

It was as if she wanted to taste every drop of him. When she was done, she rose to her feet and kissed him. Sadie took a beer from his hand and turned, leaning back against him drinking her beer. If he could freeze a frame of his life and replay it at will, Rowan would choose that moment in that special place with Sadie's sweet naked body leaning into his, just drinking a beer and watching the river flow by, the same place that had been his favorite memory all these years.

When they finished the beers she said, "I have to get back. I have plans this evening. I can't show up with sand on my knees and beer on my breath."

They walked across the field, towards the truck, side by side. Rowan took her hand and she squeezed his.

"I want this every day of my life, Sadie. I still dream of you, I've tried to forget you, but I'm still in love with you."

"I know." She again squeezed his hand. "You are an amazing lover, a wonderful man and I have no regrets about making love to you today. It was a bad idea, but I enjoyed it."

Sadie rolled her eyes and managed a smile. "I have to be fair to myself. I must do what is right. I just want to be friends with you."

Her words took the breath out of him like a punch to the gut. Here he had just made love to her, was given a second chance to be with her, and for the second time he was turned away. He stopped, took both her hands and held her to him.

"I wanna touch you. I wanna feel the way I feel when you and I make love. I want that all the time. I don't want to just be your friend. You are the love of my life, my soul mate. I have not felt like this since the last time I was with you. I want you. I want to be with you, Sadie."

"I think about us too, Rowan. I just believe that our timing is off. We will always be different people at different stages in life. I miss you, but I have found something special and as much as I want to go back there, I am engaged. I love you. I will always love you, but I found someone who is better for me."

Her words hurt, but he managed a smile.

"I've been to a lot of places, fishing, working on boats, and you were there with me all the time. I've had a lot of adventures, but I want my greatest adventure to be with you. I can be everything to you, be better for you. I missed that opportunity in the past. We said that if it's meant to be, we would meet again. Well, here we are and better than ever, I might add."

"Rowan, you are a free spirit, an adventurer. You would only be happy for a little while. Montana is my home. I love it here. I have no desire to travel. I found someone who wants the same things I want."

A few moments ago, there was a thread of hope that he could be in her life again, not just in her heart. Now, he knew she felt the current between them as strong as he did, but his strong suit had never been changing her mind. He'd talked the pants off pretty girls many times, but when it came to the one woman that he really wanted, he couldn't find the words to convince her.

She hugged him. He held her tight, but he knew no matter how tight his grip, she was slipping away, again. She pushed away from him and held his hand, pulling him towards the old truck.

Her voice quavered, "I really have to get going. Please take me back to my car."

Rowan tried to maintain his dignity on the drive back to town by making small talk. He steered the truck to the bar parking lot where Sadie had left her Saab. She had tried to lighten the mood by asking how long he would be in town, where he was traveling to next, and what his next book would be about. With tears welling in their eyes, they talked and laughed just like the first time they said goodbye years ago.

Before he knew it she was getting out of the truck, kissing him on the cheek and waving goodbye. She shut the truck door behind her and the tears welling in his eyes fell to soak the collar of his shirt. Short of being on his knees begging, he had told her how he felt about her.

He could dig in and fight for her, but the look in her eyes told him that was not what she wanted. The sex on the river was hope for him, closure for her. He saw the guilt in her eyes and knew she just wanted to move on, without him.

Rowan gathered his pack at the hotel and was on the first flight out of Bozeman. Twenty-eight hours after Sadie once again slipped through his hands, he knelt on the beach and grabbing a handful of Grand Bahama sand, he let that, too, slip through his fingers, slapping his hands together until all the grains fell back to the beach. He had to regain his footing and he knew just the place to start.

Chapter 6

Bones' Place

Rowan had been here before. He liked driving on the "wrong" side of the road. His soul was refreshed by the friendliness of the island natives and their patience with tourist traffic. Away from the airport, the condos and timeshare sharks, to the east end of Grand Bahama lies a great portion of the island lost in time.

The people of the east end cook a chicken in hopes of a hungry lost tourist wanting a piece of island life and an ice cold Kalik. The NASA Satellite Base once kept them busy, drawing in a few workers and contractors from time to time. When the economy was good and people traveled from Miami for the weekend, business had been steady; but now, the people were as much in need of patrons as their cinder block homes were in need of fresh pastel paint.

Rowan was thirsty and eager to support the local economy so he pulled the rental car into the lot of a run-down joint that looked like a good place to have a beer, as long as it was daylight.

The iron bars on the windows had been painted sea green and were the only barrier to cut the breeze as it coursed through the small plywood shack. A flickering neon beer sign hung over the doorway. A big woman black as a magician's hat greeted him on the porch with a warm smile.

"Hello, ya want to eat?"

Rowan wasn't hungry, but he knew whatever was cooking would be good and likely the same thing her family would have for dinner. Sticking to one of his top rules of travel, he decided to order the special, that rule being the more decrepit the building, the better the meal, especially when it came to soul food. Based on that criterion, this place had to have great food.

"Kalik and the special?"

"Comin' up fo ya."

She went inside the shack and yelled something into the kitchen so fast that Rowan did not comprehend, but as he sat down at a table in the shade of the porch, she returned with a cold beer. They had waited all day for a tourist to stop. If they sold a few beers and a couple of meals, it would be a good day.

He sat on the porch with a sweaty bottle of Kalik beer and a plate of barbeque chicken. The smell was inviting and Rowan realized he had not eaten since before meeting Sadie for drinks. He'd been living off airport gin and airline peanuts.

He hadn't bothered to get a motel in Atlanta, had only slept a couple hours on the terminal floor. He realized he wasn't leaving Sadie's memory behind, just carrying it with him like luggage, as he always did. His five o'clock shadow was bordering the substance of a beard; his eyes were bloodshot from sleep deprivation and a hangover. He also needed a shower; he could smell himself, and it reminded him of an airport terminal, a blend of scents ranging from ketchup to leather handbags. But the island breeze, the food and the beer lifted his spirits. Without asking, the woman brought him another cold Kalik.

With a full belly, Rowan drove past the port towns, past the resorts that touted luxury and a remote location as their attributes. He drove through the national park to where the tiny houses were spread thin, separated by lush vegetation and pines, a world away from the busy industry and port on the west end of the island.

Little ramshackle outbuildings with grills served as restaurants with hand-painted signs advertising lunch specials and beer. Black faces with white smiles appeared through the electricity-deprived doorways. Some of the people walked out to the roadway, waving, inviting drivers to stop. Their smiles proved they were proud, friendly and genuine.

Rowan turned right off the highway onto a crushed seashell street that was split into a roundabout by an old growth mango tree. Children played outside the single-story square concrete school. He made a left when the road dead-ended at the Caribbean Sea and drove to a beach with a tiki hut, an eight-room motel and modest restaurant. It was a simple place, nicer than the rest of the buildings on this end of the island with its painted cinder blocks and paved parking lot. It was a welcome sight for anyone wanting an unspoiled beach getaway.

Rowan was out of the car as soon as the wheels stopped rolling as an empty bottle rolled out of the car onto the seashell parking lot with a clink. The Caribbean waves soaked the sand within conch-throwing distance of his parking space. A few people were on the deck of the hut enjoying lunch. Whether they knew the place was here all along or they made a wrong turn, Rowan was sure they all shared the same pleasant experience of the secluded beach, a trade wind unpolluted by the sound of jet skis and a blue sky void of people screaming from parasails overhead.

The voices of those on the deck were muted by the waves, the wind and every few minutes a holler from the kitchen to deliver another fried snapper or conch salad. He just stood there for a moment taking it all in, smelling the sea. Rowan spotted a familiar face serving beers from the ice chest behind the bar; it was the owner himself, Bones. Rowan smiled at the sight of the old man. Neither hurricanes nor hunger had got him yet.

He walked up the wooden steps worn from sandals and sand to the deck and extended his hand. "Mr. Bones, good to see ya."

Bones turned, smiled and shook Rowan's hand.

"Capun Roan, how you this fine day."

Without asking what Rowan would have, Bones opened up the red igloo cooler that sat on a table behind the bar and retrieved a frosty bottle of beer.

"I'm better now, old friend. The place looks good."

"Tanks, mon. Long time, no see. You stayin'?"

"Can I have number three?"

"How long, mon?"

"Not sure yet. That all right?"

"You stay long as ya like. Short as ya want. Laugh, love, live it up, mon." Bones set the beer on the bar in front of Rowan and gave him a smile as big as his large frame, his teeth glistening in the sun.

He had a name, Marvin something or another. Tall and exceptionally thin, everyone just called him Bones. He was quiet and Rowan had never met another man with such a peaceful assurance about him. He was well respected and a minister at the community church. The people of Gold Rock came to him for solutions to their problems. Often, he served as minister and bartender at the same time. Bones had a big family but it was difficult to tell family from strangers as people drifted to and from his establishment seeking advice, help or a cold drink. He treated them all equally well.

The sun was warm and inviting so Rowan unbuttoned his shirt and draped it over a chair. He took his beer and walked across the deck, down the steps to the beach, past the lounge chairs to where the wet sand gave way to dry hard granules mixed with bits of sea shells and broken coral.

He waded in the water that swirled around his feet, the outstretched beach all he could see from east to west. The dense air fogged about him as he stood miles away from a hotel or even another's beach towel in his view, all he could see was just lonely inviting sand. He sat and closed his eyes, listening to the waves and the shorebirds.

He heard the squish of footsteps in wet sand and looked up to see a big woman in a pink dress holding out two sweaty Kaliks.

"Mista Roan, Bones say ya look like ya need anotha and anotha. On de house."

Rowan's eyes welled with tears. Bones had sized him up well. And Bones was right. He was going to need a lot of beers, time and ocean breeze.

He took the bottles and told her, "Thank you, ma'am. Thanks so much."

"Ya hongry? We got de fresh red snappa and conch."

"I'll finish these and be in for a snapper sandwich and fries."

"I'll have it ready fo ya, baby," she replied. She sashayed back up the beach, barking orders to the open window of the kitchen.

Rowan set one beer in the wet sand, twisting and turning it so it wouldn't tip over. He took in the salty air through his nostrils and felt the breeze from a thousand miles away in his hair. He turned his face to the wind and wondered what she was doing.

As he went back to the deck with the empty bottles, he noticed the girl. She shined in the sunlight like a new car, yet she was sitting with an old geezer. He watched the odd couple on Bones' deck as he finished his sandwich at the bar. Rowan studied them from behind dark aviators, pretending to look beyond her as if lost in the rhythm of the waves, as if giving his attention to the sea.

The geezer was a portly gray-haired Englishman in his eighties with a face as round as his pot belly. If he had money, he had a lot of it, but the exquisite young twenty-something seated across from him wouldn't be there for the money, unless it was Bill Gates' money, then anything was possible. But this guy wasn't Bill Gates and she was spectacular.

Rowan strained to hear their conversation over the gulls and the waves in an attempt to learn why she was with the old coot. Her accent was South African. They were having a colorful argument over South Africa's economy. She was intellectual, petite, sassy and putting the old man in his place. After a brief argument, he threw up his hands and changed the tone of his voice. She, in turn, took notes on a legal pad as he spoke.

She had thin firm arms wrapped in shiny mocha skin with an inviting face, high cheekbones and large, soft, voluptuous lips, all of it accentuated by a tiny white two-piece bikini.

Something about the old man seemed familiar to Rowan and as he listened to their conversation, it became apparent that the old man was dictating a letter. Picking up pieces of what the man was saying, Rowan soon realized he was eavesdropping on none other than English author, Ben Tapp. Rowan had read a book by Tapp about a South African farm family and he remembered Tapp's photo on the back jacket cover.

Rowan watched as the old man leaned back in his chair, apparently finished with what he had to say. One of the kitchen ladies took their empty plates. The girl closed her notepad and sipped on a fresh frozen drink. Rowan came over to introduce himself.

"Mr. Tapp?"

The old man looked up from his chair, his blue bloodshot eyes trying to focus on the figure standing between him and the sun. Ben Tapp peered over his reading glasses with a frown.

"Who's asking, lad?"

"I'm a fan of your book, Sheep Town, and an author myself, Rowan Sojourner."

Rowan extended his hand for a shake. Tapp inspected it and reluctantly shook hands. Rowan quickly deduced that Tapp didn't know of him or care to, either. Tapp only looked him up and down, as unimpressed as only Englishmen can be.

But, Mr. Tapp did introduce Rowan to his lovely assistant and that was all that mattered.

"Well, Mr. Sojourner, say hello to my assistant and travel companion, the lovely Carmen Johnson of Johannesburg." Rowan was grinning like a boy with a new balloon. Carmen returned his attention with her own grin.

As if on cue, Tapp announced his retirement for the evening. "It is very nice meeting you, Mr. Rowan Oak." Tapp laughed at his own joke. "Arguing with my assistant has made me very tired."

Rowan had heard the joke many times. It was tiring and not amusing, but some who used it thought they were the first to inform him that there was an oak tree called the Rowan Oak. Fewer still knew of Faulkner's Rowan Oak.

Rowan nodded to be polite as Ben Tapp gestured with his hand, offering his chair to Rowan. "Would you please take my place and keep Miss Carmen company?"

The old man had class, even if he possessed the dry English sense of humor, and seemed to regard himself as too esteemed to allow the afternoon to wane in the company of an American.

"I would be honored, sir," Rowan said as he turned to Carmen. "That is, if it's all right with you."

He wanted to have a drink with her. He wanted to know everything about her.

Carmen said, "I would love the company of an American author. There is not one comic book on this island," she said, laughing.

She winked while Tapp patted Rowan's shoulder, his pot belly shaking with laughter.

He walked away saying, "Hope you took your vitamins today, lad; good luck keeping up with this one."

She was a smartass, a gorgeous one at that, and she had made the first strike. His tongue felt like it weighed a hundred pounds. His mind scrambled for a comeback.

"Do you read the comic books or just look at the pictures?"

She chuckled at that, thankfully. He realized he was starting to sweat. Gorgeous women always made him a bit nervous, although he did a good job of turning that nervous energy into fruitful conversation. It was part of the excitement that drew him to the hunt, the quest.

"He tires easily," she said, "but I do not complain. It gives me an opportunity to rest and relax. He is a good man, very demanding, but a good man."

She relaxed in her chair, with one shoulder thrown back over the backrest. Her dialogue accentuated her body language. She was eager to be free of the old man. Her voice was sensual and inviting, like a song.

"How long have you worked for Ben Tapp?"

Her reply was delayed as the big lady in the pink dress set out another frozen daiquiri and a beer.

"Fourteen months, two weeks and three days," she answered. "Much longer than my predecessors, and there have been many. He's quite the diamond cutter."

Her comment had caught Rowan off-guard. He had been preoccupied studying her beauty. He was hardly listening.

"Pardon?" he asked.

"Anal retentive. Shove a lump of coal up his British bum and the next day you'd have a bloody diamond!"

They laughed together.

"I read Sheep Town. His descriptions were so vivid and rolling, almost rambling, but never tiresome. A man who writes that way, describing the world around him in that fashion, could be difficult to work for...must be detail-oriented."

Carmen's eyes opened and settled on Rowan. "Yes, that is it precisely. I've lasted twice as long as any other assistant." Carmen said this rolling her eyes and smiling.

"I imagine it's interesting work."

"That it is. We travel. We meet people all over the world. He pays me well and I enjoy the challenge of managing his eccentricities. What about you, Rowan? What do you do?"

"Whatever I want," he replied.

Carmen seemed amused at that as she sipped on her Bahama Mama.

"Seriously, I'm a guide and boat captain. I've written a couple books and am here to generate ideas for another."

"What an exciting life you live."

Carmen had a smile fit for a toothpaste commercial. The way she smiled coyly and her interest in spending the afternoon with Rowan, well, it was everything any man in his situation could want. Bones and the big lady in the pink dress brought them drinks, they talked easily despite being two people from such different cultures, and it was apparent she enjoyed his sense of humor as much as he did hers. There was a natural attraction between them as sure as the tide.

They took a stroll on the beach, continuing to talk and laugh. There were no resorts, no tourists; they had the world all to themselves. With a fist full of seashells each, they headed back towards Bones' Place as the sun was setting. They held hands and stopped to take in the last of the orange glow shooting streaks of pink against the clouds. They kissed, dropped their seashells on the sand and their clothes soon followed.

Rowan stood holding tiny Carmen against him, her legs wrapped around his waist, her arms around his neck. Her body responded to each thrust, her moans of ecstasy filling his head. His legs had quaked and his body had trembled from holding her up so long. A flash occurred as the sun disappeared and they held one another watching the last rays of light disappear into the ocean.

Rowan set her feet down on the sand, having forgotten how cool the night air was getting. They hastily put on their clothes and went back up the beach towards the lights from the motel. He led Carmen to his room. They showered together then held each other until they both fell asleep. It was romantic. It was easy, fun and unforgettable.

When Rowan woke the next morning, the sun was coming up. Before he opened his eyes he caught her scent on the pillow next to him. He felt for her in the bed. The only thing that remained was a note that read:

"R,

I had a great time. You are an amazing lover. We have to catch a boat. Put last night in one of your books.

Best Wishes—Carmen."

He reached for his wristwatch on the bedside table and sat up, looking at it. It was eight o' clock. Through the window of his room he saw a quiet parking lot and empty beach. Rowan had enjoyed Carmen's company so much that he hadn't even imagined her absence in the morning. He had met her in a whirlwind of exhilaration and then she was gone. It was as if she were an angel sent to heal his broken heart with her body.

Rowan wrapped himself in the bed sheet and walked outside on the porch. There was no taxi, no pile of luggage belonging to Ben Tapp or Carmen, not even a breeze. The morning was silent and still.

He went back inside and read the note again. It would be a good morning to sit on the sand and drink coffee. He filled the motel-room Mr. Coffee with water and took his trunks from the back of a chair. As he pulled the swim trunks on, he felt a sudden pain from down below. Stunning and sharp, it left as quickly as it had come on. He grabbed himself thinking the pain odd, but not giving it much more thought, chalking it up to over-exertion the previous night. His member swelled at his own touch and at the memory of Carmen.

If she were here they would make love and he would hold her all day. Perhaps that's why she had left without warning. Was it possible she could discern this in his eyes and in his touch? The sense of his desperation was heavy as he tried to shake the thought of her so he went outside to enjoy the morning. But his heart was broken. In his haste to make a conquest of Carmen, he'd been vulnerable. He loved Sadie and meeting Carmen had taken his mind off the current situation, but sex with Carmen had been too perfect, out of the frying pan and into the fire.

Now, Rowan sat on the sand and gazed out at the blue Caribbean. It was a silent place, beautiful and tranquil. He glanced down the beach, which went on for miles. He resumed his thoughts of Carmen and for a moment could see her standing there, her beautiful mocha skin and short white sundress. She was smiling at him. He hoped that wherever she was at that moment, she was thinking of him as well. His thoughts drifted from Carmen to Sadie and the more he thought about it, he decided that a break from women would be good for him.

Rowan's newfound bout with self-reflection inspired him to focus on his next writing project. With renewed vigor, he sat on the beach or at the bar with his notebook for weeks, building a great story, maybe his best one yet. What began as a therapy session became a daily obsession as essential to his survival as Kalik beer and conch salad.

The sun and sand, mixed with the island dialect of the kitchen staff yelling and joking with one another, further propelled his creativity. He hammered out a storyline and when his thoughts ran thin he would watch the waves roll in. While at Bones' Place, the words flowed like the incoming tide. The hot sun felt good and though his liver ached for a reprieve from drinking, his work was focused. All of it, the heartbreak, the drinking and the island had energized his mind.

The bare bones of his story became connected with ligaments of description. His characters took to their new skin and became alive on the page with heart, soul and grit. What had been a pile of loose thoughts a short time ago was now a story. Rowan was proud as he reflected on his accomplishment.

He took a long hot shower and sat on the edge of his bed wrapped in a towel, and then called his publisher, Nancy. She was happy to hear the book was ready for her and would be the first in a new character series. Thankfully, she understood his need to puddle-jump all over the western hemisphere. He told her about the land he was purchasing in Montana.

"Excellent news! Perhaps now you'll be forced to plant your ass in a chair and do something that resembles work, instead of living the life every man dreams of in this city."

"What can I say? It ain't easy being me," he quipped.

"Bullshit. When are you coming to New York?" she asked,

"I fear a trip to the city would inhibit my creativity," he replied.

Just as he was about to lean backwards on the bed, there was that pain again.

As Rowan cradled the phone between cheek and shoulder, he touched himself. Nancy was an attractive woman, but her voice was extraordinarily sexy. If she ever lost her job in publishing she could make a good living operating a phone sex line. But that wasn't why he touched himself. He'd felt the same sharp pain as he had the morning Carmen left and now the mere thought of the pain made him rub his testicles. A severed aorta would be more welcome than testicular pain. He struggled to concentrate on Nancy's words as his mind began to worry.

"You owe me dinner," she said.

As she continued talking, his fingertips ran over his testicles. He thought he felt a lump on his left side. It was impossible, he thought, to talk on the phone and give himself an exam with each duty receiving proper attention.

"Well, I'll see ya soon, promise."

He wanted to get off the phone and devote his full attention to the recent finding. Did he have a lump on his nuts? The fear of what could be wrong overtook him and he'd stuttered to get off the phone.

"That's what you say to all the girls. I'm not all the girls, sweetheart. I am your publisher and I'd better see you soon."

She was joking, but Rowan knew a direct order was coming if he did not heed the subtle warning to visit New York.

"Yes ma'am."

Beads of sweat began to break out on his forehead as his thoughts ran wild with fear.

"That's more like it. Have a great day, Rowan."

As the line went dead, Rowan threw the phone on the bed to inspect himself. He worked himself over looking at what he was able to see from his angle and fondling himself in a new way, one with scientific purpose. There was a difference in the way the testicles felt. He shook his head in disbelief. Normally, when he touched himself, he left the testicles out of it. Now, he was wishing he had more of a reference for how each one should feel. Still, there was a noticeable difference between the two. On the back of the left testicle was a small hard lump, which was different from the right testicle.

Fear again took hold and he began to think of all the horrors that may lie in wait for him. He was sweating, still steamed from the hot shower and anxious with concern for his own well-being. His heart pounded in his throat.

Rowan considered seeing a doctor here. He then thought about going back to the states to see a doctor. He didn't have a regular physician, and couldn't remember the last time he had seen one. His mind raced, and he realized he needed to relax. Then he would decide what to do. Should he tell someone? Who? What if he had cancer? He felt sick. What if it was nothing? Rowan went outside, sat on the beach and got drunk.

Rowan had bought two joints from the grounds maintenance man, Felix, who always looked high as he aimlessly wandered the grounds picking up tiny pieces of trash, pulling weeds and making himself appear busy. A few weeks ago, as Rowan lay on the beach, he caught a whiff of marijuana smoke on Felix as he walked around in circles poking at the sand with his rake. Rowan made a smoking motion with his hands to his lips. Felix nodded and smiled.

"Yeah, mon," was all he said.

He disappeared and a few minutes later, Felix returned with two joints in a small baggie.

Rowan paid him and was impressed with the efficiency of pothead Felix. The business world could learn a lot from such beachfront transactions. Pure efficiency, although it was mostly seeds and stems, tourist shake, but it was still worth it.

He lit one of the joints he'd been saving for when he completed the first draft. For weeks it had waited in his sock drawer, his proverbial carrot. He had tried getting high and writing before, the result was disastrous. Smoking pot took away every ounce of ambition he had and led his creativity in a roundabout ride, one that required a translator once he was sober. What was pure genius while high was third grade gibberish the next day.

Sitting on the quiet beach at night with only the stars, and a distant light from Bones' to detract from the feeling of solitude made Rowan feel like a very small part of the world. Getting high and looking out across the ocean at the bobbing light of a distant ship with the stars dotting the sky made him feel like it was time for another adventure, time to see more of this big round ball. He thought about building a house on the Montana property. Sooner or later, he would want a home, but first he still longed to travel. Travel invited new adventure and new adventures helped hide his heart from love's defeat. He couldn't take another punch like that. He had really fallen for Carmen. If she had stayed he would have been in trouble all over again. His new plan was fishing, writing and celibacy.

He took another hit and giggled. The darkness and weed brought a hint of paranoia, but it was drowned out by his rolling laughter, the only sound except for the noises of roosting birds that came from the bushes a few yards up the dark beach. As he sat watching the sand crabs, he named one Herman, the biggest one. Herman was trash talking the others. The littlest one, Bert, was hungry and pissed at Herman for picking this beach to scrounge for food for there was none, Felix maintained the beach too well. He made little voices for them, entertaining himself and anyone else, had there been another soul on the beach. In Rowan's warped mind, the crabs indeed talked to one another, and Rowan joined their conversation.

"May I suggest the kitchen? I highly recommend the conch salad," He said laughing as the two crabs paused in their sideways walk to stare up at him.

He burned the blunt to where he could no longer hold it in his fingers and drained the last of the beers. He gathered the empty bottles and wandered up the beach to a hammock.

When the morning sun began to sting his face, he opened one eye to see Felix raking the sand and picking up trash. The motions of the rake were delicate and had a gentle rhythm, but the hangover transformed the subtle sounds into the velocity of a train wreck in Rowan's head.

Felix smiled at Rowan. "Devil's Lettuce."

Rowan's mouth was too dry to speak. He nodded in agreement, grunted and wandered back to his dark air-conditioned room. He slept past noon.

His cell phone blared "Don't Worry, Be Happy" from the nightstand. Squinting, Rowan fumbled clumsily for it and held it to his ear as his cotton mouth excluded him from speaking the words his brain was thinking. Hello sounded like "ho," but that was good enough for Ron "Dirty" Sanchez.

"Mahalo bro," said Dirty.

Rowan smacked his lips in an attempt to extract a drop of moisture from his tongue, which was stuck to the side of his dry cheek by pot resin.

"Hey Dirty, how are ya?"

"Just making sure my favorite bookworm is gonna cut loose with us at the Lah-hiney tourney, bro."

The Lahaina Tournament was held every year in Maui at the end of October. Rowan had worked with Dirty Sanchez in Alaska. They were river guides together many summers ago.

Rowan had been so engrossed in his new novel that he'd not realized it was almost September. He had secured his spot on the boat last winter. This year, Dirty had a new boat all his own.

As he listened to Dirty explain when the other guys were flying in to Maui, he decided he could go there now and kick back, get some work done on his new book and wait for the tournament. Besides, he'd had enough alone time, and catching up with friends in Maui sounded good.

"...and you can stay with me again this year, Captain," proclaimed Dirty.

"You still shacked up with that cute native girl?"

"She threw me out. I got my own place now; new girl, too."

"Wow, new boat, new place..."

"Don't ask too many questions, bro."

It was true. Dirty had many friends and some of them were not exactly the kind of people one would invite to Sunday dinner with mom. Dirty had a knack for making friends from all walks of life and like Rowan, he had traveled. His travels had brought questionable connections and shady business deals. Dirty's friends made it a point not to ask too many questions. And Dirty was quick to protect them from what they thought they wanted to know about his cash flow.

"See ya next week," said Rowan.

He hung up, certain that good times were ahead, he would be all right, but first he needed a glass of water.

Rowan decided to visit a clinic in Freeport. He called a doctor from the phone book and explained his symptoms of pain and a lump in his testicle. He was pleased to get an office appointment that afternoon and on his first phone call.

The clinic was clean and eerily still. As soon as he sat down in the waiting area, his name was called by a very cute nurse. Under different circumstances he would have struck up a conversation with her, but his current condition seemed to overpower his sexual urges. She led him to a room, took his blood pressure and smiled as she shut the door behind her.

He was happily surprised to only wait a moment before the doctor walked in. A large-framed man, the doctor's salt-colored hair indicated he was in his fifties. He greeted Rowan with a firm handshake. The man's large paw swallowed Rowan's entire hand.

"I am Doctor Higgins and you are…Mr. Sojourner?"

"Yes sir."

"What brings you here today?"

Rowan explained his pains and lump and reluctantly waited for the doctor's request to have a look. It was inevitable. That's why he was there, after all. It was just that the doctor had huge hands, fingers like bratwurst and Rowan prayed that he didn't plan a hernia check as part of his exam. If the saying was true that a man's member could be measured by the size of his hands, with the large hands and being black, Rowan thought surely the doctor lived up to the stereotype. He was likely entertained having average-size white men in his clinic where he could treat the various venereal diseases they acquired while on vacation. Rowan dreaded showing his package even more.

"Let us have a look, shall we?"

The doctor motioned for Rowan to stand up and, well, the remainder didn't need to be stated. Rowan was extremely uncomfortable standing there naked as another man fondled his balls, not to mention the new equation he'd made with this particular doctor. As the doctor inspected his goods, Rowan wondered if any man had ever got an erection while having a testicular exam. Perhaps if the nurse did it, but right now his manhood was as shriveled as if he were standing in a meat locker. After just a moment of fondling, the doctor spoke.

"Well, dere is a growth."

Rowan was almost relieved. It wasn't in his head. He hadn't imagined it all and his fears and worry were justified.

"Please, Mr. Sojourner, I am done," the doctor said,

motioning with one hand for him to pull his pants back on. "Dere is a small abnormality..."

Rowan wondered if the doctor was describing his package or the lump.

"And yes, it is in your left testicle."

"Is it cancer?"

"Heavens no, man, it is just a cyst."

"What should I do, doc?"

"Not a ting, mon, dere is no need for panic. Jes keep an eye on it."

Rowan wondered how he could keep an eye on the back of his balls. The doctor noticed the confusion on his face.

"Continue periodic self-exams. If it continues to grow, we have another look."

The doctor's words were reassuring, there was something abnormal but nothing to panic over; a cyst was all it was. It was worth the time and money to know he wasn't a hypochondriac. Rowan left the clinic relieved and drove back to Bones'.

The wind picked up from a steady welcome breeze to gusts that hinted of what was to come. By mid-afternoon, the sun disappeared behind dark clouds and the rain came. Although the tournament was weeks away, hurricane season was nearing. Rowan left the Caribbean for Maui via New York City, of course.

Chapter 7
Billfish and Kings

Dirty Sanchez's new thirty-three-foot Bertram was sleek and sexy. Years of guiding, and a few clandestine activities, had enabled the purchase. He'd christened her *Stinky Fingers* and no one questioned Ron on the name, they'd all agreed it was fitting for Ron's boat and were relieved that he never had any children to name.

Stinky Fingers was as adept at fishing as she was at being beautiful. Outriggers sprouted from her center like anthers sprouting from a Kukui flower. The windows were blacked out, the steel was stainless and the deck was blinding white. It was a sexy boat built for fishing, but at her first tournament, *Stinky Fingers* would earn her name.

The crew led by Dirty consisted of Chance Barlow, a thirty-something bachelor and trustafarian. His father had been a developer on Oahu and left a sizeable trust fund to Chance. Tim Gustofson from Vancouver tagged along with his dad, Sid, who operated the British Columbia guide service where Rowan and Ron had met over a decade earlier. For all the men, fishing was life and life was fishing. Warm-water Marlin or cold-water cod, they loved it all.

Eighteen miles off shore, *Stinky Fingers* circled a floating satellite transmitter used by NASA to track air travel. The buoyant satellite transmitter was held in place by over two thousand feet of steel cable anchored to the ocean floor. The two-inch cable was encrusted with algae and barnacles, which attracted baitfish, which in turn attracted bigger species like Blue Marlin, Spearfish, Mahi and Yellow-fin Tuna.

Halfway through the first turn around the buoy, two rods simultaneously doubled over. Rowan took a seat in the fighting chair. He was strapped in by his crew mates. Chance Barlow quickly hauled in the skipjack tuna that had taken his light tackle squid, the first of nine big tuna for the day.

Rowan turned the Penn reel hard and fast, lowering the rod towards the back of the boat, and jerked the rod back, only to crank the reel furiously and repeat the process again and again. The big Blue Marlin jumped behind the boat. It looked like a silvery blue sea monster as it thrashed its bill from side to side and its tail danced across the boat's wake. The show was applauded by a chorus of "holy shits" by the crew and a happy Captain Sanchez screamed from the helm that the Marlin had to be 800 pounds.

After five minutes, Rowan's arms were exhausted. Every fiber of strength from his fingertips to his toes was zapped and pure adrenaline coursed through his body. Thirty minutes after the fish struck, the crew gaffed the Marlin and lashed him to the gun whale. It took all four men to secure the monster to the boat.

Shaking, Rowan struggled to pop the top on a Longboard Lager. It was a hard-earned beer. Sid opened the beer can for Rowan, whose muscles felt like jelly. He could hardly hold the beer in his hand. It was a short-lived struggle as he chugged the refreshing brew.

Tim grabbed a rod as it jerked forward. Dirty had thrown the gear in neutral and the baits had slowed, with time to sink in the water. He took his turn in the chair and reeled in a nice Mahi. It was about a forty-four pound fish. All of the crew landed at least one billfish over the minimum qualifying weight. They tagged three spearfish and released them. It was a landmark day for fishing and likely to be also a winning tournament day.

At 3:00 P.M., they listened to all the other boats give their reports. The crew had no doubt that *Stinky Fingers* was in first place. Rowan's Blue Marlin and a Striped Marlin caught by Sid would top the scales. Feeling confident, they had been easing their way back towards Lahaina Harbor for the weigh-in. With the other boats giving their final reports, Dirty ordered the lines pulled in. They would be the first boat back to the scales and win the tournament. Eager to show off the horsepower under all that beauty, Dirty set the throttle and headed for the harbor.

Rowan sat in one of the fighting chairs. As the boat struck a wave, he felt the pain in his groin again. The sharp needle-like surge was gone as quickly as it had begun, but it left him breathless. He figured that he'd strained awful hard reeling in the big blue. That's probably all it was, he thought; the strain of fighting a big Marlin. The time before, it had probably been the strain of fantastic sex with Carmen. Reassuring himself, he took another sip of water and let the painful incident drift to the back of his mind as everyone was all smiles, patting one another on the back for such a perfect day at sea.

The weigh-in was no contest. *Stinky Fingers* and her crew had been blessed by the fish gods and won the jackpot hands down. They also took second place for the number of spearfish tagged and released.

The after party was rocking and the food was incredible. Rowan was exhausted from the day on the boat. A few beers and a big dinner made his eyelids heavy. Rowan sat at the table with everyone in the crew except for Sid, who had announced earlier that he had nothing to prove at his age and nine o'clock was bedtime, celebration or not.

Dirty and his girlfriend Kai were dancing to the live sound of Moneybags and the Steel Drum Lobster Band. Kai had showed up with her friend, Irene. With a tan as dark as her perfect brown eyes, Irene sat across from Rowan and the two of them had made small talk ever since they'd been introduced.

"So, how long you in Maui?" he asked.

"Just two more days. I have to get back to San Diego."

A slow song started to play. Rowan thought of himself as a decent dancer, but he had over-indulged on the coconut shrimp and rice. Not wanting to see his food again, but wanting to dance with Irene, he had waited patiently. Two bars of a familiar Van Morrison song played and his energies began rejuvenating.

"Let's dance."

Irene smiled. She was on vacation. She was at a party in Maui and she had been attentive to Rowan, who would normally have already known the color of her underwear by this time of night, but was so exhausted he had been struggling to keep his eyes open. She was a cute girl and so he had refused to let this opportunity pass him by, even though he knew he was too tired, too full and had too much to drink to do anything about it.

Irene was petite, brunette and she pressed herself into Rowan throughout the song. Her body told him everything he needed to know. It had been a lucky day at sea and it was shaping up to be a lucky night. They walked back to their table and sat down as the band took a break.

Dirty was held up by Kai as he poured himself into the chair next to Rowan. He put his arm around his friend, letting his secret affections show as men do when they drink.

"You look beat, man. Takin' up the pen made ya soft, bro?"

Dirty was only kidding with Rowan. They were all tired, but Rowan felt it was true. It had been a long time since he spent all day on a boat, even longer since he spent a day at sea.

Rowan grinned, answering, "That was the biggest fish of my life. I'm worn out."

"Take a lotta trout to equal that big blue, bro. Even you'll never catch another like that one."

The crowd had thinned. The other captains had already left the restaurant, as Dirty was quick to observe.

"First place and last captain standing," proclaimed Dirty.

Kai pulled him up from his chair and dragged him back onto the dance floor. Irene smiled and shook her head at the sight of Dirty attempting rhythm as the band played a steel drum groove. Rowan watched Dirty for a moment then turned to Irene.

"Irene, it's been a big day. I'm thinkin' 'bout going back to Dirty's and sitting in the hot tub. Care to join me?"

"I thought you'd never ask," she said as a deviant grin broke out across her face.

The hot water felt good on Rowan's tired muscles and Irene felt even better as she sat beside him, her bare breasts bobbing on the water like life preservers. They were the most perfect tits he'd ever seen in his life. She was pretty, fresh, and the look she was giving him was unmistakable. She was all his. Nothing could stop the course of nature.

Suddenly, the sharp pain came on again and he almost doubled over in the tub.

"Rowan, are you ok?"

What was he supposed to say? He couldn't tell her about this. If anything, he needed to go to bed with this sexy young girl and prove to himself that he was all right. Again, the pain went away and he caught his breath, feeling his body relax.

"Yeah, just a muscle spasm."

He couldn't believe it; he was in Maui, in a hot tub with a beautiful girl. How he did not have a raging erection was a question for medical science. Why he could only think of the growth on his testicle, he'd never know, but it didn't help. Despite the worry of his nether-region, he felt warm, relaxed and unbelievably sleepy.

He was awoken by the sun beaming on his face and his eyes felt like an ant on the sidewalk fried by a kid with a magnifying glass. He suddenly remembered Irene and he turned to face the other side of the bed. She was not there. The sheets were pulled back and he could make out the shape her body had made in the bed as she'd slept next to him. It all came back to him; the hot tub, feeling so tired, having to admit to an attractive, willing girl that he was too exhausted to have casual sex with her.

"Oh, god, I am getting old," he mumbled.

He got up and went to the bathroom, then made his way down the hall, which was filled with the giggles and whispers of Kai and Irene sitting at the kitchen table with their coffee.

"Mornin', ladies."

"Hey, sleepyhead," replied Irene.

Kai got up and took a coffee mug from the cupboard while pushing Rowan towards the table. She poured him a cup while he sat next to Irene.

Rowan leaned into her, whispering, "I'm so sorry about last night."

"There's nothing to be sorry about. I had a great time."

"Glad to hear it, but I'm still sorry. Sorry for myself. My loss."

"Yeah, it was, but it's ok. I guess catching the biggest fish in the tournament took all your manly strength."

Rowan smiled as he took a sip of coffee.

"Dirty still asleep?"

"Oh, hell, I am sure he is. He shut the place down, but I couldn't carry his drunk ass so I managed to shuffle him down the dock and put him to bed on *Stinky Fingers*," said Kai with a chuckle.

Rowan put his cup down. "He slept on the boat?"

Kai nodded, adding, "In the fighting chair!"

"What are ya'll doin' today?

"We're going shopping. There's a giclee gallery I want to visit and then we're going to the west end for lunch. Sorry, no dudes allowed," Irene replied.

"Good for you girls."

"What about you, Rowan?"

"I'd better go check on Dirty. We'll get some breakfast and then we have a boat to clean."

Rowan took a shower and thought about Irene. He probably wouldn't get another shot at that. He felt old. Damn, he thought, it was all just too much; big day on the boat, drinks, dinner and a good-looking girl warming his bed. He was disappointed in himself. To top it all off, he continued to worry about the pain he'd felt in his groin. Did he need another opinion? He gave himself an inspection in the shower and swore that the cyst had grown.

When Rowan left the house to check on Dirty, he grabbed a phone book and sat in the car in a parking lot making phone calls to clinics. He wanted to see a specialist. Of course he didn't have a referral, but after explaining his condition to a receptionist for the fourth time, he got an appointment with an urologist in one week. Good thing, as Rowan had begun to fear the entire island would soon know of his condition if he had to explain it again.

It had been three months since he'd first taken notice of the abnormality. He believed the growth had doubled in size. The pains had become more frequent and his anxiety about the situation had now increased. He was ready to not only see a doctor, but also to pursue answers to his questions and not settle for anything less. He battled fear constantly.

The doctor's office was small. A cramped waiting room with a couch and three chairs intimately close to the receptionist's window. It was an urologist's office so there was no doubt why anyone entered; they were having plumbing problems. An old man with a cane and his frail wife had entered just as Rowan sat down. Another man about Rowan's age sat at the other end of the couch from him as he filled out the questionnaire on the clipboard. It was embarrassing to be there and so Rowan was relieved that as soon as he completed his paperwork, he was called to follow the nurse and wait in an exam room.

The wait there was typically excessive, but at least he was not in the waiting room exchanging worried glances with the other patients. After a half hour, the door opened. A boy who had borrowed his father's white lab coat walked into the room. He wasn't old enough to shave, but probably did so just to prove he could. He looked like he should be skipping classes with his friends, at the beach.

"Good day, Mr. Sojourner, I am Doctor Terry. Tell me why you are here."

As Rowan sat on the exam table, he explained his cause for concern and detailed his symptoms. Doctor Terry listened and nodded before giving him the hand wave that must be universal for pulling your pants down and showing the doctor your package.

"This is not normal," said Doctor Terry, as he squeezed Rowans testicles like a kid with play-dough. "I believe it may be a tumor."

"What?"

"A tumor and I want to remove it as soon as possible. We will run a test to see if it is malignant or benign."

Doctor Terry said something else, but all Rowan heard was the word "TUMOR." His fear was correct, he had a tumor and now he would have surgery.

"I thought it was just a cyst."

"No sir, Mr. Sojourner, I do not believe so. I am concerned and want to remove it as soon as possible."

"My testicle?"

"The tumor, although there is a possibility the testicle may have to be removed."

"You telling me I may lose a doo-dad?"

"I am just saying it is a possibility. If so, you can lead a perfectly normal life with only one testicle or, what did you call it?"

"Doo-dad."

"Right. Don't worry about that. The important thing is that we learn what we are dealing with next week, okay?"

"Cancer?"

"Well, if it is cancerous, we'll talk about treatment."

"Like chemo?"

"Mr. Sojourner, it is too soon to talk about treatment options. I will not know what we are dealing with until we have the surgery, remove the growth and test it."

"How soon will we know?"

"We can perform the surgery next week and then wait about two to three weeks for the test results."

Rowan stared at the floor in defeat and disbelief. He half expected the doctor to tell him that he just had one doo-dad bigger than the other, to slow down with the ladies, take it easy, and to curb his drinking habit.

"Mr. Sojourner, we will do our best next week. Then we'll know exactly what we are dealing with. If it is cancer, testicular cancer is very treatable."

The doctor left and the nurse returned to draw blood and get a urine sample. Of all the smart remarks a man thinks of to say when returning a urine sample, Rowan's anxiety caused him to silently leave the container with her via the cabinet above the toilet. He left the doctor's office and immediately began to think of all the questions he had not asked.

Rowan went to the harbor and sat in the fighting chair aboard *Stinky Fingers* drinking beer the rest of the afternoon with Dirty.

"That's harsh, bro. Makes my nuts hurt just thinking about it."

Ron "Dirty" Sanchez was a good friend, but Rowan found it hard to swallow that he didn't have anyone else to tell. No wife, steady girlfriend or even a dog to confide in, to share what was troubling him. This had never occurred to him until now. For the first time, he thought about his mortality. If he died, his friends would play cards for his gear, but who would miss him?

Not knowing what to say, Ron continued anyway, "Look, bro, you stay here with us no matter what, Kai loves you and we'll take care of ya. Don't worry 'bout that, bro."

"I appreciate it, man. Fact is, I got nowhere to go, nobody to go home to. Ain't been a concern 'til now."

"So, when is the surgery?"

Rowan explained the procedure that would take place on Thursday of the following week. They sat there drinking beer in silence until the sun went down. Dirty's phone rang. It was Kai checking to see where the guys were. Dirty went down in the galley to reiterate over the phone what Rowan had just told him, further reinforcing Rowan's feeling of isolation. After a few minutes, Dirty returned to the deck.

"Ya hungry, bro?"

Rowan was. After all the beer, he needed something to offset the damage to his stomach.

Kai met them at the marina restaurant and they had dinner. When she arrived she gave him a big hug and a kiss on the cheek. Later, when they returned to the house, Dirty went to the back to take a shower and Kai sat beside Rowan on the couch.

"Ron's worried. I think he's more worried than you are."

"For the first time ever, I have something to be worried about and what's weird is that I wish I had someone to share my troubles with."

"That's not weird, Rowan. You've been blessed with good health all these years. But I know what you mean. Ron told me about the girl in Montana. I'm sorry, but for now you have us and we are here for you. I can take you to the hospital next week and when you wake up, Ron and I will be there."

"Thanks." He tried to hold back a ragged sob.

A week later, Doctor Terry met with Rowan for the pre-op

appointment.

"Today we will discuss what will happen next. Do you have anyone with you that you wish to be present?"

"No, doc, it's just me. I have someone to drive me home and take care of me, though."

"All right then."

The doctor explained the procedure and that there was a real possibility that he may lose a testicle depending on the size of the tumor. If necessary and if he wanted, prosthetics were available. After that, Rowan struggled to listen. The doctor said something about tests, taking it easy for two to three weeks and the possibility of chemotherapy, but it was all talk in a tunnel. Rowan was only able to focus on living with one testicle. Would he be able to have sex? Would he be able to come or would it only be half as much? What were the ramifications?

Seeing the worry in his eyes, the doctor explained that should he have to remove the testicle, Rowan would maintain his quality of life, including the healthy sex life that he had always enjoyed.

"If we have to remove the testicle, nothing will change. Let's wait and see. One step at a time, Mr. Sojourner," said the doctor.

"Words to live by."

The nurse was looking down at him when he opened his eyes, her round brown face coming into focus. She looked as though she had been watching him for a while, waiting like a loyal pup for the moment he would wake from the surgery.

"There you are," she said with a smile. "The surgery went well, Mr. Sojourner. I'll take you back to your room soon, okay?"

When his eyes focused again, the fluorescent lights on the ceiling of the hallway went streaming by like white lines on a highway in slow motion as his hospital bed made its way to a private room. When the nurses left, he pulled the sheet back to have a look. He didn't feel any different; he didn't feel anything, which is why he had to have a look. He slid his hands under the gown, felt his groin and his fingers found the sutures. It took a moment for him to process what his fingers did not feel. He had one testicle.

His mind raced with thoughts regarding his manhood and sex. He remembered the doctor's words of encouragement that nothing would change, but doubt took a stronghold in the front of his mind and drowned out all else. The room was exceptionally quiet and lonely. The television was on but he didn't watch it, the window was open but he couldn't see past the draperies. The doctor spoke, but Rowan barely heard him. He was released and Dirty and Kai drove him to their house.

Gorging himself on Thanksgiving luau pig helped to ease his anxiety as he waited for the next appointment. Time dragged by and he counted the days until he would know the test results. It wasn't all bad. He relaxed on the beach and took full advantage of the hot tub. If ever there was a place to recuperate after a surgery, Maui was that place.

When the appointment day finally came, Rowan drove himself to the doctor's office. He waited with the other patients in the reception area. He watched an old man and woman sitting side by side holding hands and exchanging worried looks and smiles. There was no one to talk to in the middle of the night, no one to drive him to see his doctor and no one to confide in except his good friends. For the first time in his life he felt lonely in a way that could not be curbed by seducing the nearest female. He was alone.

Rowan was stoic as the doctor explained that the tumor was cancerous. He had prepared himself for the worst because that was all he could imagine and that day he was thankful for his mental preparation.

"What's next?"

Doctor Terry seemed surprised at how well he had taken

the news. He pushed his glasses up on the bridge of his nose to refocus. He could skip the bedside manner. He appeared relieved.

He explained that a shot of chemotherapy would be required. The treatment would make Rowan tired, but would forego the side effects associated with mention of the word chemotherapy. Rowan was advised to bank his sperm before the chemotherapy treatment, although he put up a brief argument that it wasn't necessary. Doctor Terry would have none of it and before Rowan left the doctor's office his appointment was made. After banking his sperm, he would have one shot of chemotherapy and a follow-up visit in three months.

"So, how do you feel about having one testicle?"

"Well, I'm here. I just want to live. As strange as it is, now that I only have one, I don't feel any different and I haven't thought as much about it as before the surgery."

"Good," said the doctor. "I only ask because if it is an issue for you, you can have a prosthesis."

"How's that?"

"It's a silicone implant that will match your testicle, a very simple surgery. You can think about it."

"A silicone doo-dad?"

Rowan was surprised at how optimistic he was about the entire ordeal. He felt good. In four days he would have his cancer treatment. In three months, he would know if he was cured. He left the clinic feeling hungry. He stopped on the way to the marina and ordered two plate lunches to go.

Dirty sat on the bait box and shoveled the pineapple chicken into his mouth. As a piece of meat hung from the corner of his mouth, he nodded his head and listened to Rowan explain his impending medical itinerary from his seat on the fighting chair aboard *Stinky Fingers*.

"So you can have a fake nut?"

"Yeah, crazy, huh?"

"Wow, man." Dirty looked puzzled as he asked, "I wonder

if it makes a different sound?"

Rowan swallowed a big chunk of rice.

"What do you mean?"

"You know, the sound of balls slappin' ass. I wonder if a fake one makes a different sound?"

Rowan wasn't as surprised or amused at the question as he was that Dirty asked it with such genuine curiosity in the scientific value the answer held.

"I don't know," laughed Rowan.

"I'll bet it's louder, a knock as opposed to a slappin' sound. What's it made of?"

"Silicone."

"Oh yeah, definitely louder, bro. You should do it, dude. Get a great big one."

"I'm serious, man, I gotta decide if I give a shit that I only got one or if I'm gonna get a falsie."

They both rumbled with laughter. It was good therapy.

Rowan decided that day on the boat that he would make the best of whatever cards he was dealt. There were far worse places to exist while battling cancer and he was thankful to have his friends. Although he was lonely, he was not alone. If the doctor gave him his blessing in three months' time, meaning that if he had won the fight against cancer, then he would spend some time in British Columbia with Sid. Until then, he would work for Dirty while getting back to his book project.

And he did. Rowan stayed busy and the weeks that he had feared would be filled with the dread of waiting to learn of his fate, instead went by so quickly that before he knew it, he was down to mere days until he would go for his blood draw and CT scan. He spent Christmas with Dirty and Kai and went for a midnight dive on New Years' Eve. He put the final draft together on the book he had started while at Bishop's Place and sent it to Nancy. He had worked with Dirty and enjoyed being on a boat again. Before he knew it, it was March and time to visit the doctor for his report.

In those months, Rowan had a lot of hours to think. He had changed. He gulped at the thought, but he had grown in many ways. He'd reflected on the ordeal and he was proud of himself and the way he'd handled it. He also decided that it was time to focus on his newfound personal growth.

Rowan entered the doctor's office promising himself that he would take whatever news he received, good or bad, with optimism and determination. The door to the clinic felt especially heavy, like he was opening a tomb or perhaps like pushing the stone away and emerging to a new life, like a stone fly. Rowan preferred the latter.

He sat in the exam room watching the clock, which ticked with painfully slow movement. Fourteen minutes and thirty-seven seconds excruciating moments later the door burst open with enthusiasm, followed by the doctor.

"Good news, Mr. Sojourner," boasted an excited Doctor Terry as he pulled his chair towards Rowan.

"Pardon?"

"Looks like you are all clear."

"Really?"

"Fish, write, have fun and come back in six months."

Rowan's eyes welled with tears. He could keep living the life he wanted. He would enjoy the thrill of new adventures ahead and keep the promises he'd made to himself.

A turbo prop took him to Port Hardy on the northern tip of Vancouver Island, his home for the summer. He was welcomed back by Sid Gustofson. It had been years since Rowan had worked for Sid and he'd always promised to come back if Sid needed help. The resort, renowned for its quality salmon and halibut fishing, had attracted some high dollar clients that Sid felt may be a bit finicky for his younger guides. While in Maui, Sid and Rowan had broached the prospect of Rowan guiding the following summer in Winter Harbor.

Rowan agreed to the work if his duties ended at the dock, meaning that he did not wish to spend all night repairing gear, cleaning fish, tying tackle and living on four hours sleep a day. Life as a fishing guide was overrated and exhausting.

Rowan loved fishing and helping clients land fish, but he had no desire to spend twelve hours in a boat and eight more hours getting ready for the next day, plus he didn't need the money. So Sid had arranged for an apprentice guide to perform Rowan's menial chores. In exchange, Rowan worked for tips and could use one of the guest houses in the fall to write and use as a base from which to explore the island. He was looking forward to refreshing his mind with the details he would need to complete his novel, and he considered the work a great exchange for some peaceful down time in the fall after what would be a busy summer. Then, he would be on his way.

Winter Harbor was isolated from the world by a narrow gravel road that wound through the lush spruce-covered mountains of northern Vancouver Island. The road was not for the faint of heart and the only thing waiting for those who braved it was a remote fish camp. Rowan relished the quiet solitude of the harbor. When the fishermen left at the end of August he could write uninterrupted, drink coffee on the dock and count more bears, osprey and sea lions than people. He appreciated the buffer zone from the outside world provided by the mountains and the countless bays and inlets.

Quatsino Sound cut deep into northern Vancouver Island. Few places of such unspoiled beauty existed anymore. Sid drove Rowan to Coal Harbor in his pickup and handed him the keys to a jet boat. A group of fishermen was waiting at the dock for the shuttle ride to the resort.

The twenty-five-foot jet boat skimmed the water as the tide went out from Quatsino Sound to the Pacific. The travel time passed quickly as Rowan watched for hazards while passing otters, osprey and black bear. He had done this often and he welcomed the familiar sights as the water seemed to welcome him home. Rowan turned the boat north as Kain Island Lighthouse came into view. He throttled the engine down and puttered into Winter Harbor where less than a dozen people lived year round, most of them working for Sid's resort.

A meal was waiting for Rowan and the fishermen. Halibut steaks, clams, rice, shrimp and steamed vegetables were there for them at the resort. Another perk of working for Sid was the food.

The guests and guides fished hard and were rewarded three times a day with the finest seafood meals Rowan had ever experienced. The cooks did a perfect job, but the secret ingredient was fresh catches. Everything was caught by the cooks and guests.

It was a good summer of fishing, whale watching and boating. Rowan spent his days on the water, leaving the docks before sunrise. He would bring the guests back to the lodge at noon for a big lunch and a nap. At four, he left for another four hours of fishing. The long days were exhausting, but the reward was in the big fish, and lots of them. Rowan was refreshing his memory with details he needed for his next book in which the main character was a fishing guide in this area. He was reliving the finer points of day-to-day guide life. Those details would win the respect of his readers.

The greatest memory of the summer would come to be known as The Kain Island King. A phrase that Rowan loved so much, he decided it would be the title of his next book.

Rowan had four fishermen from Wyoming in his nineteen-foot open bow. The eldest of the Wyoming group, a short grey-bearded man known as Pops, was excited to be there with his two sons and grandson. He made it a point to tell Rowan that he had waited a long time to bring all the family together for this trip.

They had limited out on Coho Salmon and Halibut and each of them saved a tag to try and catch a big King on their last day. The group had agreed to get up early and let Rowan take them just outside of Winter Harbor to fish around Kain Island. As the boat puttered through the foggy morning trolling for salmon, the gradual appearance of daylight exposed the lighthouse atop the Island rocks. The old lighthouse had been used to signal ships of the protective harbor. The Kain Island Lighthouse was still maintained and regarded as the last such lighthouse a northbound ship would see as it made its way up the Pacific side of the Vancouver Island coastline.

It was an ominous morning. The fog was customary for this time of year. The locals affectionately called the month fogust instead of August, but that day it had been especially dense and as the sun came up, the clouds broke the fog into chunks. The lighthouse eerily appeared from the mist only to be swallowed up by the fog again.

Rowan loved mornings like this. Just witnessing the beauty of the morning with the steady low hum of the engine as he and his clients sipped coffee anticipating a strike was a thrill. It was also great fishing weather and his favorite time of year for the area.

Off the coast of British Columbia, the King Salmon spent the summer feeding their way up the coast to northern British Columbia and Alaska. When they reached their destined river, they would swim upstream, spawn and die. The more Rowan thought about that, it seemed to him to be one of the greatest miracles of life, death and survival.

As the Kings made their way up the coast, they gained about a pound a day, which was another amazing fact about the species. By August or fogust of every year, a lot of big fish were swimming up the coastline. Rowan was hoping to get one more King for the group and considered the eerie morning to be a good omen.

Two Kings weighing thirty-five to forty pounds were theirs by sunrise. The grandson, about fourteen, caught one of the big Kings. Everyone was happy. The boat circled the lighthouse for the second time. Rowan checked the two downriggers. Two other spoons trailed behind the boat. As they circled Kain Island on the ocean side, one of the rods off the stern doubled over hard. The reel whined as the fish un-spooled it.

Only Pop's tag remained unfilled so he grabbed the rod and with help from the others in his party, managed to hold onto it. Pop's sons helped him brace against the gun whale and the fight was on. One of the sons held onto Pop's belt, afraid the old man would be pulled into the ocean.

They had a big fish hooked and it was a King. The line would peel off the reel with a blistering whine and stop. As quickly as the line peeled off with the fish making a run away from the boat, the fish would run back towards the boat, causing a frantic cry from Rowan to "reel, reel, reel!"

Pops needed help so Rowan worked the boat against the current to keep the line tight. As soon as he would throttle forward against the current, the fish would turn and he would put the boat in reverse. Working against the current and the King made a tiring job for Rowan, but he was determined to aid his client in landing the mammoth fish.

Pops would work like hell to reel in the line that was becoming slack. It was all he could do to keep up. Just as soon as the fish neared the boat and the line was tight, the big fish would make another run, peeling off the line again and taking every inch of progress back out to sea.

Pops winced in pain as his arms ached, laughing as he did. The others offered to help, but Pops would not let go of the rod. The give and take repeated itself several times before the big King was beside the boat, exhausted.

Rowan leaned over and sized up the fish, which was close to the hundred pound mark, a record fish. It was too big for the net, so he grabbed the gaff. The guys were gathered around Pops taking pictures as he strained to hold the rod. The tired fish succumbed to its fate.

Rowan leaned over the side to gaff the King and hoist him

over the side.

"Wait!" said Pops. "I'll buy the tackle. Cut him loose."

Rowan was surprised, as were the others. The fish was exhausted, but it still splashed its huge tail beside the boat, jerking on the rod as Pops strained to stand. There was plenty of life left in the Kain Island King.

Rowan wanted to make sure the old man understood how big the fish was. He didn't want the old man or his party to regret their decision.

"Right at the hundred pound mark, Pops, probably a record fish."

"Let him go," repeated a smiling Pops.

The others patted Pops on the back. His sons shook their heads, beaming. Eyebrows were raised, but no arguments offered. Pops was old, but still the patriarch of the family.

Rowan agreed, saying, "All right then."

The fish might still live, may even make the trip up the coast and upriver to spawn. Or, it may die very soon. It didn't matter to Pops. What mattered was that the fish was old and its days were numbered. Pops didn't want the fish to die at his hand. He identified with the fish.

Rowan leaned over with pliers instead of a gaff and looked at Pops one last time. Pops nodded with a huge smile. Rowan clipped the steel leader and the fish calmly sank in the water. Then, with one last swish of its tail, it disappeared into the Pacific.

Pops let out a "whew."

All of the men shook hands and high-fived one another. Pops sat down. The leader would rust out of the fish's mouth. With as much life as the big King showed, splashing away from the boat and disappearing into the Pacific, Rowan was confident the King would survive.

"Nice fish, Pops. Nice fish," said Rowan.

"Thanks, Rowan," said Pops, looking up at him with a weary smile.

"You bet."

"Would you take us back to camp? I've had enough."

"Yes sir."

The group sat at the dining table back at fish camp. The coffee was hot and welcome. The Kain Island King was the topic of conversation. Rowan had brought the camp's fish log and they all hovered over the notebook looking at the entries and pictures of fish. Someone had scribbled that the world record was ninety-seven pounds, four ounces, and everyone agreed Pops' fish was just as big, perhaps bigger.

Pops just grinned. He couldn't have been happier if he were standing on the dock beside the bragging board with the fish on a hook, having his picture taken. After lunch, Pops and the others in his group packed their bags to wait for the shuttle to take them back to Coal Harbor, then to Port Hardy. There they would fly home with four coolers of processed fish minus one large King salmon.

Just before the shuttle departed, Pops handed Rowan an envelope. It was a customary way of leaving a tip for the guide, so Rowan did not open it until he lay on his bunk that evening. The five hundred dollar tip was accompanied by a note:

Capt. Rowan,

It was a pleasure fishing with you. We were lucky to have such a fine guide as yourself and the fishing was spectacular. Thanks for not arguing with me over the Kain Island King. You see, I have a feeling this was one of my last fishing trips. I'm an old and tired man. It was good to spend time with my boys and my grandson and the big fish deserved to live out his days. He earned it.

Your friend, Pops

The Kain Island King was caught and released on August third. A month later, the season's fishermen were gone with the summer and Rowan spent his days in a rustic one-room cabin sifting through his notes and finishing his book. With no women present, there were no distractions for Rowan. He spent all of his waking hours writing. He only stopped to walk the trail that went around the shore to the resort kitchen, which remained open for a few hunters. The harbor was so quiet that he slept like never before.

Sid knocked on the door one day with a heavy envelope with extra postage. Inside, were pictures of the Wyoming group led by Pops. There was also a decent photo of the fish just before Rowan had released it.

The note was from Pops' son telling Rowan that he had just buried his father. He thanked Rowan for the memories. It was sad to think that the old man had died so soon after his vacation, but Rowan remembered the letter Pops had written him before he left camp. Old Pops knew his days were numbered. He had one last great trip just like the big King Salmon that he released. Rowan fell asleep dreaming about the Kain Island King. He too had received a second lease on life, and felt a spiritual connection to the fish. He hoped the King's last days were good ones. That night, he dreamed the big fish made it past the British Columbia Coast and all the way up the Kenai River.

Chapter 8

Tee Time

"Will you please fix the god-damn gutter?"

Jack winced, keeping his back turned to her, squinting in anticipation of being hit in the back of the head with a frying pan, or Sadie's fist. He was halfway out the door, the smell of freedom filling his nostrils, and today, freedom smelled a lot like a fresh-cut golf green. He had a tee time that started in one hour. He was so close to being free of nagging and confrontation, just for one afternoon.

The sound of her voice pierced his auditory nerves like the wail of a prison siren and she stood there with hands on hips, pissed as a prison guard on a Saturday double shift. He knew her posture and expression before he even turned around to face her. Lately, he'd felt it would be easier to live with the gatekeepers of Auschwitz than endure living under the same roof as his beloved Sadie.

"Slipped my mind, dear, I will take care of it tomorrow."

"Your mind isn't the only thing that's slipping around here."

She felt its sting as soon as she said it. She wanted to take the words back; she was being a bitch and she knew it.

"What's wrong with me?" she asked herself.

She was always flying off the handle and feeling helpless

as her cruel words and unforgivable actions plagued her marriage. She was irritable, depressed, angry, and she felt like a klutz. She was constantly bumping into things. For months, she'd staggered through life like a drunk trying to pass a sobriety test. She blamed stress for all these strange feelings.

The marriage had been good until the last several months. Sadie complained about not feeling well, but was reluctant to see a doctor. She hated doctors and Jack understood, so there wasn't much discussion about making an appointment. Jack suffered her frightening mood swings in silence, although they had become more frequent. She was also battling bouts of depression, which lasted days or weeks.

Lately, when people asked Jack how long he had been married, he replied, "Long enough that I no longer look both ways before crossing the street."

They would laugh, he would smile, but he missed his wife and he hated how their marriage had become so contentious.

He wasn't sure if her mood swings and depression were a result of his actions, inactions or mere existence. He second-guessed everything he did. Maybe she was just unhappy with him and their marriage. What he did know was that he desperately needed to play eighteen holes and come home reeking of scotch.

As for the gutter, he could fix that tomorrow. It was supposed to rain tomorrow, but he wouldn't mention the forecast to her. Anyway, a gutter could be repaired in the rain, although that was a perfectly acceptable excuse not to fix the damn thing. However, a good day of slashing, slicing and cursing at a little white round ball while drinking should be void of water, unless it is your buddy's ball in the drink. Then it is perfectly acceptable, even entertaining. So, he would golf today, gutter tomorrow.

Jack let her hurtful words roll off his back as if he had waxed feathers. He didn't have the time or energy to fight and lately it was taking a lot of both time and energy. He knew he should turn around and comfort her, but he needed to get out of the house. He was tired of fighting and trying to figure out the cause of his faults. He sighed and adjusted the golf bag on his shoulder before continuing on to the car. He was going to whack the shit out of some balls today. If he stayed home, his own balls were in jeopardy.

Jack bit his lower lip as he shut the front door behind him. He didn't want to leave her this way, but he was too exhausted to engage her and he didn't have the time. He had to get to the golf course, and a tee time is one date when a man shouldn't be late. He tossed the clubs in the open rear window of the Cherokee and with a turn of the key he was on his way.

As soon as he turned the corner, he began to cry.

Jack drove into the country club parking lot and sat in the Jeep drying his eyes. He loved her dearly. Sadie had brought him pleasure, but lately, living with her was becoming a chore. He put his shades on. Then he walked into the bar and emerged with a scotch in his hand. He loaded his clubs into the golf cart.

Sadie had watched his car disappear down the street. When she closed the door, her anger had turned to tears.

She sat on the couch and wrapped her arms around her legs, curling up into a ball. She knew something was wrong. It was as if she was on the outside looking in, and she realized that she was not taking the necessary steps to solve her own problems.

With both hands she let go of her knees, deciding to sit upright and pull herself together. She wiped the tears from her face. As she did, one hand touched the bridge of her nose with her fingertips and gently swept over her eye like a squeegee, drying itself on her pants leg while the other hand, her right hand, gouged her eye like a Saturday night wrestler on cable television.

Her eye watered and stung. "What the hell?" she thought to herself.

She set her left foot up on her right knee and inspected her big toe. She had stubbed it on the corner bedpost two mornings ago hard enough to break the nail. It was bruised deep blue and hurt, a constant reminder of her lack of coordination. She felt like a big klutz. Then, she started recounting similar instances where she did something clumsy. Was it because she was depressed? Was she depressed because she was an uncoordinated, bitchy thirty-nine-year-old wife, or was something really wrong with her?

She got up and went to the bathroom off the foyer. Splashing cold water on her face, she wanted to freshen up, start over and begin anew. She dried her face and looked in the mirror, brushing her hair, not liking what she saw. To her, the woman looking back at her was old, worn like a dishrag. She had never been happy with how she looked and excessively exercised to achieve an outward appearance that satisfied her. She covered her natural beauty with makeup, increasingly so.

Sadie smoothed out her blouse and ran her hands down her sides to her waistline. Now, she felt like a bitchy, clumsy, ugly, fat, thirty-nine-year-old cow.

Sadie went into the spare room and pulled the bed sheet off her easel. The morning light shining through the window illuminated the cloud of dust that floated from the sheet down to the floor. Over time, the dust had collected to an amount that showed the neglect she had for the art that had once brought her great joy. It had been a while since she had felt compelled to draw anything. She picked up a gray pencil and began. She started at the bottom of the paper, creating the base of a mammoth tree. She drew a line that was far from straight, so she tried again and again but could not force her pencil to complete its intended route.

Instead of a thick round cottonwood with branches that spread out to provide shade, the crooked tree trunk looked like it belonged in a Dr. Seuss book, animated, but not as memorable, and void of childlike magic. She gave up on the tree and decided to draw the river beside the tree. The lines didn't need to be straight. No matter how much she concentrated, she could not manage to make her pencil draw what she wished. She tried until tears came to her eyes. Frustration welled up inside her and let loose with a torrent. She grabbed the easel and threw it across the room. The picture landed on the bed face up as if to ridicule her.

She gave up on the drawing and ran tap water into the stainless steel teapot. When it whistled, she pushed herself off the couch and dunked the chamomile bag in the teacup, looking out the window to the world. As she drank her tea, she realized even the long-awaited hot concoction left a bad taste in her mouth. Nothing was right.

The headlights of the Jeep shined across the lawn on Babcock Street and the front bumper brushed the empty garbage can that sat on the curb, knocking it over and sending it rolling out into the street. The sound of the metal can rolling on the asphalt awoke the neighbor dogs, who barked through their chain link fence, thus further announcing Jack's arrival home.

When he had retrieved the garbage can and put the clubs back in the garage, he took a deep breath and fumbled with the keys in the door of the dark house. The dogs continued barking to ensure the entire neighborhood knew Jack Gibbons was home.

He thought about making a sandwich, knowing he would sleep better on a full stomach, but the burrito at the clubhouse was waging a battle against all the scotch inside his colon.

Sadie wasn't going to be happy that he was home, much less that he was drunk and had an upset stomach. He took his place on the couch and was thankful it was at least a comfortable one.

"Are you drunk?"

Her voice was rather unsettling with the living room light illuminated overhead blinding his eyes, like a sign from God above that Jack had screwed up so bad that divine intervention had sided with her anger. The safe haven of the couch disappeared. Now, it was just a place to take his shoes off while he was interrogated. Yes, the Lord was clearly on her side, he thought as he again stretched out on the cushions.

"I may have had some scotch with my bad golfing, yes."

"Goddamnit, Jack! Do you know what time it is?"

The level of her voice was getting louder with each syllable, a warning sign. At any moment the floor would open up and he would be sucked into the underworld.

Jack responded with one eye open, "Time for me to sleep on the couch?"

Sadie stood over him, arms folded, scowling down at him. It would have been scary if it wasn't for all the walking and cursing he'd done for eighteen holes, as then he may have felt like fighting back.

"Why don't you want to talk to me, Jack?"

Jack's natural zest for sarcasm mixed with the scotch to form a response that dripped with disdain.

"Well, gee, dear, I can't imagine why I would not yearn to partake in another round of your emasculating banter. After all, being on the golf course all day, recording my miserable score, I haven't had my daily dose of insults."

"Fuck you, Jack. Fuck you."

"That may very well solve our problems."

He looked up at her and winked to test her response. Sadie turned on her heels and stormed back to the bedroom, leaving the living room light for Jack to turn off. She slammed the bedroom door.

"I'll take that as another no," Jack mumbled to himself as he turned off the lamp on the end table. He lay there only for a moment before he passed out, still in his golf clothes.

Sadie went to bed and lay awake all night scared of what was happening to her, what was happening to her marriage, scared of whatever it was.

Her increased frustration had pushed away her normal healthy sex drive. She had never taken anything to treat depression, not even when she was widowed with two kids. She was stronger than that. She hoped that in time she would conquer whatever was wrong with her.

Months passed and at times she felt like going to her doctor for help, but her headstrong stubbornness prohibited such an act of reliance on others, so she continued to suffer, her body continued to act on its own and her relationship with Jack increasingly became a rabid game of cat and mouse. When he withdrew, she scolded him; and when he tried to assist her, or suggest treatment, she bit his head off.

Chapter 9

Life's a Beach

Four months after Jack fixed the gutter, he convinced Sadie to see her doctor. She had been reduced to tears and was, after all, depressed. But depression didn't explain her increasing clumsiness, irritability and epic mood swings. She told him she felt like she was losing her mind. Jack felt he had lost his wife. The muscle twitching progressed.

She was also having increased difficulty formulating her speech. She'd developed a stutter as if she were searching for the right words. Sadie had always been quick on her feet when speaking. Her normal fast-paced speech pattern had digressed to a slower process, especially when she began a sentence. This infuriated her and worried Jack, even more than the lack of sex.

Jack went with Sadie to her doctor visit, where the doctor listened closely to her complaints concerning the mood swings and clumsiness. She referred Sadie to a Mayo Clinic physician who recommended testing for genetic disorders, as Sadie had been adopted and had no family history. She had felt abandoned by her biological parents and never had the desire to learn who they were or how they had died.

Her new doctors performed a single-photon emission computerized tomography (SPECT) scan. Sadie received an intravenous infusion of radioactive material, which was absorbed by her body tissue. Then she lay motionless on a table while the machine rotated around her, taking pictures. The poking and prodding of the tests robbed her of what remained of her dignity. She was at the mercy of the doctors and she hated it.

Jack felt the change in her, a surrender of sorts, which he never imagined was possible from such a resilient woman.

Confirmatory test results concluded that Sadie had Huntington's Disease, or rather, Huntington's Disease had her. A family history would have allowed her the knowledge that all along she had a 50/50 chance of inheriting the gene, and in her case, she would have then expected the death sentence.

Sadie had unknowingly carried the deformed strand of DNA like an execution date. The abnormality resembles a stutter in the genetic code, where a segment of the DNA strand is replicated and causes a mutation of cells, affecting the brain.

They sat stoic, holding hands in the exam room as they listened to their doctor tell them about the disease. If either had known what was in store for them, they would have been horrified; instead, they just sat listening as the doctor explained the ramifications of the disease and attempted to prepare them for its progressive symptoms.

The diagnosis explained her uncontrolled movements, decreased cognitive abilities and the current state of her mental health.

The initial diagnosis was neither horrifying nor relieving. There was a lot to learn. Sadie and Jack knew nothing about the disease. Together, they learned about 30,000 people in the United States suffered from Huntington's Disease and another 200,000 were at risk of developing the genetic disorder. There was no cure. The symptoms were merely managed with medication.

The disease affected people differently and its progressive stages were experienced at varying rates. In many cases, and in Sadie's instance, the disease manifested itself in the host's thirties or early forties. Sadie had just turned forty, which took all the jokes out of the over-the-hill birthday tradition. She never wanted to turn forty and she sure as hell wasn't ready to manage a chronic illness.

Jack was devastated to learn Sadie's peculiar behavior was due to Huntington's, but relieved that he alone was not the source of the problem. The team of doctors explained to Jack that Sadie would continue to have less control over her emotions and that eventually she would lose control of her body movements and functions. His role as husband and lover would change to caregiver with the progression of the disease. Jack feared for both himself and his wife.

Chapter 10

A World Away

The hull glided across the Caribbean flinging salty spray in Rowan's face. He felt the power and spirit of the ocean as he sat behind the sloop's giant stainless steel wheel. The sloop rolled with the sea's waves as gracefully as her name rolled off the tongue. Rowan sailed Savannah Jane through the Northwest Providence Channel, where the Caribbean Sea mixed with the North Atlantic.

A steel drum band blared out of the weatherproof speakers mounted above the radio, sounding across the deck of the sixty-five-foot sloop. The crew busied themselves reading about the new onboard generator. There was an engineer, a dive master and two deck hands. The cook chopped veggies in the galley, his knife expertly slicing the onions with each rise and fall of the bow.

As the Atlantic trade winds filled the sails, a group of divers from Canada stowed their gear, sat in the sun drinking rum punch and visiting. For the next two weeks they would sail together in the Exumas, diving and exploring. The divers were all scientists who returned to the same dive sites year after year conducting fish counts and underwater studies. Rowan would serve as their captain, guide, and in the event someone had too much rum punch, he would also serve as den mother. He would bring them safely back to port and oversee that the vessel was ready for another tour.

Rowan had been on the Savannah Jane as a dive master and first mate years earlier. Since then, ownership of the vessel had changed, but the old wooden sloop was just as he remembered. From bow to stern, she had more character than most people he'd met.

The trip was to be her last for a while and Rowan's last trip as her captain. The new owners had decided to give her some much needed updates and minor repairs. As soon as the trip ended, she would be docked in Nassau for months. Rowan had enjoyed being back on the very boat where he'd learned so much about sailing and was satisfied to have been her captain, but it was time to move on. He found the new owners of the ship to be difficult to work with, and after sailing for almost a year, he was ready to write again.

The sights, smells and sounds of Freeport faded behind them, also taking the daylight. When they stopped for the night, they would be south of Abaco. The ship would drop anchor in places like Harbour Cay, Orange Cay, Andros and Current Island.

The group sailed and conducted dive site studies, always leaving plenty of time to relax on the deserted beaches of the Caribbean. The coral reef research project was one that he had helped initiate years ago. He'd led a group of volunteers made up of divers, boat captains and researchers to conduct studies all over the Caribbean Sea. He was proud to see the project attract international attention and funding. Over the years, Rowan led many research expeditions such as this one, as scientists studied the reef system and invasive species.

It was a great last trip as captain. In Nassau, Rowan shook hands with the crew and waved goodbye to the ship. It was time for an adventure that involved dry land and a queen-size bed. The bunk he slept in aboard the ship wasn't large enough for him to roll over, and he was excited to trade his sea legs for land legs.

He spent the night in Nassau at the bar of an oceanfront hotel. The bartender was personable, but not Bahamian, rather Brooklyn. The place was too developed for Rowan to make a nest for long. The night sky was spoiled by the glow of so many lights and high-rise hotels. He needed to get away from tourists for a while and he knew just the place. He had once been to the British Virgin Islands and especially loved Cooper Island for its solitude. Years ago, he had made a friend there.

Rowan flew commercial to Saint Thomas and chartered a float plane that flew across Sir Francis Drake Channel to Cooper Island. In the old days, he would have bought a seat on the ferry boat. With only a land payment and respectable book sales, he could elevate himself to a higher class, that of chartered flights and oceanfront bungalows.

The plane was Rowan's idea of first class and what better way to arrive than flying low over the water, taking in all the shades of blue, as the plane cast its shadow over the reefs. The plane had made quick work of the trip, and with a skilled pilot and no other passengers, Rowan enjoyed watching the water like a kid seeing it for the first time as he listened to the hum of the wing-mounted engines.

The five rooftops of Cooper Cove Resort poked through the canopy of trees. There was the main house and dining area plus four guest houses. A walking path connected them all and a private beach further guaranteed solitude from what few adventurous visitors there were to the island.

With expert timing, the pilot killed the engines and the plane drifted right up to the dock. The proprietor, Bo, extended his callused brown hand. "Rowan Sojourner, good to see you again, mate."

A descendant of slaves and pirates, Bo had been the model for one of Rowan's first successful book characters. Rowan enjoyed listening to Bo's stories of pirates, treasure, ships and bad blood, some of which had been passed through the family for centuries and sworn to be truthful. Other stories were nothing more than bullshit, the truth being decided by the listener. Truthful or not, they were always good stories and Bo and his storytelling had been the inspiration for a bestseller.

"I've a lot of work for you if you're interested. I don't suppose you would like to trade your writer's cramp for a few calluses?"

"I'm here to finish a project."

Rowan explained his need to write and was given a hut farthest away from the other guests, a pale couple from Liverpool, who spent all day in the shade rubbing sun block on each other and arguing.

Bo walked with Rowan to his cottage and they passed the couple. Rowan waved and smiled. They stopped arguing, looked at him with raging contempt and resumed their argument over which strength of sunscreen to use.

Bo and Rowan strolled past them, listening to the exchange of sharp British words between the couple. Rowan wondered if liver spots were capable of burning. If not, then why bother with sunscreen. A chill ran up his spine as he kept the thought to himself.

When they were out of earshot, Rowan said all there was to say, "Lovebirds."

"Yes, mate, with any luck we'll be viciously attacked by sharks before growing that old and fussy."

They followed a stone path, in part covered by sand, to a square bungalow hidden from the remainder of the resort by thick mangroves. The only exposed view of the hut was to the sea. The area around the house was dotted by palm trees and ferns spread sparsely on the hand-raked sand around the bungalow. The steps led to the unspoiled beach and the ocean less than casting distance from the small covered porch.

"I'm glad you are here, mate; when you settle, come have a beer with me."

"Thanks, friend." They shook hands again.

As Rowan unpacked his duffel, he reflected on how fortunate he was to travel and write and be remembered by people he considered friends, people he had not seen in years. Bo had not seen him in two years, yet he welcomed Rowan as if he'd been gone a week, never asking how long he would stay or how he intended to pay. Rowan would have been happy making a bed in the activities shack among the sea kayaks and spare mooring lines.

Rowan had two spiral bound notebooks with every page containing scribbling for his next book, the pages torn, worn and stained from salt spray and coffee, almost illegible, but an outline nonetheless. He took them out of the duffel and set them on a table by the window. He needed to finish the book and get in some face time with his publisher, Nancy. She took him to great restaurants when he was in New York. He would share his ideas with her and she would comment. Usually, by the end of a dinner, he would leave the restaurant with a mental outline of his next book idea. Rowan would disappear for months and re-emerge thousands of miles from his last known location. Nancy was the only one in the world who understood and respected his need to mix writing with travel. She was certainly the only publisher who'd put up with his extended absences.

Rowan laughed at himself. He could make more money by working harder, but was timing his writing around salmon runs, fly hatches and off-season beaches. Rowan had been getting increasing pressure from Nancy to be more dedicated to his book tour, but she recognized the motivation and ideas he received from his travels.

All he had to settle in with was a pair of pants with zip-off legs, sandals, two pairs of shorts, four shirts and underwear that looked as old as the last boat he had captained. The salt air and sea had been harsh on his clothes, which were in dire need of replacement, but that would have to wait until New York. There wasn't much shopping to be had on Cooper Island, thank God.

Having unpacked, Rowan put on a shirt and fastened the bottom two buttons, letting the breeze fill the cotton and swirl around his back. He walked up the beach to the main house to have a beer with Bo.

A few things had changed since he last visited the island; now new French doors opened to the entire ocean side of the dining hall, and what once was a thatch roof deck with a bar made of crude lumber was now a full-fledged island bar. Steel beams supported the open air rooftop, which covered a thickly lacquered mahogany horseshoe bar.

Rowan sat down running his hands across the wood. Wherever the bar had come from, it had endured a long boat ride. Bo came up behind the bar and opened two beers, sliding one down the smooth surface, where it came to a stop precisely in Rowan's hand.

Bo had been watching Rowan absorb the beautiful wood. "Hope you agree, mate, that I spent the money wisely?"

"Indeed. Nice bar."

"Judging from the check you sent, your book has been a success."

"It's done well. Your stories were an inspiration. You spent your share beautifully."

The first royalty check that Rowan received from his novel had gone to savings, new clothes and a restored 1954 five-window step-side Chevy pickup. When the second check arrived in the mail, he was stunned, and thought back to when he first had the idea for the novel that launched his career.

He and Bo were sitting at a table that was still resting in the sand nearby. They were drinking and trading stories. Rowan's stories involved his fishing excursions, but Bo's stories spanned centuries. His father and grandfather had told him many tales and Bo had always been listening, especially to the details. He was in his forties and had never watched a television show. These stories were entertainment and Bo's were oozing with characters. So, Rowan's first book idea had been born from those drunken tales on the beach at that rickety old table and he had sent a sizeable check to Bo to show his gratitude.

Rowan spent every day under the shade of a palm putting the finishing touches on the final draft of his latest creation. He resided in a weathered high-back wooden chair. When he wasn't pecking away at his laptop, he was peering over the screen at the other islands sticking up out of the water like giant tree-covered camel humps. He stopped only to charge the battery in his laptop, which coincidentally was also enough time to swim parallel to the beach, to the front of the main house, have a beer with Bo and walk back with a cold Heineken.

Mostly, he wrote all day beginning as early as four a.m. He let his ideas or the sounds of the beach wake him; birds announcing the break of dawn, the wind in the palms or some mornings the rhythm of the waves, washing on the beach. Their call was too strong for him to lie in bed, drawing him outside to the chair. The urgency to write a new novel consumed him.

The low battery icon appeared and Rowan realized he had forgotten to charge his spare. It was too nice a day to move inside and resume writing. He took the laptop inside and plugged it into the wall. He grabbed his snorkel mask and waded into the water until it was up to his hips and he fell forward with relief. He swam parallel to the island, pausing to observe a spotted drum patrolling just above the sponges and coral. The drum swam close enough to detect Rowan was empty handed, and then he slowly swam into deeper water.

When Rowan came out of the ocean and onto the white sand, he was within sight of the bar. As he walked, letting the warm breeze dry him, he heard a woman's thick English accent buzz from the bar down the beach, just as colorful as a hummingbird.

She was thin, with long arms and much longer legs. She was English, but with her dark tan, had to be a local, definitely not a tourist. As he came towards her, he heard the conversation with Bo was about ferry services to the islands from Saint Thomas. She sounded like a resort operator. Rowan sat down one stool away from the discussion that politely paused to include him.

Bo set down the glass he was drying and put a Heineken on the bar in front of Rowan, who hardly noticed the beer. He was preoccupied by the striking woman who held her chin in the palm of her hand and, with her elbow on the bar, met Rowan's gaze with a beautiful smile. Playing host, Bo introduced them.

"Rowan, meet my friend Claire."

Rowan stuck out his hand and noticed that it shook with nervous energy.

"I'm pleased to meet you, Claire." He was surprised at his own voice inflection, as he swallowed hard and tried to not sound too excited.

"Claire and her husband, Clark, own and operate a resort in Road Town," added Bo.

"The pleasure is mine," she said as she smiled. "Bo has been telling me about you."

"Well, then, it's a good thing I showed up to defend myself."

Claire laughed and it was intoxicating. She had a wide mouth, thin lips, and white smile, sexy. They started a conversation that came easy and was hard to walk away from, so neither tried. She told Rowan that she enjoyed riding the ferry once every few weeks to Bo's place, having a beer and getting away from her responsibilities for an afternoon. She was flirtatious, an extrovert with more character than a wooden sloop and as lovely as a coral reef. Brown eyes, short sandy hair escaping from under a ball cap advertising Village Resort, and nut-brown skin too smooth for sand to stick.

Rowan melted as her accent and voluptuous lips lulled him into a trance of beer breath smiles. They traded funny stories about clients and she told him about the resort she and her husband owned. She crossed her legs as she sat on the stool facing him.

"The islands would be a perfect retreat for an author to ponder his next novel."

"I could easily call this home, but I have too many favorite places," he returned.

This had been a stopping point for him to gather his thoughts and finish his book, but it would make a great home. He entertained the idea as he listened to her talk. It was such an appealing accent, refreshing, but there was a lot more to her.

When her ferry was empty of its supplies and ready for the trip back to Tortola, Claire stood up, straightening out her shorts and shirt. Rowan accompanied her to the dock and wondered why he did so.

She said she didn't want to leave, but it was the last ferry of the day. Work and a husband were waiting for her back on Tortola.

"Do come see us, Rowan," she invited, extending her hand for a shake.

"I promise."

He gave her a grin and they stood there as their hand-shake evolved into hand holding. Claire looked back at the boat waiting for her. She squeezed his hand. She had strong hands, rougher than the rest of her, from working ropes and cleaning decks. Her smile had turned lustful. Her fingertips left the blade of his hand and brushed his palm.

"Goodbye," she murmured, turning to board the boat.

"Bye."

Rowan waved and headed back to the bar. A woman like that, so full of life and charm, could make a man accept the idea of being tied down. He sat at the bar, shaking his head in disbelief. She was heavy on his mind for someone he'd just met. He had not been with a woman in a long time. Sadie had created a stretch of celibacy that had enabled Rowan to focus his energies on his work instead of women. He was eager to see her again before she was even out of sight.

On cue, Bo appeared behind the bar as Rowan sat on his stool. Bo had done an Oscar award-winning job of pretending not to listen to Claire and Rowan, appearing busy after introducing himself and showing up intermittently for snippets of conversation.

"So, you like Mrs. Dennon, do you?" asked Bo with a sly grin.

"How well do you know her?"

Bo shrugged his shoulders. "She comes over once a month or so to visit with us. She is very intelligent, asks a lot of questions, wants to know everything about everyone, but volunteers very little information about herself. I hear her husband is a drunkard, but she never mentions him or his drinking. I do know that she enjoys getting away now and again. My wife loves to visit with her as well. When they get on a roll, they are loud like two seagulls. She comes here to escape from something. Hearing the rumors, I imagine it's to get away from his shameless drinking. She says he's a good bloke. Everyone else says he's a bloody drunk."

Rowan interjected, "The poor woman is hooked on your exhilarating conversation."

"Bloody right!"

The two of them laughed. Bo's tone became more serious as if to impart information he had left out or suddenly wished to reiterate.

"She comes over here to get away from him, always goes back. Good woman."

"Yeah, well, like Bob said, 'no woman no cry.'"

Bo laughed, "Right then."

The next time Claire rode the supply boat to Cooper Island, it was one week later. Now, Claire had on make-up and her hair was braided. Her khaki Capri pants were snug and showed off her figure. When she got off the ferry, she walked up the beach to the last bungalow, bypassing a visit with her friend Bo. Rowan lay in the hammock beside his bungalow in his trunks, laptop on his bare chest, reviewing his work. Her light footsteps were obscured by the waves on the shoreline.

She stopped a few feet behind him and unbuttoned the top of her powder blue blouse. There she leaned against a palm tree and watched him for a moment before announcing her presence.

"I was thinking it's a good day for a swim."

The familiar voice shook his bones and he almost flung himself onto the sand trying to escape the rope hammock. She looked more beautiful than he remembered, more beautiful than he had dreamed of her. Before he could say anything, she held his hand and placed it around her waist. Rowan's kiss was drawn to her mouth. He couldn't have resisted if he had tried, which of course, he didn't.

She stepped towards him and he cradled her face in his hands, kissing her. She kissed back more forcefully than he expected, propelling their encounter past many levels all at once. They were kissing like reunited lovers making up for lost time. There was no need to rush, yet it was as though a train was approaching that would whisk one of them away from the other forever.

Claire pulled her blouse over her head to reveal her round breasts tucked in her white bikini top. She unbuttoned her pants and Rowan slid them down her legs as he kissed her firm belly, revealing her bikini bottom. They moved to the water kissing, like two crabs stuck together, dancing their way to the safety of the ocean.

"This is a nice surprise," he finally said.

"I've been thinking about this since I left here last week. I imagine you will soon leave and I wanted to see you one more time."

"You'll make me a home-wrecker."

"My home has been wrecked for a long time. I want you to touch me the way that you've been looking at me."

With that, Rowan put his hands on her neck and drew her close to him, the water up to their waist as he kissed her slow and hard. When they finally caught their breath, Claire pulled away from him with a smile, as if contemplating her next move.

"You didn't really ride that boat over here to swim, now did you?" asked Rowan.

Claire's look was coy. She kissed him and wrapped her legs around him as he carried her up the beach to the bungalow. When the ferry left Cooper to go back to Road Town, she wasn't on it.

They lay in bed making love, talking and laughing. Believing it wouldn't last, neither was speaking of tomorrow. He had committed adultery and the crime felt good. Rowan realized that he could feel like he had years before. He was still the man he'd always been, even better. He was proud of his performance and he'd felt her satisfaction as her trembles of exhilaration rippled throughout her body and were echoed within his own.

Claire had yearned to be touched for some time and all her loneliness had been washed away by his deft moves. She needed a man to make love to her. Her husband had touched nothing more than a bottle in years. He wouldn't even notice she was gone for the night.

They drank coffee on the beach as the sun came up. Their morning-after conversation was deliberate and easy. He made a quick breakfast in the tiny kitchen of the cottage and afterward they lay in bed again.

"I hate to leave, but when the ferry arrives, I should be on it."

"I'll take you."

Rowan borrowed a boat without question from Bo and took Claire back across the channel to Tortola. The sea was calm and the hum of the twin outboards drowned out the world. For a time, it was just the two of them alone on the ocean, alone in the world. Claire leaned back into Rowan as he sat at the wheel and he wished the five-mile boat ride had lasted forever, especially as the port, shops and people of Road Town came into view. Before she stepped off the boat, he could see she wanted to be back on Cooper Island as much as he did.

"Promise me that somehow we will see each other again," she said.

"I'll be at Bo's a few more weeks; we'll find a way."

He docked quickly and she stepped off onto the wood planks, mixing with the hustle of the market crowd, looking back once as Rowan turned the boat to the Sir Francis Drake Channel.

Rowan docked the boat and went straight back to his laptop. The past night had rejuvenated his creative process. He hammered away at the keys for hours and when he finished for the day, the night stars spread like a blanket across the sky. He lay in the hammock watching them shoot and fall. He thought about Claire and what she must be doing at that moment. He loved the way she felt, the way she talked and the way he felt with her in his arms.

He made a wish.

Chapter 11

Shipwrecked

Claire had arrived home to find Clark passed out on the kitchen floor. It was almost noon. There had been a day when she would have woke him, or at least tried. There was a time when she had spent all night cleaning up his filth, but she no longer cared to do that. She still loved him, the man he had once been, not the conch shell of a man he had become. Besides, there wasn't time to tend to Clark, there was work to do.

Claire's day began around 4 a.m. every day. She felt fortunate to live in the islands, but owning and operating a demanding resort in the Caribbean had become a living hell, even though it was smack dab in the middle of paradise.

She imagined it would be different if her husband was sober enough to fix the compressor, operate a dive boat or even clean up after himself. She had quit asking him for help and stopped yelling at him in frustration years ago. Perennially pissed, she loved and hated him and had entertained thoughts of an accident that would claim him. She saw more and more every day, he was killing himself.

Their only son, Eric, lived in Liverpool. It was difficult being that far from him. Claire felt like an awful mother, a monster, but knew he was happy there. Claire's parents were dead and she had secretly wished the same fate for Clark's parents. George and Audrey Dennon were the most miserable people she had ever met. They came to visit the islands from time to time. When they did, Claire left to stay with friends. She had tried for years to win Audrey's respect and approval, but had given up. It had been liberating for her, although one more hardship for her marriage.

Claire cleaned laundry in between answering the phone, booking guests and attending to the needs, wants and complaints of her guests. She did all this while stepping over the mound of her lifeless husband who still lay on the floor in a heap.

She understood his frustration, anger and self-loathing and imagined her understanding was what prevented her from getting on a plane, a boat or a rubber raft and leaving him to die in a puddle of piss and pity. She couldn't explain why she stayed, not to her friends, nor to herself.

Clark had once been Captain Clark Dennon of the British Royal Navy. His demise began when his ship and his title had been taken from him in a debacle of navy politics, along with a slight collision with another vessel, which belonged to an influential individual of royal descent. The last time he was sober was when he had returned home to Claire and they decided to move to the British Virgin Isle of Tortola to escape the embarrassment of his misfortune and take over his family's dive resort business.

Clark's mother and father had operated the resort for a few years, as a hobby and a symbol of status to their friends in England. They hired the labor, rarely getting dirt under their fingernails. When the novelty wore off, they yearned to retreat back to the social benefits and shopping of London. Clark's brother wanted nothing to do with the business or the island on which it stood, so Clark and Claire took over and had prospered for a few years, until Clark's drunken tirades ran off all but the most loyal of friends. They had managed to buy the resort from Clark's parents, which gave them some liberation, although George and Audrey were quick to instruct them, especially Claire, on how to do everything from book keeping to laundry. So she had learned to avoid speaking to them on the phone or in person, having mastered avoidance maneuvers to an art form.

The last time she had called upon Clark to perform maintenance on any of the equipment he lost two fingers in the flywheel of the air compressor they used to fill dive tanks. Asking for help in the islands meant waiting for days for it to arrive. Claire learned to fix things herself. She learned to take care of the business, and her own needs.

In the beginning, she had tried to stop Clark's drinking, but after a few years and more than a few fights, she just let it go. The resort was big enough to allow her to stay away from him and let him do as he pleased. Meanwhile, she ran the resort as she pleased. Leaving Clark meant leaving the resort, so she stayed.

Claire enjoyed the business. She loved the hustle of managing a resort. She loved the people who worked for her. She loved looking out her window at the orchids, frangipani and coconut palms, bougainvillea and the ocean view. But as the years passed, clients became more demanding, equipment was in need of replacement and help was increasingly hard to find. Her quick escapes to Bo's on Cooper Island were her only breaks from the demands of the resort.

When the phone rang, she was completing the payroll. She picked up the receiver and immediately regretted having done so.

"Claire, where is Clark? We have called for days with no answer. Our concern is escalating."

"Hello, Audrey."

"Claire, how is Clark? Be a dear and fetch him to the phone?"

"Audrey, your son is passed out on the floor in a deep sleep, again. I'm afraid he cannot speak at the moment."

"Oh dear, Claire. How could you let it come to this?"

"Do not blame this on me, Audrey."

"Claire, you tell Clark we are coming to take him back to England. George and Wallace are here and we will begin packing immediately."

"Will do, Audrey. I cannot wait to see you all."

Claire slammed the phone down on the cradle and screamed, "Bloody hell!"

She could cry, but there was no time. She could not withstand her in-laws mothering Clark while his brother Wallace ambled about the resort pointing out its inefficiencies. She could hang herself or run and hide. So, she pulled her hair back in a bun and went to find Ernest, the manager. She explained that the Dennons were arriving soon and that she had to leave. He shook his head in disgust. His frown softened when she offered a sizeable bonus for tolerating the in-laws.

"I'll not return until they are gone, gone, gone."

Ernest did not ask questions. He loved the resort and when Claire made a promise to him, it was always good. Her promise of a bonus for keeping the resort in operation while dealing with the Dennons was well worth it. Besides, he knew as well as anyone that she deserved better than the lack of attentiveness of her husband and the mistreatment his disease dealt her. Ernest had seen the Cooper Island boat arrive last week and watched from the market as Claire had stepped off. He had seen the American steer the boat, had watched them smile at one another and he had seen the change in her over the last week. She was in love and he was happy for her.

Two days later, Claire watched out her window as the trio of Dennons ambled up the walkway to her door. Through the walls of the main house, she could hear them complaining. Their voices carried above the birds and over the wind chimes, piercing her ears like squeals from a thousand dying rabbits.

From fifty yards away, she could see their elongated faces dripping with aristocratic pretentiousness. People like that carried themselves a certain way, as if the ground they walked on would elevate them above all others.

Her bags were packed and waiting in the boat. She had loaded the boat overnight and had returned to fix breakfast for Clark, who had been too drunk to sit at the kitchen table and eat. He was asleep on the tile floor in the bathroom. At least the in-laws would see a prepared meal in the kitchen when they spoke ill of her duties as a loving wife, while wondering where she was.

She didn't wait around to listen to any of it. Nothing would be good enough, especially her. As their voices neared the porch, she fled out the back door and down to the dock. Claire loosened the ropes and pushed the throttle forward on the Bertram bound for Cooper Island. The only pang of guilt she felt was not calling her son to let him know where she would be. She looked back at the resort and imagined the Dennons in her home. She cried all the way across the channel.

Claire powered the cabin cruiser straight to the cottage where she hoped to find Rowan. From a few yards offshore, she could see the empty hammock. The chair sat occupied only by a button-down shirt left draped over it. The laptop was open and rested on the table under the porch. He wasn't at the cottage, but he was still here.

There was a dinghy tied to a buoy on the Salt Island side of the bay just out of view of the bar. As Claire eased the cruiser up the beach to anchor point, her worries ran deep that perhaps Rowan had other company. She leaned over the bow, retrieving the buoy and anchor point with her gaff. With this came the realization that she did not need to get away from the in-laws as much as she needed to see Rowan, and hoped to find him needing her.

Rowan was seated at Bo's bar and had helped himself to a bottle of beer from the cooler. His back was turned to the beach. He was anxious to see his new home in Montana, do a quick book tour and some fly fishing, but he wanted to see Claire again. Leaving the islands was not going to be easy this time.

Claire clipped the anchor line to the boat's bow, threw her pack in the dinghy that was tied to the buoy and with nervous energy she rowed to shore.

Bo watched from the restaurant as the familiar cruiser anchored, and he recognized Claire getting in the dinghy. He walked outside to the bar and leaned over it, addressing Rowan.

"How is the book coming along, mate?"

Rowan was elated to have the question posed to him. He was anxious to talk and had been wishing he could talk to Claire.

"On the final draft now. I feel good 'bout it."

"Are you returning to Montana or planning on growing roots here?"

"I need to go."

Bo nodded. Then, as Rowan took a swig of beer, he was met with the smiling face of his friend who pointed out to sea.

"Well, mate, good luck with that."

Rowan turned on his stool, following Bo's finger pointed at the dinghy headed for shore, and saw there none other than Claire Dennon.

She tossed him the rope tied off to the stern. He caught it with a smile and slipped a knot over the dock cleat, holding his hands out to her. Claire stepped out of the boat, her heart beating fast from rowing and the sight of him. They stood holding one another, letting the breeze flow over them.

"I hope you don't mind my appearing unannounced?"

"No, ma'am. Not at all."

"I had to see you."

"I'm glad."

Rowan kissed her forehead and hugged her tight.

"I will have to go back, but I cannot stand those people in my home. And I refuse to endure the hardship of their visitation, knowing that you are here and I'm not in your arms."

He took her hand in his and they went back to his cottage.

"I want you."

"I want you too, Rowan, that is why I am here."

"Yeah, but I think I might also… need you…."

"And I need you."

She stopped him in mid stride, and with a hearty two-handed grip on his forearm, she spun Rowan around to face her. She gave him the kind of kiss that comes from unbridled passion. They stood there, their foreheads together, looking into each other's eyes.

"Yeah, but I can't have you, you're married. You may not want to hear it, but I have feelings for you, feelings that I can't hide. It's a road I don't wanna go down."

"Don't then. Do not hide your feelings."

"Girl, you'll be gone in a day or so, then where does that leave me?"

"You're not the only one running, Rowan. I believe that this was meant to be." Claire began to cry. "I cannot be strong anymore. I need you."

They left the cottage only to eat and swim, remaining wrapped up in one another like two teenagers. On the third day, Claire returned to Tortola to a home emptied of her in-laws and drunken husband. Rowan left to continue his adventures in hopes that eventually they would meet again.

A year went by and then another. For Claire there was tourist season and the off season and through it all she continued to care for Clark who returned home after an unsuccessful rehabilitation. She thought of Rowan and grew more hopeless than ever.

Snow fell and melted. Rivers swelled and fish spawned.

Rowan continued his travels and his writing. He thought of Claire often. The seasons changed but the longing for one another never did.

Chapter 12

Welcome Home

When Rowan stepped off the turbo prop in Bozeman, it was a clear spring afternoon. Now and again, a shard of green grass could be spotted in between the dead brown growth and patches of white snow. His fingers pulled a single key from his pocket, which fit the 1954 Chevy Step Side pickup waiting in the short term lot. Storm had dropped it off for him earlier in the day. A bottle of wine was on the seat with a note:

"Welcome home, friend, and happy forty-fifth. I hope you will be pleased with the progress on the house, almost done."

The old Chevy rattled down the gravel road as the sun sank into the cottonwoods. The workers were long gone for the day, but there it was, home. Small, cedar-sided with a river rock chimney and a huge deck. Rowan had pictured himself sitting on that deck many times, before the house was ever built. He thought about giving up traveling for a while and getting a good dog, maybe a Labrador. Every man needs a dog and every dog needs a porch. This one looked like a good place for a man and a dog to grow old. Maybe one day, he thought.

Rowan stood on the newly stained deck looking at the river. It was quiet and peaceful, serene. Yes, this was still his favorite place. Of all the wondrous locales he had visited while fishing, writing and seeking adventure, this was it, ten acres on the Madison River in Montana. It was still as breathtaking as he had remembered it. He had to admit that the romantic in him just wanted to keep reliving those days on the river with Sadie, many of which had occurred right here on the land he now owned. The way she made him feel, so proud and thrilled, the way she looked at him; all they had wanted was one another.

He thought of the women he'd held, hoping for a woman to make him feel like Sadie had. Claire had been a wondrous encounter. He yearned to hold her again, though she was married; he shook the thought from his mind, thinking time would fade his memory of her. He had an interesting love life, flawed as it was; nevertheless, it was exciting and he was the envy of his friends. But he was never satisfied. Rowan had long ago decided that he'd been given too many opportunities to be happy that he had passed by, and Claire was a constant reminder of that. Their timing was bad. Wherever she was, he hoped she was happy and well. Those were the two women over whom he seemed to have no control. Life's circumstances had denied him a future with either woman. He thought of Sadie again. Strangely, he could feel her presence.

He looked across the river, through the cottonwoods at a newly constructed home similar to his, but with an enormous great room with high windows that watched the river. Someone else had the same idea as he did, to build on the river overlooking this beautiful spot.

He was glad to at last have his dream home, and although he had traveled the world, his travels were far from over. He was the author of eleven books. Rowan had established himself as a bestselling author, expert on international fishing and an advocate for the preservation of natural resources. He was proud of his accomplishments and now he was wishing for someone to share his life.

Jack scrubbed at spaghetti sauce stains on the counter

and cursed. He had hired a maid to help with the chores, but she simply didn't show up a second time. Sadie didn't like her and although she could no longer form a complete sentence, she let him know that she did not approve of the woman. She would sit and stare at the woman, shooting her glare that ran right through her like a dagger. Sadie's contorted face was hard to read, but her eyes were still capable of a penetrating disdain.

Jack shook his head as he sprayed Formula 409 on the bar. Sometimes a husband does know what his wife is thinking. Through the helplessness of her deteriorating state, Sadie was still the woman of the house and Jack would have to find someone she approved.

It was her house, the one she had worked for and dreamed of. Jack just went along with the building process because that was what she wanted. He had been happy living in town; as nice as it was living on the river, he still missed visiting with neighbors across the fence and being invited to golf on a regular basis. He missed the social benefit of their old house in town and had let her have her way with building a new one, hoping the new home would lift her spirits as she struggled with Huntington's Disease. The best part of the new house, however, was its close proximity to great fishing. It was the river that made the house a home and he thought it to be a great trade for the over-the-fence visiting and driveway greetings that make up suburban life.

Sadie's chair was parked in its usual spot by the window. Outside, robins were fighting over the birdfeeder. Sadie watched them cocking their heads, pecking at one another, chirping and flying around the yard. She wondered how long it would take her to die. Would she waste away to nothing? Would she die of some other disease? Or, would she choke to death on her next meal? It was a concern now that Huntington's had disabled her ability to swallow efficiently. She was imprisoned with her thoughts, unable to walk, talk, or move of her own volition. It was painful for her, and a burden to Jack.

If she could drive herself off a cliff, she would have done so a long time ago. Sadie wished that she would have when she first learned that she had the disease. Back then she had no idea what was in store for her or Jack. The degeneration progressed quickly. Some people live with the disease as victims of the involuntary muscle movements that make them look as if they're doing some satanic dance. Their arms and legs and facial muscles flail about of their own free will in every direction. This debilitation is commonly referred to as Huntington's Chorea.

In Sadie's case, she had lost her coordination and the ability to walk. Then she had trouble moving her arms to reach for things. Her depression progressed and she aged rapidly. Her once beautiful skin turned yellow and loosened around her bones. She looked decades older than her fifty-four years.

In the beginning, she quit looking at herself, the changes in her appearance too shocking and rapidly deteriorating for her to accept. But now she would occasionally look in the mirror when the hairdresser came over to fix her hair. It was a treat that Jack felt was good for her spirit. She wasn't able to go to the beauty parlor, or to town for that matter. They had quit those excursions long ago, unable to tolerate people staring at them. She could hear their cruel whispers. Those that knew her did their best to avoid her, crossing the street or acting too busy to talk to her when she was able to go into town. She had stopped leaving the house long ago. At one time, it was too much trouble for them both, but now it was impossible. She sat in silence with her thoughts, watching the robins and listening to Jack curse in the kitchen.

His foul language was reassuring, telling her that he was there. Listening to him curse to himself and at inanimate objects made her comfortable. It was cute, the way he stormed about the house declaring war on grease and grime, burning eggs and breaking fragile wine glasses. He had a god-given talent for breaking wine glasses. He broke one earlier in the morning washing dishes and was still picking up the thin slivers of glass all over the kitchen. He directed his next proclamation to Sadie.

"This god-damned faucet is a chunk of shit, Sadie. I can never get the water temp just right. Either too damn hot or too fucking cold, son of a bitch."

If Jack had been looking at her, he would have seen her attempt to smile. It was funny to her, the way he mumbled curse words around the house. It was good for him to vent and he did so without upsetting her. His words never varied more than an octave or two, almost in a monotone. It was just the way Jack communicated. If he was speaking, he was likely cursing.

He was the only man she ever knew that said goddamn whether he was happy or mad. "Goddamn, it's good to see you," or "Where's my goddamn keys," was proclaimed with the same level of enthusiasm. Jack made cursing an art form.

Jack stepped back and surveyed the kitchen with great satisfaction. "Motherfucker is clean now."

He needed to find more help around the house, and missed going fishing. He wasn't living the retirement that he and Sadie had planned, neither was she. With the exception of the house, they had lived a frugal existence and planned to spend their winters vacationing in Europe. Now, their savings were quickly depleted by doctors, home health nurses and other caregivers.

Jack whipped the kitchen towel from his shoulder to wipe his hands as he came to sit beside Sadie.

"Goddamn birds are having a field day, aren't they?"

Sadie moaned what Jack understood as agreement. She unfixed her gaze out the window and stared at the pack of cigarettes on the table nearby. Jack picked up on her change in focus, he was good at that.

"Want a smoke, dear?"

Sadie blinked her eyes at his question so he lit one and put it in her mouth. He lit a cigar and they sat there smoking together. Jack had to make sure that she didn't burn herself. Smoking was the last thing she had any control over. More and more she could not eat whole foods, and she had to give up drinking wine. She had once been a busy woman, involved in various social events, so being confined to a chair was excruciatingly painful for him to watch. All she had left was smoking and she smoked more than ever, secretly hoping for cancer. She smoked the cigarette and then she had another.

"If it's all right with you, dear, I believe I'll go fishing this evening," said Jack as he watched a purple smoke ring evaporate overhead.

Sadie appreciated the way he included her in his thoughts. She wanted to touch his hand and tell him that sounded like a great idea, but she couldn't. She loved him for acting as if she could stop him, like she would ever say no.

Rowan worked the fly low over the Madison and aimed for a rock protruding from the water. The Royal Wulff set on the water between the ripples like a real bug. It began to swirl on the current as it floated toward the granite rock, which sat in the middle of the river, dissecting the current and creating a calm pool of water downstream. As the fly floated beside the rock, it disappeared with a violent splash.

Rowan set the hook as the line stretched and the fly rod bent. The Brown Trout made a run upstream. Dominant and hungry, she'd seen the fly enter her domain by the rock and had gobbled it up. Unfortunately for the fish, this fly had a hook in it. The fight was on.

The brown made a fast run, peeling line from the reel. Then, as quickly as it had fled with the current, the big fish swam back downstream faster than it had run away from him. Rowan wound the reel to keep the line tight while the fish tried to shake free of the hook. He dug the felt soles of his waders into the gravel river bottom, the current pushing against the sides of his knees. Rowan continued to reel in the line and the big fish began to tire.

The rod bent and doubled over as a flash of color appeared under the water just a few feet in front of him. She had to be five pounds and fat as a football. Rowan held the rod in his right hand and un-slung the landing net with his left. He leaned forward with the net in the water and pulled the rod behind him to inch the fish closer. With one last splash, the brown trout shook the tight line violently and with a snap, the line uncurled loose and coiled up on the surface of the water. The fish was free.

Rowan stood holding a straight rod with stretched mono-filament line. The distorted line resembled broken thread that once held a button to a shirt, as it floated on the water swirling around his knees. The big fish would live another day in the Madison.

"A good fight," said the voice from across the river.

Surprised, Rowan looked up to see a fisherman who had arrived during the excitement and instead of taking up a spot on the river for himself, had stopped to watch. The man was dressed in waders and a red plaid shirt with a tattered fly vest that had to be as old as the wearer's fifty-something years. His entire wardrobe was ripped and torn, most likely from crossing through barbed wire fences in order to reach his fishing destinations, a sign of a tried and true sportsman. Poking out of his white beard was the red stub of a smoldering cigar, glowing and dimming like fire from a friendly dragon's mouth.

"Good fish. A picture would have been handy," Rowan replied.

"I'll serve as your witness. You had him until he saw that damned net, probably seen that before. Look at it this way, you're educating the fish."

"Yeah. No fish left behind."

Both men gazed at the river, which had returned to tranquility. The man puffed the cigar as Rowan wound up the loose line from the water's surface back onto his reel. They paused to look at the water for a moment, the current carrying away the sediment that Rowan had disturbed while standing in the river, evidence that this fishing hole had been thrashed enough for the afternoon.

Rowan was more than halfway across the river now, which was a bit wider than a two-lane highway, the June water thigh-high on him, pushing strongly against his legs. Rowan stared out at the river, the bearded man and the roofline of the new home behind him through the trees.

"That your place?" asked Rowan.

"Belongs to my wife. She lets me live there. Sometimes I even get to sleep inside," replied the smiling man.

Rowan took the sarcastic banter as an invitation and he carefully picked his way across the Madison to meet his neighbor. It was a short walk that became easier the closer he came to the opposing shore. Rowan's felt soles went up and onto the sand bar and crunched the gravel.

The old man extended his hand. "Jack Gibbons."

"Rowan Sojourner. Good to meet ya, Jack. I'm your new neighbor."

Jack glanced across the river and nodded. "Nice house. Perfect location."

"Thanks. I always wanted to move back here and live on this stretch of river. Fond memories."

"You sound like my wife. For years she insisted we buy this place, said it was a very special place to her. Then, she became ill. So, you from here?"

"The short answer is no. But this has always been home to me. I went to school here, financed the downtown bars some years ago."

"So you're a banker?" Jack asked.

"No, just spent a lotta time and money there."

Jack led the laughter that they shared. "I understand," he

said as he bent down and extinguished the stub of his stogie on a river rock. It had become short enough to singe the hairs on his beard. "What do you do now?"

"I'm a writer, but to keep starvation at bay, I was a river guide for many years," he replied.

"I'm not a reader, so I am impressed by anyone who can read a book, much less write one. My wife on the other hand reads quite a bit." Jack looked at the ground, adding, "At least, she used to read a lot, not so much anymore."

Inside her home, Sadie watched from her wheelchair. She could hardly see Jack through the trees as he stood on the riverbank. He appeared to be talking to another man fishing in the river. That was Jack, she thought, always chatting it up. He had been given the gift of gab and she was instantly attracted to his incessant banter; it was a rare thing in a man. His gift had been handy now as her affliction had all but completely obliterated her ability to speak. Her speech had quickly digressed to mumbles and slurred words and then suddenly, almost overnight, it had become non-existent. Now, he spoke for both of them, a task that perhaps he'd been born to perform.

She communicated her needs by looking at objects and blinking her eyes. Jack's ability to talk and ask questions resulted in her having only to blink her eyes quickly at the phone when asked if she wanted Jack to call the kids so they could talk to her, or she would stare at the remote when she wanted the channel changed.

Sadie's condition had digressed rapidly since she turned fifty. The last few years had been a living hell. She'd not been able to work in a decade. She felt like a burden to Jack and her caregivers. She knew what housework had to be done, but all she could do was sit, stare and wait for Jack to do it.

As Sadie was left with her thoughts, watching her husband through the window, she saw on the shelf in front of her a book by her old love, Rowan Sojourner. One of her caregivers had left the book for Sadie to read, but before she could do so, her disease had taken away her ability to hold the book. She started the novel, fell ill with the flu and in the interim of setting the book aside, had lost the ability to hold a book open, something even a child could do. She wanted to read the book her old lover had authored. She at least wanted someone else to read it to her, but her nurses were busy caring for her, she didn't want to burden them any further. Jack wasn't a reader; she knew it would be tortuous for him. So, the book sat on the window sill, dust collecting on its fading cover. She looked out the window again.

Rowan pointed the tip of his fly rod upstream. "I haven't thrashed the water up there in that big hole and am ready to call it a day, so it's all yours."

Jack replied, "Well, I'll go see if I can't get a piece of that action."

He dug inside his fly vest and produced a cigar still in its wrapper. Jack held it out to Rowan. "Here, neighbor."

"Hey, thank you very much," Rowan smiled. "Nice to meet ya, Jack, and good luck."

"You too, Rowan, see you on the river again soon."

Rowan made his way back across the Madison as Jack walked the shoreline upstream. Jack seemed like a decent fellow. He may be a good neighbor and if not, there was the river to separate them. He grinned as he hiked back up the bank and through the trees to his home. The sun was settling in the western sky and its light filtered through the large windows of his home. Rowan set his fly rod down on the deck, went inside and grabbed a bottle of beer. He returned to the deck to watch the sunset.

The granite and pine on the distant Spanish Peaks turned pink for a moment before the last rays of the sun left the Montana sky. Four beers and one hand-rolled cigar later, it was dark and the stars were one by one showing up for their night shift. Rowan felt a peace fall over him. It was a peacefulness that he had could not remember having before. The memories he made here long ago were just that, memories. Now, this had become his special place, though the reasons were twisted. It was home now, a good place to grow old, but at times like this he wished he had a woman to share it with.

He heard the breeze rattle the aspen leaves near the river then he felt the cool night breeze crawl over him, refreshing at first, then eventually forcing him into the warmth of the house.

Chapter 13

Good Morning, Sunshine

Jack dumped a half cup of fresh blueberries in a blender. He cut up a pancake and added it to the blueberries. A few seconds on the puree setting and the bluish concoction was ready. He carefully poured it into a plastic cup and shook a can of Reddi-whip. Jack squirted the whipped cream on the top of the slurry and stuck a plastic straw in it.

Her food needed to be pureed to avoid her choking. It was hard for Jack to prepare the food for her. He hated the thought of feeding her food from a blender. They used to go out to dinner a lot, they enjoyed great food together. She was also an excellent cook and he often thought about all those wonderful meals they had together. Now, it was like trying to feed a baby bird.

"Good morning, sunshine."

Jack pulled the down comforter back and positioned his wife upright. Just a few months ago, she was able to lift herself up, now he had to hold her. Her body was a rigid twitching alien to them both.

"Breakfast is ready," he said, helping her slide her legs off the bed and into the wheelchair. "How's blueberry pancakes sound?"

She sounded out a weak and garbled "yes, good" that broke Jack's heart. It was more of a mumble, unintelligible to anyone else except Jack, like only a parent can understand a toddler learning to make new words. She used to be such a morning person; now, Jack had to be the morning person.

Jack hated mornings.

Sadie smiled. It wasn't the bright smile that he remembered from years ago. That smile had given way to mood swings and depression. Many times, Jack had to close his eyes and remember how beautiful her smile had been. But it was a reminder that his Sadie was still in there somewhere.

His love for her ran deep and he liked caring for her, but when a man dreams of growing old with a woman, he thinks of daily walks which over time become shorter, spoiling grandchildren together and arguing over the thermostat. He never thought that he would be the primary caregiver, dispensing medications and scheduling doctor appointments. He was irritable enough when he had a head cold. Sadie was the strong one. She had been sick for years and the diagnosis she endured had come over a decade ago, but he continued to adapt to his ever-changing role as her condition spiraled toward complete incapacitation.

Jack pushed her wheelchair up to the dining room table. He sat beside her and held the cup of breakfast.

"Reminds me of those tropical drinks in Hawaii," he reminisced.

Sadie leaned forward. Her eyes were set on the straw, but her body, her head, her mouth would not go where she intended. This was the hardest part of the disease for Jack. This strong woman so full of life and independence could not even drink through a straw without help. It crushed him, but he did his best to hide his heartbreak. There was no time for it anyway, too much to do. He'd hired the nurses to bathe her, he had done it, but it broke his heart seeing her naked and helpless and he had gladly relegated that duty to others less intimate with her. He was busy enough cooking and cleaning.

He held the straw to her mouth.

Swallowing solid food had become a task. One Sunday morning, a month ago, they were having breakfast when Sadie choked on a piece of sausage. Jack had given her a few pats on the back and it became dislodged, but he started thinking about how dangerous it was for her to eat solid foods. A feeding tube would be next. They were fifteen miles from the hospital, much of it gravel roads, and an ambulance may not be able to reach her in time. He cringed at his own dismal thoughts.

Jack needed help. The home health nurse stopped by three times a week, but it wasn't enough. Sadie needed more care than he could give. A nursing facility was out of the question. He wasn't at his wit's end and even if he was, a nursing home would not be an option for Jack. Putting her in a home was akin to throwing his wife away. He was going to have to draw more money out of retirement in order to provide better care for her.

Jack had always felt that Sadie had chosen him. She was so strong. Her mental and physical prowess so abundant, she had always dominated her environment. It's what made heads turn when she walked into a room, it's what opened closed doors for her and it was what made Jack instantly fall in love with her. She floated around a room like a butterfly, mingling with the powerful, and making the wallflowers of the room feel comfortable. Wherever she was, she owned it. He was still in love with her, but he missed that strength in her.

Jack knew that soon she would lose the ability to control her bladder, her last stronghold of dignity, and that her dementia would get worse. Though she seemed to communicate enough to fulfill her needs, he missed their conversations. It had taken her condition time to gain momentum, but now she was deteriorating rapidly. Still, he realized her condition was mild compared to the battles with Huntington's chorea. Instead, Sadie just seemed to be losing control of herself, an irony that seemed so unfair since she had always been in control of everything. It made Jack sad, yet he was thankful to be able to care for her, this miraculous shell of the woman she once was, still his beloved wife, though often unrecognizable to others closest to her.

Sadie sipped the blueberry pancake concoction through the straw. She had lost her ability to tell him exactly how grateful she was. She was certainly unable to show it, but she was still a woman. With an uncoordinated hand, she clawed at Jack's arm and tried to smile, but it was more like a grimace. It worked, though. Jack smiled back at her and kissed her on her forehead.

"I love you too, sweetheart," he said. "Now, can I get you anything else?"

Sadie tried to shake her head no as her torso moved uncontrollably side to side. Jack understood. She was finished with breakfast. Jack unlocked the wheels and moved her to the big picture window overlooking the backyard and the river. Sadie stared out at the tall grass bending with the breeze, through the cottonwoods and aspen to the Madison River. The sunlight filtered through the leaves fluttering in the wind and the rays of light fell onto the water, sparkling like diamonds in the morning sun.

Chapter 14

Fishing Buddies

Rowan had watched the old Jeep Cherokee roll into the drive from the county road. He wasn't sure who it was and he didn't care. He was sitting on the deck in the late summer sun, soaking up the warmth like a turtle on the sandbar, more than halfway through a bottle of Argentina Malbec.

"Howdy, neighbor," said Jack as he stepped onto the deck.

Rowan sat up in his chair, ignoring proper etiquette when guests arrive. He was too baked by the sun and wine to stand and act chipper. Then, he saw it was the neighbor he'd met on the river two days ago.

"Hey, Jack. How ya doin' today?"

"I'm great. Too nice a day to spend inside. Thought you may want to go fishing, but it looks like you are doing all right."

Rowan looked up at Jack squinting from the overhead sun. "Where ya wanna go?"

"Well, if you have the time and another bottle of that wine, I'll drive us over to Cottonwood Creek. I hear they are hitting caddis flies and this afternoon should be perfect."

Rowan lifted himself out of the chair with a groan and stepped inside the sliding glass door just long enough to retrieve a glass for Jack and fill it with malbec.

"Lemme get my gear," said Rowan as he went back inside.

Jack stood holding a glass of wine below his nose, inhaling the fumes as his gaze went through the trees and across the river to his own house. It looked great from here. He had not enjoyed the view to his house from across the river. It made him proud. The way the cedar and glass reflected the sunlight warmed his heart. He wondered if Sadie could see him on their neighbor's deck. Was she watching? Could she even see that well anymore? Or, was she with the health nurse, Judith? She was probably getting a bath.

Jack wished he could have Judith come to the house every day. A nursing home was starting to make sense. Caring for Sadie was emotionally draining and he had always been challenged when it came to domestic chores. He also needed time to be a man, have some space, visit with a neighbor, drink wine, fish and escape. He felt guilty fleeing the house, but it was something he needed. If she could see him standing on their neighbor's back deck, she would be happy for him.

Jack's guilt session was interrupted as Rowan emerged from the house wearing his fishing vest with waders draped over his shoulder, a rod in one hand and a bottle in the other.

Rowan topped off both their glasses with the bottle that sat on the railing. "How far a drive is it?"

"About one bottle."

"Glad to meet a fellow Montanan who knows how to properly measure the length of a trip in ounces rather than miles," Rowan announced with a smile.

They loaded Rowan's gear into the back of the Jeep. Jack drove and talked about his recent trip to the fly shop downtown. Rowan listened as he took in the scenery, his head heavy with malbec.

"New line and backing, eighty-five goddamned dollars! Christ!" cried Jack. "At least I got some good information on these flies. I always wanted to fish this stretch, just never made time."

Allen Andrew Cooper

Rowan could not count the times he had fished where they were going, but it had all taken place a long time ago when he was in college.

"Been meanin' to go in there, maybe get a new rod."

Jack continued crying, "Well, let me tell you, they can smell a goddamned dollar from a mile away. Saw me and my money coming and took it, man. You would think if you buy a new reel, they would put the goddamn line on it for you... free!"

Rowan imagined the young store clerk sizing up Jack and concluding that he was incapable of efficiently spooling the line on the reel and so he didn't offer the service as an option, but as a necessary measure to ensure his client could be on the water soon instead of spending all day creating nesting habitat for birds, and returning to his store dissatisfied. He kept the thought to himself.

Jack downed his wine like a thirsty frat boy happy to be away from home. Rowan wondered what had driven Jack out of the house on such an unplanned venture, but he didn't ask, only guessed; after all, Jack was married. The man just needed his space. He had long ago learned not to ask those questions, they usually came with lengthy answers requiring attentiveness, care and concern. If Jack wanted to talk about it, he would say so.

Rowan watched a flock of Mallard ducks taking off from the water, splashing and kicking their way into the air and flying over the water just inches above the surface. Then there were the pelicans floating downstream. Rowan's favorite bird, because sitting there on the water, they looked completely without grace, but in flight, the great white pelican is the epitome of grace, the B-52 of the bird world. The two men drove in silence, watching the river as much as the roadway before them.

This stretch of the Madison was beautiful. He had not been this far west on the river in years, not since his early days as a guide. They drove past the landing where he and Sadie had floated their inner tubes. That had been over twenty years ago and it was so vivid in his memory that he once again felt as if she was there with him. They turned off the highway as Rowan reached in his vest for the wine opener and pulled the cork out of the new bottle.

The river was peaceful. The summer crowds and tourists were gone, leaving the water, fish and the last rays of summer light to the local fishermen who kept honey holes like this one a secret.

The Jeep arrived at the public access parking area just as the sun dipped in the western sky. The air cooled. As the trees and setting sun cast shadows on the river, the water began to bubble with fish hitting the surface. Thousands of Blue Winged Olives were flying around, some settling on the water's surface only to be gobbled up by rainbows, browns and brook trout.

With Rowan's first cast, the fly disappeared in a fury of fins and water. As quickly as he could unhook the fish, he made another cast and soon had released four fish in a row. It was a spectacular sight; fish jumping and bugs swarming in the last light of a waning afternoon.

Rowan stood in the river taking it all in as Jack appeared. He had been busy getting his new reel ready and was eager to fish. Jack walked downstream and eased into the waist-deep water. He peeled some new line and cast to the opposing bank, careful to let the fly land lightly on the surface and swirl under the earth where the river had carved its way under the bank. The splash was so loud that it caught Rowan's attention fifty yards upstream. And, if that wasn't loud enough, Jack began to laugh in excitement as the big trout ran up and down the river.

"Ha ha, yes! Goddamnit, yes!"

Rowan wound up his line quickly and waded to the bank. He traversed the rocky shoreline towards Jack. This would be a good one to watch. He stood in the river a few feet behind Jack, as the line stretched and the rod jerked erratically when the fish swam for deep water and switched directions.

It took several minutes, but the well-hooked fish began to tire and Jack reeled it closer to him. Rowan grasped his landing net in his left hand and eased it into the water beside Jack then stood there motionless, waiting to scoop up the brookie. A healthy specimen, fat from feeding all afternoon, it looked as if it had swallowed a football. Jack released it, puffing on his cigar.

Light was fading fast. They had only been out for a couple hours, but the fishing had been good and the catching had been even better. They climbed up the riverbank back towards the Jeep and together took one last look at the river. A cloud of insects swarmed over the water as the crickets began their evening chorus from the tall grass that lined the bank.

Jack let the tailgate down and retrieved the bottle from the front seat. An afternoon out of the house was just what he had needed. He was rejuvenated. That glorious fish had given him a new attitude and a refreshing outlook. Rowan watched his new friend silently gloating.

"Nice one, Jack. Well played," encouraged Rowan.

"Thanks. Thanks for coming along."

"I wouldn't miss this for anything. Easy to forget little treasures like this place. They're all around us. I'm glad to be at a place in life where I can take the time to enjoy it," said Rowan as he poured a dose of wine into a Solo cup.

Jack nodded in agreement, saying, "Yeah, I know what you mean. Too many years I spent working and not taking the time to spend an afternoon like this one."

The two men watched the last of the sun disappear over the mountains. Each of them still wore their waders and fishing vests. Jack unzipped a pocket on his vest and retrieved two cigars. He held one out for Rowan.

"Don't mind if I do," said Rowan.

They drove slower on the way home, the sense of urgency

no longer in Jack's right foot as he kept under the speed limit. He could feel the wine in his head and wanted to be extra careful. There were deer everywhere and several crossed the road in front of the Jeep.

It was well past dark when they arrived at Rowan's house. They agreed to do it again soon. There are few things finer in life than catching fish and getting drunk, thought Rowan. It was good to bond with one another fueled by alcohol and at the expense of simpler organisms such as fish and grapes. Rowan revisited the spectacular afternoon of fishing with his neighbor and new friend. The stars were out in the clear sky so he sat on the deck, taking in the peaceful surroundings and keeping a red wine headache at bay with more red wine. Life is good, he thought. Life is good.

Jack entered his home elated and unsteady. He hadn't had that much to drink in years; he'd simply been too busy. He sure as hell wasn't accustomed to drinking the good hooch that Rowan had served up. The young nursing student was on the couch watching television. She graciously accepted the hundred dollar bill he handed her. His time out of the house and worry-free care for Sadie was worth every penny, as he explained to her.

"Can you come back Monday?" Jack was a bit embarrassed as he realized the question was more enthusiastic than required. He felt guilty for having a good time away from Sadie.

She sleepily nodded yes and Jack was already planning another fishing trip with his new friend. He opened the bedroom door and watched Sadie sleeping soundly. Soon, he would join her, but not before a sandwich.

Across the river, Rowan admitted he was haunted by Sadie's memory. All his life he had wanted to build a home here at this very spot. He thought of today's drive along the river. While listening to Jack bitch about how much money he had spent, Rowan's thoughts were filled with the memory of a day on the Madison those many years ago. He felt her presence all around him. It filled his head with memories, some of which made him smile, but the clearest memory of all was her slipping through his fingers.

When the night air made him shiver, Rowan went inside and sat on the couch inattentively watching a re-run of a college football game. Sports Center came on and his mind drifted to Tortola, to Claire Dennon.

He changed the channels until he came to the ten o' clock news. A black bear had destroyed a cabin east of town, effectively robbing the cupboards of jars of peanut butter and several bottles of Marionberry wine.

The homeowner, a woman with a New England accent as heavy as the bags under her eyes, was upset that her cabin window had been broken and her cupboards clawed open. A police officer explained that the fish and wildlife department would trap and relocate the bear. He looked like a department veteran who wanted nothing to do with the absurdity of getting upset over something as trivial as a bear in the house. The microphone was shoved even further into his face. "Trapped and relocated all because he likes peanut butter. Who doesn't like peanut butter?" he asked with a grin as he patted his paunch.

This took Rowan's mind off women and suddenly he became hungry. The bear had a good idea, he decided, so he made a sandwich.

Rowan's peanut butter sandwich paired with an already open bottle of Shiraz was satisfying. The sweet berry flavor of the wine acted like liquid jelly for the sandwich, a good blend since he was out of milk. Yes indeed, peanut butter and wine, too bad he couldn't compare culinary tips with the bear. He decided that he'd go to the store in the morning. Maybe he needed to clean up the house, get groceries and make it a well-stocked home. That would boost his spirits. Whatever he was going to do, it would wait until tomorrow. He fell asleep on the couch with the television on.

Chapter 15

Looking Out My Back Door

Rowan woke to an infomercial selling an abdominal exerciser. The house was dark, the remote still in his hand. He yawned and smacked his dry lips. The peanut butter residue had formed a hardy caulk inside his dry mouth. A very fit and young man with a ponytail was talking excitedly to his television audience. Rowan turned off the T.V., got up and made a cup of coffee. Today, he would do something productive, or maybe he would just go fishing.

That's it! Fresh trout for breakfast, thought Rowan. He drank a cup of coffee on the deck, assembled his gear and ambled down to the river. His jeans were dampened from the dew on the morning grass; his open-toe sandals filled with cold wet grass seeds. He did not care. He was going fishing right behind his house, time to reap the immediate reward of living on the river.

In a few minutes, he was casting in one of the deeper pools downstream from his house. Sunlight had yet to permeate the canopy of cottonwood leaves that covered the river. He tied on a fly that resembled a mosquito and three casts later, breakfast was on the line. The Rainbow Trout was an eight-inch fish, just the right size for a fry pan and enough to pair with two scrambled eggs.

He stood on the gravel shoreline with his pocket knife

relieving the fish of its entrails. A Clarks Fork Nutcracker flew by and lit on the ground like a Central Park Pigeon waiting to be hand fed, pecking away at the gut pile, showing little concern at the presence of a human.

The Nutcracker picked up a beak full of breakfast and flew off as a much larger magpie landed nearby. The black-and-white bird kept a safe distance from Rowan, not as trusting as the Nutcracker. Magpies were wary birds, while nutcrackers are commonly called camp robbers, for their bravery wherever food is involved. He trudged back to the house as more magpies gathered, pecking at the entrails and at each other.

The river is life. It gives and it takes.

As Rowan ate in silence, he decided fresh trout for breakfast isn't a delicacy spoiled by regularity. It is reserved for a few special times. There is a draw to a fish-and-egg breakfast that fulfills the primal instincts in a man. It makes a man feel like a man to catch and eat his own breakfast, except for the egg, thought Rowan. Chickens are incredibly messy and eggs would just have to be purchased at the store. It was also good to turn on the gas stove, as opposed to being forced to build a fire. Primal instinct's good, modern tools better.

Rowan devoured the pink meat with his eggs and toast. Breakfast was interrupted by a rap on the door. As he walked towards the front door, Rowan could see the front grille of the Jeep parked in his driveway. A rush of panic swept over Rowan as he wondered if his neighbor was going to be more of a pest than fishing buddy. He opened the door and welcomed Jack inside.

"Excuse me if I'm interrupting…."

Rowan shook his head, "Naw, naw. Just finishing breakfast. Come on in."

Rowan opened the door wide, motioning for Jack to step inside. Jack removed his hat; he was smiling like a kid with a new plan for a backyard rocket ship.

"I really enjoyed fishing yesterday and wanted to know if

you would go again?"

"Well, lemme think," he said drawled, while still chewing trout, "I've an awful lot to git done…sure, where ya wanna go?"

"I have a nurse to stay with my wife overnight Thursday. If you're up for it, we could drive over to Ennis, get there in time to drown some flies, stay overnight and fish the morning before coming home," said Jack, eagerness showing on his face as he waited for Rowan's reply.

"Well," said Rowan, "I can't imagine anything on my calendar more important than fishing."

Jack, long deprived of male companionship, added, "There's something else…."

Rowan quit chewing his breakfast. He moved a thin bone to the corner of his mouth and slid it out the corner of his lips, then discreetly removed it and set it on his near empty plate.

Jack wasn't sure how to ask his new friend into his home. It was something people do every day, but Sadie's current condition made it difficult. He didn't know how Rowan would react to his frail wife twitching uncontrollably and unable to contribute to whatever conversation came up. On the other hand, Rowan seemed to be open-minded and he didn't want to apologize for his wife. She was the love of his life and he wanted Rowan to meet her.

Here it comes, Rowan thought to himself. He's known me a couple of days and he's going to ask me to help him in the yard or chink the logs on his home. There was awkward silence between the two men as Jack searched for words he had already rehearsed while the fear of tree trimming, leaf raking and plumbing projects filled Rowan's head.

"I would like you to come over this evening for a drink, meet the wife."

Rowan was relieved he wasn't being asked to help Jack stain

the logs or some other horrid chore. He was being invited over for a casual get-together. Thus, his response was more excited than socially required.

"Sounds great. What time?"

Jack still seemed nervous. He twirled his brown ivy hat on his fingertips.

"I just want to tell you in advance that my wife is very ill. She has Huntington's Disease, which denies her the ability to move freely, talk and recently, chew her own food. Some people, close friends even, cannot tolerate the sight of her. If you're comfortable with it, if you don't mind—"

Rowan interrupted him. "Jack, thanks for the invitation. I would love to meet your wife. What time?"

A relieved Jack replied, "Five."

Chapter 16

Meet My Wife

Rowan knocked on the stained glass and cedar door. He heard footsteps on the hardwood floor inside and was met by Jack's welcoming smile ushering him inside.

"Welcome neighbor, thanks for coming over."

"Thanks for having me," replied Rowan.

Rowan stepped inside, handing Jack a bottle of Australian Shiraz.

"Thanks Rowan, I'll pop the cherry on this right away."

Rowan was immediately surprised to notice that the home's open floor plan resembled the plan he'd chosen for his own house. In the center of the home was a fireplace embedded in river rock that was strategically piled up to the twenty-plus-foot ceiling. The cabinets, trim work and floor were hardwood. The place should have smelled like a sawmill; instead it smelled of cigarette smoke. The enormous west-facing glass windows invited guests inside like rays of light. As the sun was setting, shadows fell across the floor inside the living room. Jack proudly guided Rowan to the kitchen bar and poured wine.

As Rowan entered the kitchen area, he could see around the rock fireplace and through the huge windows, the sun setting across the river behind his own home.

Sadie sat in her wheelchair by the windows. She was excited to have company and having a neighbor over for a drink would make Jack feel normal for a while. She had listened with interest as Jack had talked about their new neighbor, a writer. Of course, Jack had not told her their neighbor's name, he'd forgotten it, and then forgot to tell her. She was eager to meet Jack's new friend.

She heard the voice enter her home talking to Jack at the door. The voice had a pleasant timbre. It was a familiar voice she had not heard in years, although she had replayed it in her mind many times. Could it be that he had returned to the river just as she had?

Sadie recognized the unmistakable soft spoken southern drawl of Rowan Sojourner. The man at the door was their neighbor, the author, her old love. Her body twitched to its own rhythm as she thought of how fulfilling it would be if she could walk over to him and give him a hug. The most tortuous thing she had encountered thus far was not being able to talk to Rowan.

Sadie knew the man well before he realized who was seated before him. Years of fighting a losing battle with Huntington's made her appear much older. She had quit looking at herself in the mirror years ago. When they had company such as tonight, Jack would have a hairdresser come over and fix her hair, put on makeup and eventually let her look in the mirror. Jack would compliment her and she enjoyed, as he put it, being all dolled up, but no amount of cosmetics could hide the devastation that Huntington's had unleashed. Her skin resembled that of an old woman, her tired eyes told a tale of devastation.

She tried to flash a smile but could not. Sadie recognized the familiar split second of horror in Rowan's eyes. She had seen it before whenever anyone looked at her. She'd seen it in her family's eyes, her friends, even in her own children's faces. They would consciously correct their mortified gaze to resemble that of a sympathetic and friendly soul, but everyone's first look at her, that split-second unconscious reaction, was always the same. She couldn't blame them; after all, she could not stand to see herself in the mirror. Time had not been kind.

Something about the woman was familiar to Rowan. Her eyes, blue eyes that once orchestrated the desires of men, were now weary, but still beautiful. No other woman in his life had those eyes. Blue the color of the Montana sky just before a summer rainstorm.

Rowan took both of his hands and managed to trap her flailing right hand as Jack introduced them. He held her hand and mustered a smile. It was hard to smile, he wanted to cry. This was why he'd felt her presence, she had been just across the river all along. This realization was dawning on him as Jack introduced them.

"Rowan, this is my wife Sadie. Sweetie, this is our neighbor and my new fishing buddy," said Jack.

Sadie saw the questions in her old lover's face. Did he recognize her?

Rowan responded with, "Hi." He wasn't sure what to say.

Rowan could not believe what he saw. So many times he had thought of his dear Sadie, how she was doing. How were her kids? Where was she? Each time he had remembered her stunning beauty, healthy mind and loving heart. Could this be that woman?

"You have a lovely home. Thanks for having me."

Somewhere inside that body that twitched uncontrollably, it was her. Oh, how he wanted this day to come, to see her again, but he never dreamed it would be like this. Yet it was undeniable. His forced smile broke into a hearty grin when he saw the necklace she was wearing. It was a necklace he had given her years ago. It was made up of turquoise and cat's eye stones. Here she was, his Sadie living just across the river from him. He trembled with nervous energy.

A slave to her disease, she was no longer the tall powerful woman she once was, but the eyes are the windows to the soul, and Rowan seemed to read her heart. He was certain that she wanted to say so much to him, as he did to her. He wanted to tell her how her departure from his love life had been the catalyst that propelled him forward to become a successful author. He wanted to tell her about his travels, his thoughts of her and he wanted to hear about her life.

Elated and devastated, he squeezed her hand in the polite handshake that a man gives a stunning woman. Jack invited Rowan to sit down and he did, right beside Sadie.

Rowan scanned the room, the dusty bookshelf and saw the faded jacket cover of his novel on the shelf beside her. She noted that. With all her focus, she stared at the book.

Jack felt at ease that Rowan seemed comfortable sitting in his home, let alone sitting near her. Some visitors, despite Jack's preparatory speech about his wife's condition, simply were not comfortable. Jack saw that Sadie continued looking at the book. She was communicating with Jack. Rowan took a drink of wine that emptied his glass.

"Do you want that book, dear?" Jack reached for the novel and held it in front of Sadie.

"Oh, it's our neighbor Rowan's novel," said Jack with excitement.

Her eyes flashed from Rowan to the novel and back again. She wanted to ask. She wanted to point. But, all she could do was use her eyes. Jack had become quite adept at her only form of communication.

"Dear, do you want Rowan to sign your novel?"

Sadie looked out the window into the dusk. It was a clear "no" to Jack. Rowan watched her, not sure what to do or say.

Jack knew what she wanted. "About a year ago, this book showed up here. I think a nurse left it for Sadie to read. She started the book and then the disease took a sudden turn for the worse. She hasn't finished it and I have not done a good job of reading to her."

"That was my first novel, I will gladly read it," said Rowan, and realizing he had sounded a bit over anxious, he looked at Sadie.

"I'll read to you."

Sadie's head cocked and her eyes darted around in her head, eventually focusing on him and she managed an upturn of her lips.

"Are you sure?" asked Jack.

"I'd love to," said Rowan as he took the book in his hands and opened the bookmarked page number forty-seven.

"I see you've just come to the main character, Carter, and how he falls in love with the ever-exquisite Danielle Shannon. Yes, she is quite the vixen, and holds the key to his heart. Oh, you girls are an evil lot," he teased as he tried to relax.

"I'll second that!" cried Jack from the kitchen.

Rowan and Jack giggled. Sadie rolled her eyes.

Rowan was about to read a love story to Sadie, a love story that he wrote, a story in which the character names and places had changed, but the story was theirs. Sadie knew it. That's why she wanted to finish the book. Now, Rowan, the author and lover known in the book as Carter, would read their story to her. She wanted to give him a hug, but she could not move of her own volition no matter how much she tried. She wondered to herself what she had done to deserve this torture.

Rowan read:

"The August sun scorched the river rocks along the Madison, so much so that Danielle winced as her bare feet danced across the sun-baked rocks from the cool, sandy spot to the river's edge. Carter stuffed the empty beer cans and potato chip bag into the rucksack and also left the reprieve of the willow tree's shade to chase after Danielle. She was playful today, and being out in the sun made her want to be chased, grabbed, held and kissed by Carter and no other.

"Carter caught up to her as she entered the cool water. He grabbed her and swept her off her feet, held her in his arms as they both laughed. With a heave, he tossed Danielle into the deep pool and waded out to her. Their feet no longer touched bottom and they swam together to where the current barely swirled. They exchanged flirting smiles until they reached the other side. It was a game that led them to the sand of the far bank exchanging kisses on the hot sand."

Sadie watched Rowan read. She remembered the day as if it were yesterday. The way he held her, his touch, his scent. That had been one of her all-time love-making favorites. She was watching Rowan read and then she closed her eyes. Her head bobbed uncontrollably up and down and twitched side to side.

"A fish jumped, a magpie squawked and the river water rippled like the synchronized sounds of a well-orchestrated symphony, but the two lovers made their own music and nothing else mattered until they lay breathless on the sand. Neither of them wanted to let go for fear that releasing the embrace for a moment may lead to forever."

Jack poured Rowan's glass full and sat across from him and to Sadie's right. "Dear, let's not make him read, let's visit."

Rowan dog-eared the page and closed the book as he held the glass of wine. "I would love to come back and read to you again, Sadie. I've forgotten how silly this comic book is."

"Did you hear that, dear? Our neighbor, the best-selling author, will come over and finish reading his novel to you!" Jack said as he held her hand. "That would be great, Rowan. You two have a lot in common. Sadie here is a wonderful artist."

Rowan choked on his wine as he almost blurted out that he already knew how great an artist she was. Jack's excitement over Rowan being there was feeding Rowan's paranoia. Was Jack being sincere or was there a hint of sarcasm. He wondered if Jack knew their history. Surely he did not.

"Want to show off some of your work, dear?"

Sadie stared at the cabinet in the corner of the room and blinked her eyes. Rowan's reading had brought back a flood of old memories and she wanted Rowan to know that she shared those memories. She had kept a journal of her own. Even though she loved another man, those days on the river were special to her.

Jack saw that Sadie focused on the cabinet and was blinking. He got up from the couch and opened the cabinet. He returned with an artist's sketch pad, which he handed to Rowan. Rowan opened the heavy paper cover to reveal the first sketch of a river with a young man and woman fly fishing side by side, the river's current swirling gently around their legs.

Rowan's heart stopped. It was a drawing of the day he had shown her how to cast a fly rod. He remembered that day well and it was the chapter preceding the passage he had just read to her today. She had drawn the picture just as he had written about it. After fishing, they had a picnic and then made love on the river. Rowan lost himself in the pencil drawing.

Jack broke the silence. "So what do you think, Rowan? She's pretty darn good, huh?"

Rowan looked up at Jack. His eyes were wet. He watched Sadie. Jack did not know about them. If he did, Rowan felt that Jack would make a friendly joke about those days or give some other signal that he knew. Should he say something? There was no good way to do it. There was no right time, especially not now. He felt uneasy.

Rowan turned to Sadie. "I love it."

He gazed into her eyes and she into his. Her head bobbed like a cork on the ocean waves and eventually she was able to focus on Rowan. He hated that he was such a superficial man, but even so, he saw through the devastated shell of this woman and into Sadie's soul. She had returned to the river just as he had. She had drawn their days together on paper. He'd never seen these drawings. She had completed them after they were lovers. Jack was her husband, but Rowan held a special place in her heart.

Jack swallowed a big gulp of wine and said, "Sadie's painted and sketched for years, mostly images of the river. That's how we met. She was at the riverside not far from here. Her easel sat on the rocks and she was painting. I was fishing. We started talking and I guess I just wore her down until she eventually gave up the fight and agreed to date me." Jack was beaming at the recounting of the memory.

"Yep, wore her down like a big trout 'til I could land her in my net." Jack chuckled as he crossed his ankles on the coffee table.

Rowan managed a grin to acknowledge Jack's humor as he felt a chill. Could it be that Sadie was painting a memory of him when she met Jack?

Rowan processed it all as fast as he could and asked, "When did you paint this one?"

Jack spoke up for her. "About fifteen years ago. See the lines, they are perfect. She was an exceptional artist. I have an idea of when each of her sketches or paintings were done by how well the lines are drawn."

Jack got up and retrieved more sketch pads from the cabinet and set them on the table. Rowan studied the drawings in his lap like the student of a famous artist trying to go inside the mind of the creator.

Jack continued, "Before she was diagnosed with Huntington's, Sadie spent her free time as an artist. She became frustrated about eight years ago when, among other things, she had difficulty drawing. The drawings show the progression of the disease until, through that frustration, she gave it up years ago."

Jack took another drink and held his wife's hand. He set his glass down and smiled at her. Rowan was lost in a world of pencil-drawn scenes. Each picture brought back a memory of Rowan and Sadie. Whatever he had not written about their love that summer, she had drawn, and she hadn't missed a single detail. He wanted to run out the door crying and he wanted to see more. Rowan solemnly set the pad down and picked up another as he smiled at Sadie.

The second book of drawings was beautiful. Some were in color. Most of them were of her and Jack. His crow's feet and toothy grin were trademark characteristics of her sketches of him. Other drawings were of the river itself. The river was important to her. Whether it was because of Rowan or Jack or some other unknown factor, the river was her sanctuary. It showed in her peaceful sketches.

"They are beautiful," said Rowan.

Sadie stared at the pile of sketch pads. She blinked furiously at one pad in particular. Jack noticed her fixation and leaned forward from his chair. Rowan watched in fascination as Jack ran his forefinger across each book in the pile. Jack watched for her reaction. Slowly he touched each book one by one. As his finger ran across a thin green notebook, Sadie's eyes suddenly blinked furiously. Jack's finger stopped.

"This one, dear?" he asked.

Sadie's eyes continued to blink.

"Yeah, that's the one, huh?"

Jack looked at Rowan as he watched with his mouth slack-jawed. "She wants to show you this book of sketches."

He handed the book to Rowan, who set it on his lap, nodding at Sadie.

Rowan opened the notebook and there on the first page was a color pencil drawing of a man standing behind a woman on the rocky shoreline of a river. The man pointed over the water at the fly line coiled in mid-air. His other hand rested in the small of the woman's back as if he was coaching her fly fishing endeavor. They were both wearing ball caps and their jeans were rolled up around their knees.

Rowan remembered the day well. The two lovers had a picnic on the Madison, floated on inner-tubes and swam and played in the river. One day, as they sat in the shade watching a boat float by with two fly fishermen, Sadie remarked on how graceful it looked to cast the line and have it drop on the water so smoothly. Rowan told her he would teach her how to fly fish. By the end of the day they returned to the river and within minutes, she was making good casts and having a blast.

That had been a proud day for Rowan, one of his best. He'd showed off his skills as a fisherman and a teacher to the woman he loved, prompting his desire and natural ability to teach and guide fishermen. She had kissed him right there and gave him the look he'd always wanted from her, the look that gave him butterflies.

Rowan returned his attention to Sadie as he tried not to weep. She was focused on his eyes now. She was not blinking wildly, just watching him. He looked past her towards the river outside. The picture in the sketch pad was of the very place where he had taught her to fly fish. Their homes were situated directly across from one another very close to that wondrous place of memories she had drawn.

"It's very special," said Rowan in a whisper that squeaked with stress.

Her eyes were wet. Jack wiped a tear from her face.

"She is honored to have you look at them and enjoy the pictures. I had forgotten how precious her art was to her. In our day-to-day activities, I forget about her artwork. I'm so glad you came so that we could see them again." Jack wiped a tear from his own face. He smiled at Sadie and squeezed her hand.

Rowan turned his attention back to the pad. He gently turned the page to the next drawing. A beautiful girl sat on the sand staring at the river. Her knees were drawn up under her chin and her arms wrapped herself up tight. The picture was positioned from the river looking back at the girl with the blue sky and aspen trees behind her. The girl appeared to be sad and deep in thought.

Rowan looked deep into Sadie's eyes. She was trying to tell him something. Was it that she had loved and missed him all these years? She had been very blunt with the truth when she told Rowan that she wanted another man. She had made it clear that she wanted more from their relationship, that she yearned for a touch he never gave, a loving touch that fulfilled her, a touch that was not his, but Jack's.

Sadie continued to stare at Rowan. When he looked up from the page, she was blinking at him. Rowan smiled back and turned the page. The next picture was of the back of a naked woman in the river. Her bare breasts were only visible to the lucky bastard in the drawing who treaded water in the middle of the river, only his head visible on the surface. He remembered that day too. He smiled.

He flipped through the pages for more, but that was all the sketches there were. He set the book down and took another from the stack. Rowan opened the sketch pad and noticed the lines in the drawing were more erratic than in the previous drawings. With each page turned, the sharp contrasts and detail gave way to blurred lines, as if the artist had become drunk. The trunks of the trees were less straight while Jack's smile was almost comical; the details of the river's fish and birds were childish. The leaves on the aspen were swollen and distorted. Rowan flipped through the pages a little more quickly than the other pictures. He set the book down and smiled at Jack, then Sadie.

"I love your work. I adore it, brings back memories," said Rowan. Sadie flashed a smile which again distorted into an eye-squinting menace. "I should go home."

"If you must, but you're welcome to have another drink," responded Jack, standing up as Rowan rose from his chair.

"Thank you for having me," he said to Jack as he shook his hand.

Rowan then turned to Sadie. She looked up at him. Rowan trapped her hand in his and held it.

"She doesn't want you to go," said Jack. "Please come again and read to her anytime."

"I will." Rowan's eyes were on Sadie as he spoke. "I can come back tomorrow and read to you until my eyes are crossed." He then turned to Jack, offering, "And if you need to go to the store or run an errand, I will be more than happy to read while you are gone. Anytime."

Rowan squeezed her hand, then turned and marched towards the door. There were too many emotions he was experiencing. Some were bound to come out of his eyes at any moment. He had to get out of there. At the door, the two men shook hands.

"I'll call you in the morning."

"Thank you for coming over. We both enjoyed it."

Jack waved goodnight from the doorway. Rowan headed down the drive and his face filled with tears as he opened the squeaky door to the old Chevy. The flood of emotion that he had been able to hold back came pouring out. He had not wept in years, but was making up for it now. She lived next door. She and her husband had built their home on the same stretch of river where she had playfully loved him so many years ago.

The secrets in a woman's heart are unknown, but looking at the drawings, Rowan knew the moments they shared were as dear to her as they had been to him all this time. And as if it wasn't enough to discover Sadie, he had been awestruck by her physical decline and disease that now rendered her powerless.

He wiped his face as he shifted the gears of the Chevy motoring across the old bridge. The headlights of the truck cast a dim glow down onto the black water of the river and the tires made a rhythmic thumping on the wooden boards. He turned the wheel left towards his house and then again into his driveway.

Rowan pressed the clutch and turned the ignition off. He shifted into neutral and let the five-window Chevy glide into the yard with only the sound from the squeaking of the old truck springs. He tapped the brake pedal lightly and the truck stopped. He put her back in gear and sat there in the dark crying.

When his eyes were empty, he went inside. He took an open bottle of wine on his way to the recliner and sat in the dim room drinking and reminiscing. He had often thought of Sadie even though he had not seen her. It was only natural for him to remember her beauty, her inviting smile and confident gait, especially when she wore her favorite pair of jeans. Lord, that woman could fill a pair of jeans.

It wasn't just the physical deterioration that devastated him, Rowan was overwhelmed by how much her life and Jack's life had changed. Hearing Jack tell him about the progression of the disease and the drawings, he surmised they only had a few good years together before their lives started to change.

He wanted to see her again and read to her. He wanted her to know that without her devastating breakup with him, he may never have lived on the rivers of the North West, picked up the pen and created the comfortable life he had today. He wanted her to know what his feelings were then, feelings that he should have made clearer to her. It was his fault. He knew he had never gripped her arms and told her he didn't want to live without her. He wanted her to know his side of the story and how much he still adored her. He could do that now by reading his first novel to her. The irony was that she could not appropriately respond other than blinking her eyes or attempting to smile. He could read the whole book to her and not hear from her, only hope that she understood what he was reading.

And what should he do about Jack? Tell him their history and possibly destroy their newfound friendship? Maybe it was best to just let things go. He tried to imagine telling Jack his history with the man's wife. It would be pompous and rude. Rowan decided to keep his mouth shut, at least for now. It was unnecessary and in light of their current situation, uncalled for.

Rowan felt betrayed by Jack. They had become fishing buddies and now were friends. All those meaningless male conversations they had and he never put the pieces together. The two men had talked about trout flies and fishing holes, but they had never really spoken. Only men could spend weeks together and not truly know anything about the other.

Rowan cracked a smile at the thought of the possibility of two women going fishing for a single day. No doubt they would know every detail about each other, their loved ones, family, kids and color of their kitchens. Forget a whole day; they would know those details about each other by the end of the supermarket check-out line. Life is odd, though sometimes also sadistic, twisted and cruel.

Chapter 17

Spruce Moths

The leaf springs under the Wagoneer squeaked from the strain of the weight of the drift boat trailer and bags of gear; rain gear, extra clothes, spare rods, reels and tackle, most of it belonging to Jack. It could have been a two-hour drive to the river, but they stopped along the way at the bar in Whitehall and Three Forks, so by the time they reached Dillon, the chance of fishing the Big Hole in the afternoon diminished with the daylight.

A few more drinks and a steak dinner drove them back to the hotel by nine. They shared a bottle of aspirin and Jack ripped the plastic seal off a new bottle of Pepto Bismol. He poured an equal share into the flimsy plastic hotel cups.

"One more thing about aging I hate is having to plan for the hangover," said Jack.

"Here's to heartburn and acid reflux," toasted Rowan.

They were there to immerse themselves in the annual Spruce Moth hatch on the Beaverhead, the best-kept secret in fly fishing. Every year in late summer, moths hatched in the trees above the river and fluttered down to the river to drink. Many were trout meals. Fishing the Beaverhead morning and evening during this event brought rich rewards for the few who experienced it.

When the alarm rang at 4:00 a.m., it felt as though they'd just gone to bed, but they were eager to be on the water. The morning was calm; cool air, no wind, not a cloud in the sky. The surface of the deep pools were smooth and inviting when the sun came up. The only ripples were made by moths and rising trout hitting the water. Rowan enjoyed being back on the river maneuvering a boat. He and Jack took turns casting and rowing the wooden drift boat. In long stretches of calm deep water, the rower could get in a few good casts so, Rowan locked the oars and whipped the line out to drag a fly behind the boat as Jack stood on the bow casting.

Rowan watched Jack at the very front of the bow smoking his cigar and setting the fly on the edge of a little eddy that formed downstream from a rock near the middle of the river. Before the fly was wet, it was gulped by a trout that went straight for the bottom of the river. It was a rocky bottom frequently seen, but here the river was deep and dark. Jack pulled the fish towards the boat.

"How about we anchor?"

"You're the captain," answered Jack.

As Rowan tossed the river anchor behind the boat, his rod was jerked back towards the stern. Rowan grabbed the rod as it teetered on becoming lost to the river. He set the hook.

"Fish on. Looks like you are on your own."

Rowan freed one hand to toss the landing net to Jack, who fumbled to keep the line tight and scoop the big fish from the river. The two grown men giggled like little boys. If either had a worry in the world a moment ago, it was eclipsed by the trout on the hook.

Jack pulled the fish from his net and quickly removed the hook from its lower lip. The fish was still full of life and Jack set it back in the water where the cool water flowed over its gills, and in a second it wriggled from his loose grip and was gone.

Jack turned to watch Rowan reel a cutt of equal size up to the boat. Rowan reached down into the water, grabbing the fish, unhooking it and releasing it in one fluid motion. He stared down into the water at the reflection of himself watching the fish slowly fin its way into the deep water. There are good fishing days and there are great fishing days. In his reflection he saw himself grinning. It was a great day.

They fished from the boat, on occasion stopping to wade and by noon, they had lost count of those fish netted. Countless others had set themselves free just before being scooped up. The calm of the morning gave way to a breeze from the northwest that quickly turned into a steady wind with gusts that spun the boat on the river's current. What had been a cloudless morning was now engulfed by dark rain clouds.

Jack hooked a big fish that made a hearty run downstream. Rowan fought the wind and current to maneuver through some shallow rapids in between rocks. The rocks were just large enough to dent the boat, so he wanted to hit the rapid just right. His river skills were good and the boat had few dings to prove so. Rowan had bought the cedar boat from his friend, Woolly, who had built it.

Woolly claimed that he could shoot the hull point blank with a .38 caliber pistol and the solid construction would not be pierced. Rowan had never felt like testing the claim, instead putting his full faith in his friend's craftsmanship and attention to detail.

The fish was headed for the fast water. It was a good one and Rowan didn't want Jack's line to snap so he stayed with the fish, slowing the boat with backstrokes of the oars just enough to help keep Jack's line tight. Using the boat to tire the fish, he was positioned to maneuver the boat through the rocks.

Jack barked orders from the bow and cheered Rowan's river skills. As the rapids closed in, Rowan realized they would inadvertently hit a rock he hadn't noticed on the right side of the boat. He warned Jack, who was looking in the other direction, oblivious to the rock, focused on the big cutthroat swirling the surface of the water.

"Brace yourself Jack, rock! Rock!"

Rowan worked the oars furiously to straighten out the boat but the boat was headed for the rock and approaching fast.

"Hold on, hold on, Jack!"

Jack was standing up as he had most of the day, a fresh cigar clenched in the corner of his mouth. He was peeling line in frantically and laughing like a wild man as he watched the big cutt roll beside the boat.

Jack cried, "Ha ha, you big beautiful bastard!" He never heard Rowan's warning.

The boat sideswiped the rock, sending a shuddering thud through the laminate of the cedar construction. It would be enough to dent the gel-coat, a war wound is all. Still, the rocking it caused combined with Jack's unsteady stance as he peered into the water at his would-be prize cutthroat was enough to knock Jack off balance. Like a cartoon character on a cliff, he waved his arms frantically in an attempt to regain balance. In a heart-stopping splash, he flailed in the water, screaming, cursing and crying for help, but never letting go of the fly rod or allowing his lips to release the hand-rolled Cuban.

The water was cold, even for late summer, so it took Jack's breath as he sputtered and fought against the water chilling and filling his waders. Rowan could no longer see the river rocks on the bottom. He needed to help his frantic friend, but he didn't want to lose the boat so he threw an orange floating seat cushion for Jack to catch it as it floated by.

"Jack! Catch!" The cushion almost hit Jack in the face it was so close.

Rowan grabbed the bowline, a twenty-foot piece of rope tied to the front of the boat, which had a loop in the other end he used as a handle. He put his wrist through the knot. Rowan felt strong enough to hold onto the boat and get Jack to shore.

He hoped he was right.

Jack flailed and splashed towards the cushion floating

towards him. The cold water had frightened him and the panic of not being able to swim well, especially in water-logged waders, was preventing him from reacting to the situation as a grown man should. The cigar still clenched in his teeth muffled his cursing and screaming, which came easier than formulated thought. Fear makes a man do stupid things and no man knows if he will panic until the situation presents itself. The cushion floated towards him and in his frantic search for it, he missed it as it floated just beyond his fingertips.

"Goddamn," grunted Jack as the flotation device escaped him. He took in another mouthful of water.

Rowan quickly put on a life jacket and as he did, he could not help but think of how funny and cruel life could be. Here he was in a position to allow the bastard that Sadie had chosen over him to drown. No witnesses. But, Sadie needed the man more than ever and Rowan was never the nurturer that she needed to care for her. Rowan shook the thought from his mind. Of course he could not allow the man to drown now, but there was a time he would have done it, even holding Jack's head under for good measure.

"Help!"

Rowan jumped in as the top of Jack's head went under, his wide fear-filled eyes disappearing from the surface. The cold water had robbed him of his frantic energy. He was no longer panicked and was giving up when Rowan grabbed him from behind.

"Easy, Jack, easy. I got ya."

Rowan's boat experience had prepared him for the possibility of assisting a drowning victim. He had the good sense to instinctively throw the cushion and still have a spare jacket.

"Relax, buddy, I got ya."

Rowan swam around behind Jack. He grabbed a fistful of shirt collar, talking calmly and quietly to Jack.

"O.K. Jack, can ya hear me? Can ya hear me, Jack?"

"Yeah," said Jack as he coughed and spit water.

"Good. Then stand up."

During the drama, the current had pushed them towards a sandbar in the middle of the river, which got shallow fast on approach. Jack still spat water and coughed, the Cuban stuck to his lips.

As the two men got their feet under them, Jack stood and reached down into the water. His hand came up with his fly rod; the line had tangled around his waders and it was taut. Jack felt the tug at the end of the line as he untangled himself.

"Fish on!" screamed Jack.

Rowan could not believe it. Jack was near death a moment ago and now he was reeling in the very fish that had attributed to his near death experience. The man had all the luck in the world. He was reeling in a trophy pig of a trout.

"I can't believe it! Can you fucking believe it?" cried Jack.

"No, Jack. No, I can't," said Rowan as he shook his head and laughed.

He let go of Jack's collar, giving him a pat on the back, and pulled the bowline towards him, grabbed the stern and gave the boat a shove onto the sand bar just enough to prevent it from floating away. He unsnapped the landing net from his fly vest and watched the scene unfolding before him.

The rod doubled over and the reel screamed as the fish made another run downstream, peeling line off at a frantic rate. The big fish had taken advantage of the near drowning to recapture some spirit. Somehow the line tangled in Jack's feet had stayed tight enough to keep the trout hooked. It was nothing short of divine intervention that the fish had remained on the line. Rowan fully expected the fish to have natural markings resembling the Virgin Mary on its side, the miracle fish.

Jack played the fish, keeping the line tight and allowing the trout to make several runs up and down the river.

Jack started reeling the line in and now the fish was tired enough to play with. After several minutes of give and take, the fish was pulled reluctantly back towards the sandbar. A huge splash right in front of them and the big cutthroat rose enough for Rowan to scoop it up from the water with the landing net. It was hard to believe how big the cutt was.

"I'd say ten pounds, Jack."

Jack reached down and wiggled the hook loose from the fish's lower jaw with thumb and forefinger. He was amused by how easily the hook came out. The big cutt wiggled in a last-ditch effort to get away.

Jack patted his pockets.

"God-damned camera is at the bottom of the river," laughed Jack. "Just let her go, pal."

Rowan lowered the net in the water. He held the huge tail then slowly moved the fish forward and backward. The water ran over the gills and breathed new life into the creature, which disappeared with a splash.

Jack's water-logged cigar drooped so he unzipped his fly vest and procured two hand-rolled Hondurans from a Ziploc bag. He handed one to Rowan, bit off the end of the other and shook water from his gas lighter. The two of them stood in the river without a dry stitch of clothing between them smoking cigars, thankful to be alive and grinning from ear to ear. It began to rain.

Rowan had paid a rancher's kid to drive Jack's Jeep and the trailer to the take-out point. They were relieved to see the kid had followed directions. They were ready for dry clothes. As instructed, the key was left in the door to the gas tank.

They loaded up the boat and headed home. Jack insisted he was fine and that he drive. The warm clothes waiting in the Jeep felt good. As soon as they'd changed clothes, they were on their way home. With the sun shining through the passenger side window, Rowan fell asleep as the Jeep turned north. When he awoke, Jack had stopped at a liquor store and was returning with a paper sack.

Soon, the headlights of the Jeep illuminated Rowan's yard. Rowan stepped out of the Jeep to turn on the yard light while

Jack turned into the horseshoe-shaped driveway to drop the boat trailer. Rowan unhitched the boat and shoved it under its shed with the efficiency of a one-man pit crew, eager for a hot shower.

"I owe you a drink for saving my life today."

Rowan turned from the boat to see Jack holding a bottle of Macallan single malt scotch.

"I'll drink to that."

Chapter 18

Happy Birthday

The next morning, Rowan showered. He still smelled like fish, so he sliced a lemon and scrubbed his hands with it. He stood in front of the mirror shaving and staring at the man in the mirror, wondering how much he'd changed in her eyes, what she saw when she looked at him. Time had changed them both. His fingers traced the tiny creases around his eyes. His youthful complexion was taking on the weathered texture of an old mariner's map.

After a breakfast of orange juice, a banana and three cups of coffee sweetened with Bailey's Irish cream, Rowan knocked. Jack met him at the door as he said goodbye to someone on the phone.

"Good morning, Rowan."

His head pounded intermittently from the previous night's wine, and his failure to have an aspirin chaser and glass of water before bed. Regardless, he smiled at Jack.

"Mornin', Jack."

"Sadie is excited that you are here. If you don't mind, I need to run into town and pick up her birthday present, it's today, snuck up on me again. Our son, Toby, just called and reminded me of her birthday."

"No worries, Jack."

For years, Rowan had remembered her birthday on

August 27th, writing it on calendars stuck to refrigerators, fishing camps and captain's quarters, but as time passed he had quit writing down the date and naturally forgotten.

Jack patted his shirt and pants pockets, looking for his keys. "I procrastinate terribly; I'll only be an hour or so."

"Jack, don't worry 'bout it. I may be an author, but I'm a slow reader. Take your time."

"Thanks, pal. She is all set. You won't be called upon to do any caretaking. I appreciate your being here and will take off as soon as I find my god damned keys."

Jack patted Rowan on the back and led him towards the living room. Again, Sadie was seated by the windows. She was watching several magpies peck at a bowl of dry cat food outside on the cedar deck. Rowan watched, too; it was hard to tell what got pecked more, the cat food or other magpies.

Rowan pulled the book from the window shelf and sat in the chair next to Sadie. He opened the book and looked over the page at her.

"Comfortable?" he asked.

She blinked her eyes at him.

Jack spotted his keys. "There you are, you bastards."

He picked up his keys from the kitchen counter and promised, "Back in just a few."

Rowan continued looking at Sadie. "Take your time, Jack."

The door slammed shut and an engine turned over in the garage. The garage door opened, the engine noise rumbled and the garage door closed again. Then, the crunching sound of tires on gravel faded as Jack's Jeep drove away. Rowan continued looking at Sadie. She continued looking at him. It wasn't the longing sensuous gaze of long ago, but it was tender. Her eyes, though fogged with suffering, still told a story and Rowan was about to read that story back to her.

"There's so much to say to you, Sadie. I've had many great adventures and you were with me on every one. I spent many sleepless nights dreaming of you and restless days remembering you. You've been the reason I can't sleep, the woman who wakes me without being beside me and the queen of my soul. I'm happy to read to you. The main characters of this book evolved from us."

He leaned forward towards her. "You have a page book-marked. Want me to start there?" he asked.

Sadie grunted.

Rowan asked, "The beginning?"

Sadie's eyes blinked rapidly.

Rowan said, "Well, O.K. then, from the beginning."

Rowan flipped the pages of the book and cleared his throat.

In his best deep voice he pretended to read, "In the beginning God created heaven and earth."

Sadie rolled her eyes in mock suffering.

She was still in there, unable to tell him what she was thinking or laugh at how goofy he could be.

"I'm just kidding. O.K., here goes."

"Their first trip to the Madison together was with friends. Floating, as it was called, simply riding down the lazy river on inner tubes. Preferably, you used the ones from truck tires. They were big enough to let your butt drag.

"She had glowing skin that captured sunlight and turned it into bronze summer sun-soaked skin. She never burned, just got darker as the days passed. Her presence was as com-manding as she was gorgeous. Everyone watched her, a treat for the eyes. Carter was awestruck and speechless when she had invited him to go to the river for a day with her friends.

"The second trip to the Madison was just the two of them. It was where he fell in love with her. It was a second date and he was hopelessly in love and she knew it. Though he didn't dare tell her, it was obvious by the way he looked at her. She was intrigued by him also, although in any relationship someone always loves the other more, it's never equal, at least that's what she used to say. Well, Carter knew from that day on, his heart held majority over emotions between them and he wouldn't have had it any other way."

As he read to her, she either watched him read or occasionally he would see her close her eyes. He imagined that his writing took her back with him to relive those days. As he read, he heard a clock in the hallway chime twelve times. They had been sitting and he had been reading for about three hours, but it had passed by quickly. He continued.

"Her words cut him in two. One half remaining alert, trying to process her emotions and make sense of what it was she wanted. The other half was already curled up in the corner crying and hiding. Carter listened to her, tried to reason with her in a last ditch effort to persuade her to stay. But he knew her well enough to know that when this woman's mind was made up, it would be easier to drain the Madison of its June water than change her mind."

Rowan read his first novel to Sadie, words with memories. It had been close to two decades since he wrote the novel. Although he could quote entire pages of his own prose, he had also forgotten some. It all flooded back to him now and he realized what he had omitted and how much better the book could have been. He had read it to himself as he wrote it and read select passages to his editor, publisher and at bookstore signings, but he had not revisited the book in years.

The Jeep's tires crunched the gravel and the garage door opened to let Jack in. Rowan dog-eared the page and closed the book.

He said, "Let's continue tomorrow, I bet we can finish it in no time. Happy Birthday, Sadie."

Sadie rolled her eyes is if to say big deal. However, it was good to see Rowan again. If only she could have made herself up for him, hugged him and held his face in her hands as she told him how much she had always cared for him, how much she had wanted him and how good it was to have this time with him again. Instead, her gaze was empty, her voice silent and her frustration deafening. She felt as if she was being buried alive with nobody to hear her scream. She still had so much to say.

The door from the garage opened and Jack came in holding a beautifully wrapped gift. He came over and set the gift in front of Sadie.

"How was the visit?" Jack asked.

"Great, Jack, not sure who enjoyed it more."

"Well, we both appreciate your coming, reading and watching after my Sadie while I go to town."

"My pleasure, Jack."

Jack turned to his wife. "Happy birthday, sweetheart, I hope you like it. I could only think of one thing to get you."

Jack opened the gift, a plush pink flannel robe. On most days, that was all she wore with nowhere to go, no one to impress.

It was big and soft and looked comfortable. Sadie's eyes blinked wildly. Rowan had read to her, but he felt bad not having a gift to give to her. Once again he had been outdone by Jack Gibbons.

Jack placed the robe in Sadie's lap and held the soft arms of the garment to her face for her to feel. She tried to speak, opening her mouth and closing her eyes in concentration, but she could not form a word. She looked up at Jack and blinked.

Rowan leaned over and gave her a hug. "I enjoyed reading to you and can come back tomorrow while the story is fresh."

Sadie looked at Rowan and blinked wildly as if to say, "Yes, yes!"

"Well, there's your answer, Rowan," said Jack, extending his hand for a shake. "Thank you for staying with her. Sadie has a nursing assistant tomorrow afternoon. I'd like it if we could go fishing for a couple hours."

"Sure. I'll come over in the morning to read and be ready

when you are," Rowan said as he walked towards the door. He turned and waved to them both, but he focused on Sadie and mouthed 'goodbye' as he closed the door behind him.

Jack sat next to Sadie. "Did you enjoy your visitor?" he asked.

Sadie's eyes blinked furiously at Jack, and then she turned her attention to the pack of cigarettes on the coffee table before her. Jack picked up the big blue ribbon and red wrapping paper and put it in the box where the robe had been. The store clerk had done a wondrous job of wrapping the gift. It was a shame he was the one who had to unwrap it.

"How about some T.V.?"

Sadie continued to stare at the cigarettes. The last thing she wanted was to watch a television drama; she had just relived the greatest drama of her young life as her old lover released a flood of fond memories in her.

Jack looked at Sadie for her answer. Rapid blinking was a definite yes. If she looked the other way it was no matter and if she closed her eyes it was a definite no. But Sadie just stared at the cigarettes and Jack eventually saw it.

"Oh, sweetheart, you want a smoke, don't you?"

Jack got up and reached for the pack and a lighter. "In my haste this morning, I forgot to tell Rowan of the possibility that you may want a smoke. I'm sorry."

Sadie had not even thought about the cigarettes. For the last two hours, she forgot they were right in front of her. She had been completely absorbed by the reading, her memories flowed like river water over her body. The hurt that had propelled him to write was her doing, and it cut her like knives. Their lives had taken different directions and merged again.

Her love life had been fulfilling. Her married life had been better than that of her girlfriends, but the good years had not lasted long enough. Her disease had robbed them of a long happy marriage. They had not had the opportunity to make the kind of life they had planned.

Jack was patient and kind and put his retirement plans aside to care for her. She could ask for no more and no better, but having her old lover in her home reading a story that closely resembled her long-ago love affair had rekindled cold embers within her. She wasn't the woman she once was, but she sure as hell wasn't dead. She needed a cigarette.

Jack never smoked cigarettes, never liked them, but Sadie had always found peace in an occasional cigarette, especially after a great dinner or sex. He had accepted it and often would sit and watch her smoking. It was sexy to him. It was sensuous to watch his woman put her lips on the cigarette and blow smoke. He liked the way she would hold the cigarette and smile at him coyly. She in turn liked the smell of a good cigar.

These days she just smoked to have a cigarette. It was about the only pleasure she had left. She could hold the cigarette between her lips most of the time. Jack would sit next to her, placing it in her mouth. Smoking was the last and only activity she could do herself. She smoked more than ever now. Jack bought them by the carton. What difference did it make? Huntington's disease wouldn't kill her, just render her completely bedridden. Unless she succumbed to some other fate, her condition would deteriorate and she would develop chorea where her body twitched ever more violently. With nothing to lose, lung cancer would be a blessing.

Jack just lit it for her and put it in her mouth. She would smoke while he did other things. Not being a smoker, he once forgot about the lit cigarette and it burned right down to her lips. Jack felt like such an asshole that whenever she wanted a smoke now, he would put aside whatever he was doing, just sit with her, and make certain she didn't get burned.

He would Joke with Sadie, saying, "You're just trying to get me to smoke. I haven't felt this much peer pressure since high school." He would then laugh. He was a good sport, a good caregiver and a great husband.

Sadie drew on the cigarette that Jack held for her. She felt the nicotine course through her veins and just for a moment, she felt like a woman again. She thought of Rowan and the words he had read to her. She thought of those youthful days when they made love on the river just outside her window. She had followed through with her marriage to Jack despite being in love with Rowan. She'd never had sex like that day since. The cigarette tasted good, like an after-sex smoke.

Jack held the cigarette for her. She thought of what a patient and understanding man he was. She imagined that Jack was worrying about caring for her enough, scheduling home health nurses or paying bills. She hoped he was thinking about fishing.

The Marlboro was about burned to the filter. Jack stubbed it in the ashtray. Sadie glanced out the big windows towards the river. On cue, Jack wheeled her to the window. Together, they looked out at the bear grass and granite rock in their landscaped yard. It was a beautiful bright summer day, a day too nice to be inside.

"Dear, would you like to sit outside in the sunshine?"

Jack leaned down to look at Sadie, who met his question with blinking eyes and a contorted smile. Jack opened the door to the deck and wheeled her over to the railing. He pulled up a chair beside her and sat down with the mail. It was a perfect day, not too hot or too cold, warm enough to sit in the sun with his wife.

"Oh look, a letter from Bree!"

Jack held the colored envelope in front of Sadie for her to see. Then, he opened it and read the birthday card:

Mom and Jack,

I hope this arrives on your birthday; I will call in the evening. There is only one phone in the village and when my shift ends it will be too late to call! Hope you are enjoying the summer and that all is well. I have enclosed some pictures of me and some of the patients in our clinic. Love you, mom. Happy Birthday.

Love, Bree

"Well, dear, she sure sounds happy. I know you are proud of her."

They sat looking and listening and their stillness was rewarded with an onslaught of birds chirping and feeding in the yard. Hummingbirds buzzed their heads, hovering at the feeder Jack had set out. He and Sadie enjoyed watching the hummingbirds. There were several regulars that frequented the feeder so it had to be filled almost daily.

Jack had to take the feeder in the house at night or else the black bear that lived in the woods would destroy it. She had destroyed two feeders in the area, pulling them down, ripping them apart, wanting the sugar water inside. She would break open the feeder and lick up what spilled on the ground, on the deck or glass, making a mess and scaring whoever happened to be on the other side of the glass. That's what bears do best; scare the hell out of humans.

The first and only time it happened to Jack's feeder, he was making coffee one morning and standing at the window over the sink. They had just moved in and set out the feeder. As he watched, a huge pink tongue licked the window right in front of him. Barely awake, he ran screaming back to the bedroom, woke a bewildered Sadie from bed and returned to the kitchen just in time to see the bear ambling off the lawn in search of another bird feeder.

Since then, Jack had taken the feeder in at night so as not to tempt the bear onto the deck. He also led a campaign among the homeowners in the area to do the same. If a few people complained about smashed feeders, lawn furniture and licked windows then the bear would be trapped and relocated or worse, euthanized. His efforts had paid off. Since that time, the sow returned to the river every spring to bear-proof garbage cans and responsibly tended bird feeders. This spring, she had returned with two cubs.

The hook waited in the jaws of the vise as if to plead, "Let's go fishing." Rowan wrapped the thread around the tip of the pheasant feather, attaching it to the hook. The feather was from a rooster he had shot during the previous year's hunting season not far from his home.

A bigger portion of the feather, the hackle, was then tied to the hook and the bare metal barb began its transformation into a fish-attracting Woolly Worm. Rowan was tying a few extra flies for the trip with Jack the next day.

As he wrapped the chenille around the hook shank, he thought of Sadie and how much she had once loved to fly fish. He had been the one that taught her, feeling as much joy and elation watching her cast as she did the first time she actually caught a fish. Now she was unable to enjoy almost everything she had once lived for in her busy life. Sadie had been an active woman and now she was held prisoner by a disease that most knew little about.

Had she changed inside? She could hear, think and feel. She just couldn't do for herself. With a heavy heart, Rowan sighed at the thought of not being able to walk down to the river, cast a line or even sit on a rock and watch the world float by. How could he and Jack get her out of the house and down to the river? Could it be done? What if they did and she could sit on the bank in the sunshine and perhaps feel a little more like the woman that once stood in that very spot so full of life, energy and love? He would find a way to present his idea to Jack. He thought of this as he wrapped another fly, losing himself in its intricate detail.

Chapter 19
That's What Friends Are For

Rowan finished assembling his rod, pulling the line through the guides and setting the hook into the cork of the rod handle. He examined his box of flies like many would study a restaurant menu. The previous night he tied a handful of Orange Humpy's and Grasshoppers. He studied the row of Humpy's he neatly stowed in the case, all lined up in a row, their hooks stuck into the Styrofoam liner of the case to prevent them from tangling with the other collection of flies, easier to identify and find his preference while he was standing in a river.

Jack tied an Elk Hair Caddis to his leader.

"I want to thank you for coming over to our house, reading to Sadie and giving us both some sense of normalcy," said Jack

"Don't mention it. It was good to read my gibberish aloud. I enjoyed it and it gave me some perspective on the battle you and Sadie wage every day."

He relished the thought that his fly box was the only organized aspect of his life. He'd made the Humpy's reddish orange hackle extra thick near the hook eye, no reason, just the product of drinking an entire bottle of Walla Walla Cabernet while fly-tying. If he put little plastic eyes on it, the fly would resemble a tiny lion. He ran his fingers across the flies and settled on a Chernobyl Grasshopper, its body made of fluorescent green hackle and bright orange wings with white rubber legs. It was alien in appearance, its natural colors exaggerated, yet irresistible.

"That's why I say thanks, Rowan." Jack said as he put a fresh cigar in his mouth. "Even our close friends have disappeared. They can't stand to see her like this, it just makes people uncomfortable. You cannot believe how alienating this disease is. Days go by, the phone doesn't ring, we aren't invited out, and nobody drops by for a visit. I think that is the worst, the isolation."

Rowan hung his head in silence. There was nothing to say to that. He knew what a social butterfly Sadie had been and imagined that part of her aching as she aged.

Jack took the cigar out of his mouth and pointed it at Rowan. "It took a lot for you to sit and read, watch her, more than most are willing to do, and I thank you."

Rowan thought it may be as good a time as any to present his idea to Jack. "Can I say something without risking being out of line?"

Jack just nodded, curious, looking at Rowan with one eye squinting in the sun as he lit his cigar.

Rowan continued, "I was just noticing as I read to her that she has a certain fascination with the river. She seems to respond to it. The drawings you showed me are her depictions of the river. It's special to her."

Jack nodded and spoke as he drew on his fresh-lit cigar. "Yes indeed. It's where we met. She loved to fish, picnic or just lay on the sand drawing. We traveled a lot, but this is home, and that river was her favorite place of all."

Rowan cinched the knot on the grasshopper and asked, "When was the last time she went to the river?"

"She hasn't walked in almost three years," said Jack. "The last time we went to a public access, she could walk well enough with my help. It's impossible now. I can't push that god-damned chair across the fucking river rocks."

Tears flowed from Jack's eyes. He sounded helpless as a flood of emotion overcame him. Rowan kept talking to stop the dam of emotion from breaking him, too. He didn't think he could handle crying and fishing. They would wind up at the Manhattan bar in nothing flat.

"What if I helped you clear a path through the grass, make a trail over the rocks to the river. You two could have a picnic; sit by the river in the sun."

Jack stared at the ground and wiped his eyes underneath his shades. He had been so overwhelmed caring for his wife's daily needs that apparently he had not even thought of doing something so time consuming. He mentioned that he had a small tractor with a brush mower and a blade, adding, "It's a nice thought, Rowan, a lot of work though."

"I know, but I'll help. In a couple months, it will be too cold and once winter sets in, impossible. We can get to work as soon as we return." Rowan was excited.

Jack puffed on the cigar and scratched his head. "I could blade the yard and spread gravel to the river, but what about the river rock? Not even two of us could get her near the river. It's too rough to roll the chair and too far to carry her."

Rowan smiled, "I was thinking that we could build an elevated walkway so that you could push her out your door and right down to the river."

"Rowan, I'm a bit of a builder myself, but they don't give away lumber. That's a lot of money and I'm so busy taking care of Sadie that I really don't know how much I can do, physically or financially. I'm stretched pretty thin."

"I understand, but I don't have a wife. I'm in between books and a little bored and we've become friends. Friends help each other. I'd like to do this."

"I will not take a handout, Rowan, of your time or money."

Rowan kicked at the gravel and smiled. "I know."

They walked to the river as Rowan explained the details of

how they could suspend the walkway over the rocks and make it effortless to take Sadie out to the water. If they started soon, she could have her feet in the river once again to enjoy the last days of summer and early fall.

Jack cast the caddis. It landed like the real thing and floated under a lodge pole log that had fallen halfway across the river.

Rowan reveled in the fact that Jack often took his lead as to what fly he himself would use. It was hot and dry, the Caddis was a good choice, but the hopper was better. The late summer grasshoppers were everywhere and the ones that Rowan had tied last night were irresistible, at least he thought so. Late afternoon was coming on strong and the day was cooling, shade was beginning to cover the river and the air hit Rowan's face, signaling it was time to focus on fishing.

Chewing on the half-lit cigar, Jack puffed, cussed and continued to cast around the log. If he could not entice the trout to bite then maybe he would aggravate the fish into swallowing the menacing fly. It was a tactic that Jack used often, to Rowan's amusement. Though, sometimes it actually worked. Many times, Rowan had stood amused at the spectacle of Jack thrashing the water with his rod tip while spitting verbiage like that of any sailor worth his salt. He had actually entertained the thought that quite possibly the fish may be attracted to the sound of a man cursing at them and swearing to himself. Rowan had witnessed more skilled fishermen at work, but few of them were as good for entertainment as Jack. However, Jack was not to be dismissed as a good fly fisherman, he was good at casting the line.

Rowan made his way downstream on the gravel bank to a quiet pool fed by water that ran up under a dirt bank. It was a shady spot, a cool hiding place for a big fat trout that would dominate such an ideal hideaway, often chasing off others while watching to gobble up what looked good enough to propel him from his position of comfort and safety.

Rowan unhooked the hopper from the cork and dabbled

some fly dressing on it for flotation and to help mask human odor. He stripped some line off and shook the line loose from the rod guides as he studied the far bank. It was thick with knee-high Timothy grass, the tops so burdened with seeds that the stems hung over the water while the river carved away at the dirt under the grass.

In a flash, he was casting under the bank. The hopper landed lightly and he let it ride the slow ripple of current for a moment. As the leader straightened out, he mended his line with an exaggerated waving motion of his arm before the hopper began to drag unnaturally against the current. Just as the fly reacted to the mend, a fish hit the surface where the hopper had been.

It was a good splash made by the big rainbow that Rowan imagined must live there. He had the fish's attention. He made some low teasing casts over the water, letting the hopper flash over the surface without hitting it, as if the grasshopper was looking for a suitable place to land on the bank. Rowan's hopper glided just above the grass on the opposing bank, almost hanging on the seeds at the end of the long grass stems. His down stroke was full of grace as the hand-tied hopper glided towards the surface, a perfect presentation.

The surface of the river was untouched by the hopper as the water erupted underneath and the fight was on. After missing his quarry and seeing it flash over the water, the big fish was agitated and hungry, aggressive as he took the hook hard, determined to rid his space of the menacing yet appetizing insect.

The rainbow splashed and thrashed across the surface in an acrobatic dance of fins and fly line. True to its name, the Rainbow Trout caught all the rays of light the sun had to offer, showing off its vibrant colors.

The sound was so reverent that Jack looked upstream before Rowan could say "fish on." Down to the bottom he swam, tugging the line and making the rod jerk bend into a

C. Then, with equal speed, back to the surface the fish came, continuing its dance in an attempt to throw the hook.

Rowan guessed the fish to be large enough to break his leader so he was careful to use the right amount of line and rod pressure to tire the creature. The fish surfaced and dove repeatedly. Rowan pulled the rod back and reeled as he lowered it, inching the fish towards him.

He stood in the middle of the river as the catch turned on its side reluctantly relinquishing itself to an ill fate. Rowan slid the net towards the fish, but with one last slap of the tail the hook came loose and the fish was gone.

It was good action even if he didn't net the prize. It would be hard to top that one so Rowan waded back to the rocky bank and sat down as he tied on a new leader. He thought more about his project proposal to Jack and mapped it out in his mind. Sadie could no longer move at will. All she could do was blink her eyes, smoke cigarettes and form a remnant of the smile she once had.

Her physical abilities were non-existent, but her mind was still sharp. She understood the conversation around her though she could not participate. She was able to make decisions about what she wanted to watch on television, whether or not she wanted a cigarette, and she had her memories, as Rowan had watched her reactions to his reading. For her to be at the river's edge once more would mean as much to him as the sights and sounds of the water would rejuvenate her soul.

Chapter 20

Take Me to the River

Four days after Rowan had pitched the idea to Jack, they had started work. Jack wasn't going to let Rowan pay for the lumber so Rowan had devised a plan to work around Jack's pride. Rowan had the boys at the lumber yard deliver a truck full of redwood that they stacked in Jack's yard. Across the river, Rowan watched from his kitchen window as Jack stood in his yard holding a cup of coffee in one hand and waving the other arm wildly at the truckload of lumber.

Rowan imagined Jack was cursing and it amused him.

Realizing he'd lost the battle before it began, Jack accepted the free lumber.

Jack sat next to Sadie with two glasses of lemonade. She stared ahead at the birds fluttering about the yard. Within a week, Jack explained, he would be able to wheel her off the deck and across the yard to the elevated walkway that he and Rowan would build. The walkway would serve as a bridge over the river rocks and uneven ground. As Jack explained the project to her, he wasn't sure if she comprehended what they were doing.

Sadie listened to Jack tell her what they planned. It sounded crazy. Jack had no idea how much she had wanted to just be closer to the river, much less be able to feel the water on her feet once more. The pain was becoming unbearable as her condition worsened. Maybe this would make her feel better, if only for a moment.

They worked all day every day, putting their weekly fishing trips aside in order to finish the project, taking advantage of the warm weather. Rowan had the platform framed two days after he started.

The walkway was wide enough, and strong enough, to carry her, and it sloped from the yard towards the river with ease. At the end of the walkway was an eight-by-ten foot platform with railings. The entire platform and base was constructed of redwood cedar. From its conception, Rowan imagined his old love sitting there enjoying the shade and closing her eyes to the sound of the running water, as she was taken back in time. And he imagined the cedar railing where her pack of cigarettes would sit. All of this was to be made with his hands and the thought gave him joy.

Rowan saw one screw was missing, the last deck screw needed to be drilled. He took one from his tool belt and handed it to Jack, who stood there with his hands on his hips, also delighted, inspecting his handiwork.

"Here ya go. Last one," Rowan said, pointing to the place where the screw needed to be drilled into the decking. "You do the honors."

Jack knelt down and put the last screw in the deck. He stood and the two of them shook hands as a chorus of crickets sounded, welcoming the evening. They gathered up their tools and headed back towards the house.

"How does a cold beer sound?"

"Best idea you've had today," replied Rowan.

The next morning, Rowan pushed the wheelchair with ease across the wooden walkway. Her chair rolled over the planks, high above the rocks, branches, leaves, all natural obstacles that would have otherwise prevented her from being here.

Rowan spoke in soft tones, "I know how much the river means to you. It means that much to me. Seeing your pictures, I realized that a part of you still loves me just as I still love you. You made a good choice in Jack. He's a great man, a lousy fisherman, but a good man nonetheless. I always wanted to live right here where you and I spent those wonderful days; those memories are good ones. I always wanted to return to the river and am happy that you did too. I helped your husband build this walkway so you can once again be close to the river. I'll always love you, Sadie."

Rowan continued to push her chair across the planks, so he didn't see the tears on her face. But Jack did as he waited at the end of the platform with a fistful of flowers. He saw her trying to smile and her tears of heartache and joy. She was closer to the river than she had been in years, the smell of it, with the breeze that floated across it; in the sheer beauty of the river, even the bugs darted and swarmed in the morning light, as if to welcome her back.

Jack gave her the flowers, daffodils, her favorite. There were none growing in their yard or anywhere else around here for that matter, she thought. He had planned ahead. He probably had to order them in, meaning that he had to go to the florist days in advance and pay a premium, knowing they were her favorite. Jack set the bundle of yellow blossoms in her lap. Her fingers brushed across them as she wished she had the ability to hold them up to her nose and bury her face in them, closing her eyes and inhaling them. Jack kissed her on the cheek.

Sadie moaned what should have been excited high-pitched laughter at the work they had done for her. All she could do was moan and twist in her chair, unable to kiss and hug them and give a thousand thanks. Jack knelt beside her.

"Dear, let's get you down to the water."

Jack slipped off her house shoes and tossed them on the bank. He guided her wheelchair off the platform decking, down the ramp and onto the shoreline. The two men held each side of the chair to ease her down to where the water was shallow, just enough that the front wheels were submerged.

The fresh cold river water was exhilarating. She could not move her legs, but she still had feeling. The muscles in her face twitched with activity. She was trying to smile and laugh. Tears of happiness streamed down her face as she closed her eyes and felt the river current on her feet.

Rowan stood barefoot in the river, his pants rolled up to his knees. He was as proud today as he had been so many years ago when the two of them stood near that very spot as he taught her to fly fish. And he was happy to see Sadie's reaction. She seemed renewed. Her memories, hopes and dreams all seemed to come back to her as she sat there with her feet in the flowing water.

Jack stood beside Rowan in the river and patted him on the back. Rowan smiled and put his arm on Jack's shoulder. The two men stood there in silence watching Sadie. Her face changed from smiles to frowns as the muscles in her face did as they pleased, but the underlying joy was there all along. She just closed her eyes.

Rowan considered how strange life can be. Here he was, back here with her again, this time with his arm around her husband, and he didn't even want to drown the man. After all those years, he was able to do something for her.

Jack thought of how fortunate he was to have made so many wonderful memories with such a phenomenal woman and he was saddened that they couldn't share them the way he had planned. But he was grateful to Rowan for the suggestion and his hard work and friendship building the walkway that got them here today. He could tell that Sadie loved it. It would make her a happier woman and that was his job.

Sadie opened her eyes and looked at the two men standing

there watching her. She closed her eyes again and reveled in the feel of the cold water that had traveled down the mountain from the snowpack high above and miles away. Her days of telling stories and showing emotion were done, she was dying as her body deteriorated more rapidly from week to week, but her mind was still vital and the water was rehydrating her memories.

In the span of less than half an hour that her legs twitched and feet splashed in the Madison, Sadie was a young girl splashing and playing in the water. She was a young lover, a mother, a woman unsure of what lay ahead for her but willing to accept her fate and make the most of her life. She had been all of these things. Now, she was still here fighting. She had two of the most significant men in her life with her, still caring for her. For a minute or two, all her suffering was drowned by the river.

Sadie looked at Jack and blinked her eyes at him. Her feet were getting cold and between the water temperature and the flood of emotions coming back at her, she had the chills.

"Are you ready to get out, dear?"

Sadie blinked.

Jack and Rowan grabbed the chair and pulled it from the river. Jack slipped her shoes back on and the two men guided the chair back up the ramp to the platform. Jack dutifully took the cigarettes and held them in front of her. She blinked her eyes and Jack grinned.

"Need a smoke, huh?" He put the cigarette in her mouth and lit it. Sadie dragged on the smoke and Jack sat beside her.

Chapter 21
Sail Away

Clark died on a Sunday morning, a lethal combination of drugs for which he had no prescription and a deadly amount of rum that sent him to bed one last time. Before Clark's ashes could mix with the Road Town sand, there was an offer to buy the resort. As much as Claire loved Tortola, it was time for a new adventure. The offer was respectable. She had squirreled away a chunk of cash in the years she had run the place. She felt it was her bonus for keeping the business going and not killing Clark. The proceeds from the sale, savings and Clark's life insurance would be enough to travel and explore locales for a new home. Their son, Eric, was out of school, grown now and chasing dreams of his own. The thought of returning to England never occurred to her.

Meanwhile, the sand felt good between Rowan's toes, feet that had not touched the hot Honduran sand in years. Almost three thousand miles away, Montana was buried in ice and snow. The Madison was covered in sheets of ice piled on top of one another like giant misplaced Lego blocks. He imagined the roof of his home hosting a couple feet of snowpack and a deck that desperately sought the relief of a snow shovel. With his eyes closed and that in mind, he grinned.

The air was wet and heavy with the salty ocean breeze

that swept off the sea, cool and refreshing. This was the way to spend winter. If he had stayed in Montana, he would have tied a thousand flies and drank himself into a cabin fever coma. Here, he worked in a dive shop near Frenchtown a few hours a week, just to maintain some resemblance of a social life. He fished and relaxed on the beach, reading and reflecting.

Seeking a winter refuge from the bone-chilling Montana winter, Rowan had settled on Roatan for its diving, consistent weather and friendly natives. Of course, the fishing was good, too. He purchased a two-bedroom condo overlooking Shipwreck Cay. Monthly association fees were atrocious but the beach was a short barefoot walk through the canopy of trees that hid the condominium complex from other developments. It was a pleasant stroll, not even long enough for a beer to break a sweat on a can. Best of all, he wasn't required to cut the grass and he could leave for months at a time without the homeowner hassles of maintenance.

Rowan was still surprised that he lived half of the year in a condo. The close proximity to others had never appealed to him nor had staying in one place, but he had never been fifty years old before. He felt fortunate enough to have two homes now with the luxury of traveling in between the Caribbean and Montana. It was the best of both worlds.

While most of the tenants chose to swim in the pool that separated the condos from the sea, Rowan chose to take his daily drink in the bay, often swimming out to Shipwreck Cay. It was a hundred yard swim that he enjoyed and he liked having coffee with the family who lived there, bringing gifts of fruit, tea or anything else he could place in a waterproof container tied to his waist.

Ernesto and Ana Valenzuela lived on the cay with their young son, Luis. The cay had been handed down from generations to Ernesto. If they left the cay, it would be the property of whoever decided it was theirs. By consistently occupying the island, the family maintained their continuing claim over it. The cay had been noticed by developers and rumor had it that offers had been made, but none accepted, at least not yet.

Ana cooked in the lean-to shack and made jewelry while Ernesto worked at the nearby shipping yard. Their narrow flat-bottom boat served as their only means of transportation, taking Luis to school, Ernesto to work and Ana to town twice a week.

Rowan often swam out to the cay to have coffee with Ernesto or just visit for a moment before swimming back to the lounge chair-lined condo beach. He relished the fact that despite the development of Roatan, a certain friendliness along with untamed portions of the island still existed, such as the cay.

This morning he had just swum back from the cay and was lying in the sand with his feet being washed by the lapping of the saltwater. Rowan was reflecting on Sadie's relationship with Jack. He'd long been ready for a love like that, which had escaped him all of his life. He was lonely. When he went to town at night for a drink with the other locals, he wished he had someone to walk home with.

In the time that Rowan had been Jack and Sadie's neighbor, he had learned a great deal about love by watching Jack care for Sadie. He began to think that he was ready to love and nurture a woman. He had never been a nurturer; hell, he'd never been accommodating. But he was ready to love a woman like Jack loved Sadie.

The simmering sun dried his skin, leaving traces of salt. He sat up on his elbows and looked around at the empty beach. He studied the gray hairs on his chest, outnumbering the black ones by a depressing margin. Either he was getting old or turning into a wizard. He preferred the latter. After all, he had become wiser in his old age.

When he arrived at the dive shop, Rowan propped his bicycle up against the back of the building with no need to lock it. He greeted Jorge the gardener with the usual mix of broken English and Spanish. They agreed to go fishing the next day. Jorge's brother had a good boat.

He checked the day's schedule then drank his coffee while completing the inventory of dive tanks. He didn't need the money. Rowan worked there part-time as a reprieve from writing at his computer. He loved the owners, the staff and enjoyed the guests that filtered in and out of the resort. Work was a social event for him.

Glenda had worked in the resort's kitchen as long as anyone could remember. She came over from the kitchen on the flat deck ferry that shuttled staff and guests of the resort back and forth across the bay to the island. She was Rowan's favorite in the group.

She had the biggest smile Rowan had ever seen and a friendly personality to match. Glenda was part of the reason Rowan worked there. He had met her years ago when he was looking for a place to rent, long before he became an author with a bank account. She knew everything that happened before it occurred. Glenda had found him his first place to rent. She was his oldest friend on Roatan. She always had an ear to the ground.

"Good morning, Rowan baby," she said as she set down a tray of fresh fruit and coffee between them.

"How's Glenda this fine morning?"

Rowan reached for the carafe and poured a cup for both of them while Glenda set a plate beside him. There was island-grown cantaloupe, watermelon and orange slices.

Glenda sat down next to the glass-top wooden table, across from him. "Rowan baby, what keeps you here?"

The cantaloupe was so juicy that he had to wipe his chin before answering her question. "Fresh Fruit."

"Baby, why you here?"

"I like spending time here, especially the winter months."

"No, baby, I mean why you just sit around here on this island like an old man?"

"I am an old man," Rowan replied with a wink. Glenda rolled her eyes.

"I've traveled my whole life. I'm just taking time to relax and think about what I will do next."

"Forgive me, Rowan. I'm a curious woman. December through April, I watch you and I wonder why there is no Mrs. Sojourner. You don't need the money, but you keep coming back here tinkering in the dive shop. You should have a wife making a honey-do list for you."

Glenda meant well although she had no idea how much her prying hurt. Aside from the to-do list, he'd been having the same thought. He had lived a full life of adventure, floating from one fishing excursion to the next. Women had easily come and gone throughout his life and finding someone to share his days with had never been a priority after Sadie. His memories of women were comprised of moments spent with them, and what he wanted now was to make a future with a woman.

"Glenda, there were many women. When I was a young man, I focused on the conquest. There were three I think of often; one died with my child, one wouldn't have me and another was married. I've made my own bed and I accept it."

"Forgive me, baby, I just worry about you."

Rowan leaned over and kissed Glenda on the forehead.

"I'm lucky to have you worry for me."

When he rode his bike back to the condo later that day, he thought of the conversation with Glenda. He had made plenty of friends on the island through the years and they had all welcomed him when he decided to call Roatan home during the winter. He was finally ready for true love. He had felt something surge within him when he made love to Claire on Cooper Island, but she was married. Nevertheless, he thought of her often. Rowan accepted the realization that he may have wasted too much time seeking pleasures for himself instead of seeking someone to share those pleasures with.

He held the phone in his lap for an hour before working up the courage to call. What if her husband answered the phone? What if she didn't appreciate his calling?

He dialed the number and listened to the connection crackle and buzz as the lines spanned across the ocean floor.

"Taylor's Resort, this is Amy. How may I assist you today?"

It was a pleasant enough voice, but it certainly did not belong to Claire. It lacked soul, thought Rowan.

"I am calling for Claire Dennon?"

"I'm sorry, sir, she sold the resort."

"Well, do you know where she may be reached?"

"No sir, I just work here. The new owners might have that information. They are away for the season. May I take a message?

"Thanks, but I'll try back later."

Rowan hung up and sat wondering, where was Claire?

Morgan Singer, the Director of Singer Funeral Home and Crematorium in Bozeman, Montana held the Folger's Coffee can out to Jack with a disconcerting look. Jack laughed and cried as he took the can. Sad and funny mixed together like Sadie's ashes and a few remaining coffee grounds. The ashes in the coffee can had been something she had made him promise years earlier. Her frugality coming into play, she had argued with him that there was no need to waste money on an ornate urn when her final wish was to have her ashes spread in the Madison River.

Jack had said maybe that was a waste of a good coffee can. He told her he could use the can to store bolts in the garage and that he should just use a McDonald's sack. Sadie laughed and said that he could go get a cheeseburger and eat it on the way to the crematorium, pick up her remains and have them scooped into the sack, after he finished his fries, of course. Then, he could drive across the river bridge and toss her out the window on his way to the fishing hole. They had laughed, but Sadie insisted he keep his promise of using a coffee can, remarking that the paper sack may get soggy from the French-fry oil or a carbonated drink, thus spilling the ashes. Then he would be forced to clean his Jeep.

Sadie died at home, years after the urn jokes they made. She died in her sleep, which is all anyone can ask for. The February snow was piled up on the window sill and through the frosted glass he could see the river was frozen in huge ice cubes the size of cars all piled up like a crash. Now, Jack placed the coffee can on the seat of the Jeep and drove home.

He set the makeshift urn on the kitchen counter. He then thought he should find another location to set the urn until the river thawed and he could fulfill her final wish. What if someone made coffee from the wrong can? He laughed as he cried. He knew she was laughing with him. He moved the coffee can to the window where Sadie loved to sit and watch the current streaming over the rocks.

Jack had taken her down to the river morning and evening. There, she would sit on the platform, close her eyes and listen to the birds in the trees and Jack cursing. Jack took her to the river until winter set in. When she sat inside looking out the window, he imagined she was remembering her time outside. As her condition worsened, Jack wasn't sure what she remembered, but he hoped the walkway he and Rowan built helped soothe her by bringing back remembrances of the good times.

The cancer diagnosis was sudden, severe and a blessing. There was no need to fight. Huntington's had already taken her life. She was ready and had been for years. Jack was ready, too. Anyone could see it in his weary eyes. He had been forced into the role of caregiver just as she had been sentenced to live in that body that was no longer hers. He was sad, had been for years, now he was just relieved.

The coffee can urn held Sadie's remains until the first of May when the river was coming to life again. There was still snow in the high country and heavy wet snow still frequented the valley, but the firm grip of winter had loosened and there was increasingly more sunshine now than snow. Sadie's final wish would be granted soon.

A few friends had called and stopped by, most of them Jack hadn't seen in years. They too were set free. They no longer had to approach cautiously or pretend to be too busy to stop by. Jack had gone down the list of people that he and Sadie had known for decades, calling and informing them that her struggle was over. Now, it was time to invite those he wished to be there when he finally set her free.

He thumbed through his little black book. There were only a few that he thought would put down what they were doing and fewer still that he wished to come. He and Sadie had been so alienated by their friends.

There was one friend at the top of his list, his neighbor, Rowan. But he didn't have to invite Rowan or even tell him what he was planning. Rowan called frequently to check on them and as if he'd sensed the end of her life, he had called just moments after her death. He had offered to come back to Montana earlier than planned, but Jack insisted he wait for spring.

A few people stood behind him as he held the coffee can. Toby and Bree stood closest, each of them with a hand on his shoulder as if to silently give their approval.

Rowan stood on the platform, hands on the railing, quietly saying goodbye. Sadie was dead and still he felt no different than he did thirty years ago. He had rediscovered his lover with her ailment and he had felt no less love for her. He was watching her husband readying to toss her ashes into the river and realized that he had spent all these years loving her.

He was here to support his friend who years earlier had won Sadie's love. The river where he and Sadie had loved, laughed and played had brought them together and today it continued to bond them. They had built their dream homes on the river exactly opposite one another, never letting go of the fond memories they shared here on the Madison.

Rowan watched the ashes drift through the air. The way they had been tossed from the coffee can, they arced like a giant rooster tail, settling on the water in a cloud of sprinkles, making a faint sound like so many tiny diamonds hitting the water. It was too late for goodbye, that was already done, but now she was about to be truly gone, all of her, forever, only able to return as rain like the billions of drops of water that swept her downstream now. Her ashes clouded the air over the water and swirled on the surface of the deep.

In seconds, her remains were scattered all over the river current, heading for shallow rapids. A muscle in his leg twitched as a small part of him wanted to jump in and hopelessly scoop up what he could from the river, but he found peace in knowing that now she was forever part of the river she had loved so much.

A few ashes still floated on the surface, as stubborn as his memory of her, as if they too were saying goodbye back to him, not wanting to let go.

This is what she had wanted, to have her remains given to the river. All her life, she had lived, loved and laughed on the river, building relationships with others and with nature, raising her children. The river gave and gave to her. Now, she gave it all that was left of her.

To Rowan's surprise, Bree and Toby each gave him a hug and thanked him for building the walkway. Toby stuck out his hand and smiled.

"Thanks for taking me fishing when I was a kid. I'll never forget that."

He patted Rowan on the back and walked towards the house with everyone else. Rowan was speechless that the kids who were by no means kids anymore had remembered him.

Quietly, the small herd of friends and relatives filtered back into the house. Rowan reached inside his vest and retrieved his flask. He leaned on the railing and took a sip and offered it to Jack as he approached. Jack accepted the flask in silence. He took another look at the river, with no sign of her now. He looked at Rowan and the two of them shook hands.

"There is plenty of food inside. Please come in and visit," said Jack.

"I will, but I want to just sit here a minute. Bad part about funerals, they remind me of my own immortality."

"Well, don't dilly dally; there are a couple of available females your age."

Rowan gave him a wry smile, quipping, "You mean they're still alive?"

"Sorta," snickered Jack. "Depends on how long you stand around out here, better act fast."

The two of them were silent for a moment watching the water where her ashes had fallen.

Jack took another healthy pull from the flask and handed it back to Rowan. Then he said, "I want to thank you for being so good to us."

"That's what friends do," said Rowan as he put the flask back in his coat pocket.

"No. You were more than a neighbor to me, more than a friend to Sadie."

Rowan stared at Jack, whose eyes met his gaze of disbelief. Rowan tried to speak, but words wouldn't come.

Jack put his hand on Rowan's shoulder.

"I know about you and Sadie. I know that is a big reason why she wanted to live here. I know that is part of why she wanted to have her ashes scattered here. I saw through it all and in the process, I found a friend in you."

"How long have you known?" asked Rowan.

"All along." Jack smiled at the surprised look on Rowan's face. "That woman could have any man she wanted. She chose me. There was no reason for me to be jealous."

Rowan was speechless. He watched the water, searching for words.

Jack started laughing.

"I'm just fucking with you. After she died, I started reading. I read the book, your first novel that you started reading to her that day I went to town. See, when I got back from town that day you read to her, she smoked a half a pack of cigarettes. Took me a while, but I put it all together."

"Jack, I should have said something earlier."

"Like what? I knew Sadie was reluctant to marry me. I knew she loved men very much, but in the end she did choose me. I can't be jealous of every man she met before me. You have been the only friend we have had in years. I hope that friendship continues."

Rowan, still speechless, offered his hand and Jack shook it and then shuffled back to the house.

Rowan took another pull from the flask and let the single malt glide down his gullet. The tears flowed like river water. Although she had been gone in some aspect for years, it was not any easier. Now, she was completely gone with nothing left but her memory and what he remembered most was this very spot. It was where they had spread a blanket by the cottonwood, which was still there. They had a picnic and let the cool shady breeze flow over them one hot August day. It was on that day at this very spot she had promised that she would love him forever and he promised the same to her.

Rowan wasn't sure if Claire Dennon was married, where she was or how to find her. He didn't know what he would say to her, but he wanted to see her again. What he did know was that he was wasting time and there was no more time to waste.

Chapter 22

River of Return

The ferry docked in front of Bo's Place on Cooper Island. Claire Dennon stepped off the boat and gave Bo a hug.

"How are you today, Claire?" asked Bo.

"I'm better. I have money, and most of all I have the spirit to get on with my life."

Bo smiled. "Good girl."

Bo then nodded his approval. He was friends with Clark and Claire Dennon for many years. He had watched Clark drink himself to death and supported Claire when he could.

"Did you fulfill his last request?"

Claire answered, "I did. I spread his ashes on the beach. I even sprinkled some of them on a piece of bread like he asked and it was gulped down by at least a half dozen gulls."

Bo laughed. "Then I'd say wash your hands of the bloke. Have an adventure. Find a man that recognizes all you have to offer."

Bo put his long dark arm around Claire and they strolled up the beach to the bar. Bo's wife, Anne, brought a fresh pot of coffee with a big hug for Anne and the three of them sat under the thatched roof, enjoying the morning breeze.

Anne asked, "So, where will you go first?"

Claire had a sheepish grin. She brushed the chestnut hair from her face and smiled at Bo. "Well, that is part of why I am here."

"Oh?" said Bo, sitting up in his chair.

"Your friend that I met, the writer...."

"Rowan Sojourner?"

"Yes. I want to see him again."

Anne nodded at Bo and grabbed his hand. "Where is he, love?"

Bo scratched his beard. "He splits his time between Montana and Honduras like a bloody hummingbird. This time of year he's getting ready to go back to the states. He works in a dive shop for something to do and has a condo there. He comes and goes with the seasons. I don't have a number or address, but if you make it to Roatan, check with the dive shops or find a fishing boat. That will lead you to him.

Glenda finished folding the clothes. The trash needed to be taken out. Rowan had left to go to Montana for the memorial service and would be gone for the summer. In his haste to leave, he had forgotten the trash and the aroma of the rotting banana peels permeated the entire condo. Glenda stopped by to check on the place every other week. She had a key and Rowan insisted that his good friend use the condo when he was away, though she never went inside except to clean. Sometimes she would sit by the pool and visit with some of her friends who worked there, but she never went for a swim or so much as sat in the sweltering sun. Rowan was a clean person, but he was a man. Glenda enjoyed dusting the bookshelves and doing the light cleaning that was always needed. It never took much of her time to give it a woman's touch and the chore was a great excuse to visit her friends on the south side of the island.

Claire Dennon cleared customs with a drove of dive vacationers and the group made their way outside to the portico where cabs, vans and buses awaited. She was approached by a young cab driver who spoke good English.

"Taxi?"

"Yes."

"Where would you like to go?"

Claire wasn't sure how to answer so she started at the beginning. "I am looking for Rowan Sojourner. He is an American. He lives here."

She could see the disinterest in the young cab driver's eyes. This was no easy meal ticket. This woman didn't know where to go or how big the island was. He started to walk away.

Claire stopped him, grabbing his shoulder. She opened her purse and handed him a fifty dollar bill.

"Half now, half later. Take me to the nearest dive shop."

With rejuvenated spirit, the young man replied, "Ok, lady."

The first dive shop they stopped at was only a couple minutes from the airport. It was hardly worth riding in the car on the narrow paved road. Cars and light trucks met each other blind on the curves and hills, disappearing from view as soon as they appeared. They turned off the road and Claire went inside alone to ask the young girl working the desk if she knew Rowan.

"He is an American, a dive master, an author."

The girl shook her head no. A man's voice croaked from the break room behind the desk.

"You looking for Rowan?"

An older gentleman, perhaps the manager, appeared from behind the desk, still wiping his lunch from his face.

"Yes, yes, you know of him?"

"Sure, he owes me twenty dollars, terrible poker player, works out of Coral Bay. Tell him Miguel says hi and that I want my money."

The man cackled and sat back down with his sandwich.

They drove back onto the narrow road, and when they turned off, it was a few more miles this time. Jorge was raking the sand around the palms he'd recently planted at the entrance to the resort. He noticed the tall woman approaching without luggage.

"Excuse me. I'm looking for Mr. Sojourner."

Jorge stopped his raking. "No here today."

"Well, where is he? Can you tell me?"

Jorge looked her up and down. She had nice legs. Too bad Rowan wasn't here; he would be disappointed to have missed her. The next time Jorge saw him, he would tell his friend about the woman with great legs that was asking for him.

Thankfully the young cabbie got out of the car and spoke briefly in Spanish to Jorge. After a friendly greeting, they laughed before being interrupted by the Englishwoman.

"Uh, excuse me, can you tell me where Mr. Sojourner may be found?"

Jorge rattled a string of vocabulary that was part Spanish mixed with enough English that the meaning wasn't completely lost on Claire, but she still wasn't sure where Rowan was. At any rate, he was near, these people did know him. Jorge looked Claire up and down in approval. The cab driver motioned for them to leave.

"Don't worry, lady, I know where he is," said the cabbie.

Claire hadn't realized that she looked worried. They drove back out to the highway and continued farther away from the airport. When they turned off the highway, the cab stopped under the shade of the entrance to a complex of condominiums. Claire walked in with the cabbie in tow.

A receptionist and security guard were having a colorful conversation that Claire imagined involved anything but work. They saw her coming and the guard stood and greeted her.

"Welcome, how may I help you?"

"Hi. I am looking for Rowan Sojourner."

The guard also looked her up and down. If she was trouble, he seemed to have concluded that it came in a well presented package. "Is he expecting you, ma'am?"

The question caught Claire by surprise. She had pondered

how he would react. She'd considered attempting to call him by phone and profess her intentions, but she wanted to see his face when she told him that she wanted him, that she missed him and that she had been in love with him since they met. Hell no, he wasn't expecting her. As a matter of fact, she was the last person he would expect to see.

"I certainly hope so," she replied in a matter-of-fact voice.

The guard walked back to the office and whispered something to the receptionist, who picked up the phone and dialed Rowan's condo.

Glenda didn't usually answer the phone when she was cleaning, but the receptionist didn't usually leave a message. Recognizing the receptionist's voice on the machine, Glenda answered.

"Hola, Lucy."

"Hola, Glenda. There is a woman here for Mr. Sojourner. I thought he was in Montana."

"Si. He left yesterday. Who is she?" asked Glenda.

The receptionist looked back at Claire.

"English, pretty, came here in a cab. Should I tell her he's gone already?"

Glenda did not know who could be asking for Rowan. Any woman living on the island that he had courted, however fleeting their romance may have been, would know where he was and where to find him. So, whoever this woman was, she was not from here.

"Send her up."

Claire knocked on the door. She was surprised to see Glenda and even more surprised to see her smiling and inviting her inside. "Hey baby, come in, come in, I am Glenda."

"I am Claire. I am looking for Rowan."

Well, thought Glenda, here she was. In all the years she had known her friend Rowan, he'd mentioned few women in their coffee conversations. She knew Claire existed and secretly had hoped she'd look Rowan up again. Glenda had once pried the information out of him like a pearl from an oyster shell. She tried to contain her excitement, knowing how happy he would be that she had come to find him.

"No, baby, he's in Montana, just left yesterday."

Glenda could see her news let the air out of Claire. The girl appeared to have traveled a long way to see him.

Claire wasn't sure what the nature of Glenda's relationship with Rowan was. She didn't want to ask but struggled with the awkward silence.

Claire set her shoulders back. "Forgive me. I met him years ago. Then, I was married. I was hoping he might wish to see me again."

Glenda smiled at Claire. She put her callused hand on Claire's shoulder. "Oh, girl, I've heard of you. He would love to see you."

Claire's face expressed hope as tears welled in the bottom of her eyes. "He's spoken of me?"

"Yes. He's a wonderful writer, but getting him to talk about himself is a chore. He was very fond of you though, baby." Glenda affirmed.

Claire began to cry. She had no way of knowing if he'd ever thought of her again since Cooper Island, but she had thought of him. Those dreams of him saw her through some rough times. Her body had ached for him, never knowing if he even remembered her name. She sat down on the sofa guided by Glenda, who took a seat beside her, offering a tissue.

"He goes to Montana in the spring. This year he left a few weeks early, his neighbor died. They were good friends and she is the only other woman I ever heard him mention, other than you."

Claire sobbed. "I feel foolish, like a schoolgirl chasing the quarterback."

Glenda put her strong arms around Claire. "Don't feel that away, girl. Dogs chase cars. Now, that's foolish, but people, people chase dreams. You can stay here until you get a flight to Houston tomorrow. He's only a few hours away. You want to call him?"

Claire explained to Glenda her motive for surprising Rowan. His eyes would tell her if he was happy to see her again, if he still wanted her. If she alerted him that she was coming, she would lose the element of surprise that she counted on having. After listening to Claire, Glenda agreed that she would honor Claire's request not to reveal the surprise.

It was a bright sunny spring day, a warm one by Montana standards, almost fifty degrees. For those who had endured the weeks of endless cold and snow, the warmth felt good on their skin, but for Claire it was cold. She walked out towards the taxi cabs. In the minute it took to find a friendly cabbie and for him to put her luggage in the trunk, she thought surely she would freeze to death. She gave the cab driver the address Glenda had written down for her on Rowan's stationery.

Claire hurried back inside to the terminal. A blouse and Capri pants weren't enough. She had noticed the gift shop when she'd arrived. A few minutes later when she returned to the cab, she was peeking out of a blue-and-gold sweatshirt hoodie with letters across the front that read, "Montana." Her sweatpants matched.

According to the nametag pinned to the car's dashboard, the cab driver's name was Jeff and he talked nonstop for the duration of the twenty-minute drive. He was a native Montanan and operated the only cab service in the Gallatin Valley. As he talked, Claire rehearsed what she would say to Rowan. Of course, what she would say depended on how accepting he was of her. As the cab turned off the highway onto a gravel county road, she began to fear that she would be deemed a stalker. Or, she imagined he would open the door, not remembering who she was, as another woman met her there, putting her arms around him. Claire began to doubt herself. This was crazy. The driver continued talking.

Though the silence was non-existent, the scenery was breathtaking. Patches of green grass sprung up amid the piles of snow that still clung to the half-frozen ground. Gophers scrambled through the grass chasing one another, just as pleased with the warmer weather as any human. A herd of deer grazed alongside the road, never so much as looking up at the green cab rolling by, leaving a cloud of dust hanging over the road. The mountains were clad in white and green.

The driver fell silent for a moment, but only a moment as he said with surprise, "Oh, this is Mr. Sojourner's place."

Claire was also surprised. She leaned forward in the back seat. "You know him?"

"Yeah, everybody 'round here knows him."

The cab stopped in the driveway. There were no other vehicles in the drive.

Claire stepped out, her eyes taking in the cedar home. Her palms were wet. She was so nervous.

The driver carried Claire's bag to the front door. Claire stood there. Here she was, now what? She had hoped he would meet her at the door.

"That'll be thirty-five."

A sea of fear had drowned out the words of the cab driver. Claire just stood there staring at the house.

"Pardon?"

"Thirty-five dollars. Please."

She was brought back to the reality of her current situation by counting the money and tip. She handed it to the driver.

"Doesn't look like anyone's home. Want me to wait?"

"No, thank you."

"Well, all right then, but if you need me, here's my card."

Claire gave him a half wave as the cab backed out of the drive. She rang the bell and no signs of life came from inside the house. She tested the doorknob and it was unlocked. She looked around. There was no reason to lock the house; she was in the middle of nowhere. Hopefully, he wasn't far away.

Entering the home would be crossing the line.

She decided to wait on the deck. The air was crisp with the scent of pine, quiet and peaceful. She closed her eyes and imagined his response to seeing her, what he would say, what he would do.

She walked around to the back of the house and stood on the back deck, gazing at the open space behind the home, and noticed the river through the trees. The sun shone on the water, as though the surface were sprinkled with jewels. It was beautiful and inviting. She had stood there waiting for a half hour and she was growing restless. She noticed the well-worn footpath that led towards the trees so she followed it from the house to the river. The knots of nerves in her stomach released as she took in the soothing sights and smells of the water.

Birds glided in above her and the scent of so many grasses, pine and flowers overwhelmed her senses. She stayed on the path and it led her to the water's edge. There, she looked downstream where the water disappeared around the bend. She could hear the rush of distant rapids. The water was muddy and fast moving. Logs and branches floated past her in a rush to pile up miles downstream from their origin.

"If you came all the way here for a swim, you're outta your rabbit-ass mind."

His voice froze her in fear. She turned around to see him standing up from the old chair where he'd been sitting, watching her. All the rehearsals of what she would say and do were lost. Just who had surprised whom, it was difficult to say.

He was coming towards her now, dressed in blue jeans and a flannel shirt. She'd never seen so many clothes on him. The breeze was cool there in the canopy of the trees, but that wasn't where the chill came from that coursed through her. He began to smile. Whatever he'd been drinking in the blue tin coffee cup, he tossed on the forest floor.

He seemed pleased.

Rowan had sat in the chair drinking wine from his cup as

he often did in an attempt to clear his head. It was his favorite place to watch the world go by. A flood of emotions roared through him. They'd held the memorial service for Sadie yesterday and Rowan had made up his mind that he would return to Tortola to find Claire. He wanted to see her again. And now, here she was right in front of him.

"Well, I figured if you were never going to stop by and say hello, I would just have to come find you."

"I'm so happy you did."

The embrace was what each of them had imagined since that day on the beach of Cooper's Island. They stood holding each other, neither of them wanting to let go, not even for a moment to speak or ask questions. Rowan never let go for another nineteen years.

Chapter 23

Return to Madison River

When Rowan did let go of Claire, it was in room 170 at Bozeman Deaconess Hospital. He felt the life leave her brittle hand, worn thin and frail from a weary battle with cancer. A battle fought by Claire that had destroyed them both.

Rowan hid his diagnosis from her and fought off his worries by giving her his support. He didn't want her to die worrying about him, knowing that he had colon cancer. So, he didn't tell her, a secret he only had to keep for a few weeks. He sat in the orange vinyl chair looking at the thin sheet that covered his wife. He remembered how beautiful she was until she became ill. He waited until the chaplain arrived with two hospital orderlies to remove his beloved Claire to the basement morgue.

"Mr. Sojourner? I'm the Chaplain. I am sorry for...."

Rowan stood and walked out the hospital room door, brushing past the men as straight as possible although he wanted to crawl from his heartache of loss and the pain of his own cancer-ridden body. He had no interest in what the chaplain had to say. His regard for others, his patience, and his life were gone.

He and Claire had long ago agreed to be cremated. The arrangements had been filed with the local mortician. While enjoying a Bali sunset several years ago, they had scribbled their last wishes for Claire's grown son, Eric. They wished for their ashes to be scattered in various places from their home in Montana all the way to Cooper Island where they had first met. There was nothing left to do. Rowan just wanted to go home.

Once there, he took two Percocet and sat in the recliner. He slept for the rest of the day. His mind was heavy with worry and fear, but his body was taxed from staying up with Claire. Her final stay in the hospital had lasted two weeks. When he woke, the sun was low in the sky, sinking to kiss the Spanish Peaks as it did every evening.

Rowan watched Sports Center and choked down a microwave dinner. He had grown accustomed to being spoiled by Claire's cooking. For the last year, she had been too sick to cook and he had begun to miss her cooking and her vibrant company months ago. In fact, he had made up his mind days ago that he was not interested in living without Claire. He had lost Sadie when he was a young man, only to find her and see her slowly succumb to her illness. He felt lucky to have Claire and she had completed his list of adventures. Without her and with his failing body, he now had little interest in living.

Rowan's prognosis was grim. He had witnessed the ill effects of chemotherapy on others, mostly his wife. He was depressed thinking of the treatments. He missed Claire and felt an empty void about him that he'd not experienced in years. He was not looking forward to battling cancer alone, didn't want to grow any more frail than he'd already become and spent his days and nights turning the pages of memories in his mind as he sat in solitary silence.

Jack was in a nursing home. A stroke had forced him to rely on others for his daily needs. Rowan had visited him in between his own doctor appointments and time by Claire's side. On the last few visits, Rowan felt ill. The stench of the nursing facility had forced him back out the door to vomit in the parking lot. When he saw his old friend Jack, he had to remind him who he was, and when he spoke, Jack just stared blankly at the wall. Rowan was scared that even if he survived the chemo and battery of invasions by doctors that the same fate would lie in wait for him as it had for poor Jack.

The waders hung on a nail in the garage. They were covered in dust and fit tighter than the last time he'd fished in them. Rowan was winded by the time he'd pulled them on, further confirming his feeling of uselessness.

Walking the dirt path to the river's edge was a chore as well. All he carried was a fly rod, but the short walk he'd made a thousand times before now felt like a climb to the peak of Everest. He hurt and he felt weak. He didn't like it, didn't like being an old sick man, and he didn't like the idea of returning to his home and not having Claire to greet him there with a kiss, as she always did. However, he did like the idea of going fishing on the Madison one last time, while he still had the faculties about him to do so.

He had to rest, sitting on a tree stump by the river's edge and catching his breath, before he could peel enough line off the reel to make his first cast. It had been several seasons since he'd fished the deep pool under the willow. The spring runoff was swift enough to keep the water murky and make Rowan maintain vigilance over his footing. With his strength so poor, he would be at the mercy of the river, a reality Rowan had never let worry him. He'd fished every salmon stream in the northwest and never been at the mercy of any water anywhere.

The rainbow gulped the elk hair caddis. Rowan's reaction was slow, but it was enough to hook the fish. The flash of colors expressed its namesake as it danced across the Madison, capturing every ray of light along the way.

Rowan held the line tight and began to reel in the line. The fish fought back, stripping the drag, and forcing Rowan to inch some line in when he could. The fish was big enough to pull him off balance so he shuffled his wading boots on the river rock for balance. Suddenly, Rowan realized he was standing in waist-deep water. The river pushed at his legs and he worked his heels to dig their felt soles into the river rock bed. The water pushed and Rowan pushed back. With a good fish on the hook, he felt stronger than he had in a long time.

Rowan pulled the big Rainbow in within reach of his net. As soon as the fish saw Rowan, he was rejuvenated with life and made a fast run downstream, taking the floating line all the way down to the backing. The drag on the reel sounded like a siren. When he stopped the run with his hand on the reel, he rocked forward and suddenly Rowan felt his feet leaving the rock bottom. He was reeling in line almost as fast as he was being swept downstream.

The mid-June current was strong. A lightning-struck lodge pole log floated in front of him, bobbing at the mercy of the Madison. The river washed him farther downstream, right past the spot where over fifty years ago he had held a loaded gun in his mouth. He had done a lot of living and he was living now as he fought the current.

The cold water forced him to take short shallow breaths, but as frigid as the runoff was, it was no match for the painkillers, the adrenaline rush of a big fish and the numbness to life itself. A numbness known only to a dying man content with his life's achievements. Tied to his vest, the landing net trailed in the water behind him as the rushing power carried him. He gulped muddy water and spat it back out, reeling and struggling to stay afloat, while grinning at his own defiance of death as the river swept him away.

The cedar on Rowan's house was faded and discolored from years of fighting the sun's rays with stain, and allowing a few lazy summers to go by without getting all the chores done, like staining the house. When your wife enjoyed travel and fishing as much as you did, there was always something better to do than stain the house.

The weeds were no more overgrown than ever, as Rowan's strong suit had never been yard work. There had always been a fish, an adventure or a glass of wine to keep him from being a slave to his lawn. But these were the only signs that told a passerby that nobody lived there. The drift boat still rested under the shed, shaded by the spruce. The log furniture still waited on the deck to give the pleasure of a cozy refuge to watch a sunset.

All the other houses had manicured lawns landscaped from house to curb and there were many now. So many houses that the elk refused to winter on this side of the Gallatin Range, preferring the solitude of deeper snow in another valley, versus sharing their once-habitual winter range with humans, their barking dogs, curbside recycling and exhaust fumes.

The old five-window Chevy pickup sat sheltered in the garage blanketed by sheets and tarps, encapsulated by a thick coating of dust, like a time machine waiting to give a ride.

The car now parked in the drive belonged to Claire's son, Eric. He was there to clean the place up with his wife and seventeen-year-old son, Tom, who always called Rowan grandpa even though he wasn't Tom's biological grandpa. It didn't matter; Tom loved him more than just a man known as the one who married his grandma.

Rowan had accepted Claire and Clark's grown son Eric as his own, as Eric accepted Rowan. Shortly after Claire married Rowan, Eric and Elise were pregnant and little Tom was well cared for by his grandpa Rowan.

The hallway was decorated with pictures of Rowan and Claire in every corner of the world. The couple hugged, kissed and smiled in the foreground of dozens of photos whose backgrounds included beaches, yachts, mountains and fish, lots of fish.

Eric and his family were boxing up the personal effects and preparing the house to be shown by a realtor. The biggest task for Eric and Tom, and the most lucrative, was to move the book collection. Rowan had acquired a personal library of fine reading and reference books and there were many first editions. The will had left them all to Tom and he and his father decided they would go through them one by one. Those that were of particular monetary value could help fund a college education. The dry Montana air helped preserve the valuable first editions. But there were many books that Rowan felt were necessary for a young man's reading list, which he had written down in a note to Tom when he signed his will.

"Count of Monte Cristo, The Old Man and the Sea, To Have and Have Not, these are must reads. Promise to read them, not to me, promise yourself. If you have, then read them again. Make a study of the character of those men, you'll be enriched. Read my books too, they will give you insight. I wanted to write a love story about how I met your grandmother and our irreplaceable moments together, but I got too old too fast. The notes for the would-be novel are in this library somewhere in a diary, which I kept until I got so damned senile that I forgot where I put it. I encourage you to keep a diary, everyone has a story. Eventually, you too will get old and forget. The fortuitous details of our lives left undocumented all too often are obscured by the unfortunate worries of the day. As for the books, keep the ones you want. There are enough books here to travel the world. They are all yours. Live. Take good care of my truck."

Love,
Grandpa Rowan

Elise wiped the counters while Eric and Tom boxed the books. The first editions went into a box all their own. The paperbacks filled many boxes. They pulled these from the shelves, carefully inspecting them. Beside a first edition of "Don't Stop the Carnival," Tom found a green diary with dog-eared pages and what looked like red wine- and coffee-stained pages.

He sat in a chair and opened it. There were reflections of fly fishing, diving, travel, but every day there was mention of his love for Claire and a moment they shared, with every page full. Tom read the rough handwriting, scribble no doubt recorded in between travel and husbandly duties, but the almost illegible ramblings were rich with prose and oozed affection and adoration for his wife and their love together.

"Dad, I found it!" he exclaimed as he leafed through the diary.

Eric sat beside him. They looked the book over together. "Son, your grandpa Rowan was a good man with a full life of his own before he met my mother. He and mom loved each other and they were an active and adventurous couple. Not sure what's in that book, but my advice would be to take good care of it. I've read your writing, son, it's good, and someday you may become a writer like your grandpa."

Tom liked the thought of being a writer. He envisioned himself as his grandpa, pecking away at a keyboard while sipping coffee. He saw himself casting a fly to a trout on the river standing in the middle of the stream, wearing his grandpa's old fishing vest and thinking of his latest work in progress. His thoughts floated to the river and settled on its surface like a hand-tied fly.

Tom walked out the back door and down to the river. It was still peaceful despite a dog barking down the street and a lawnmower engine running in the distance. Standing beside the river, though, all the noises of the neighborhood were drowned out by rippling water and the crash of distant rapids.

A Dipper flew down and landed on a rock sticking out of the water, and then dove into the river where the black bird disappeared for several seconds before flying out of the water downstream, magically reappearing like a hat trick. The cottonwood trees still gave shade and the smell of the water-drenched bank was an awakening reminder of the life that the river gives and takes.

Grandpa Rowan's old wooden chair sat atop the river rock, crooked and half-hearted, like a disabled ship thrown onto a beach by a hurricane. Tom brushed the leaves out of the seat with the back of his hand, knocking loose chips of blue paint, and sat looking across the river, at the cedar plank walkway that wound towards the water.

Now, it was broken by falling trees in places and appeared forgotten with moss and wood rot. His grandpa had told him about a very special lady that once lived there. Grandpa Rowan had built the structure for her so that her husband could push her down to the water in her wheelchair.

Tom listened to the constant soothing sound of water flowing over river rock. He remembered catching his first fish, a small rainbow, just a few feet from where he sat now. He didn't know who was more proud that day, he or his grandpa. Grandpa Rowan had taught him a lot about life and everything about fishing. The river had wound through his young life, entwining itself within his very marrow, carrying memories, love and comfort.

Tom studied the old walkway and was surprised to see a girl walking barefoot on the planks towards the river, towards him. Her long blonde hair was pulled back from both sides of her face, her skin dark from sunny summer days, as she held her white summer dress up with both fists, watching for slivers or exposed nails in the old boards.

She brushed the hair from her face and didn't notice Tom sitting there until she was standing on the old moss-covered platform. Their eyes met. She waved.

He waved back at her. She was tall and thin, about his age. The sunlight permeated the canopy of trees and shone on her like a theatre spotlight. Her face glowed from across the water and her wide smile was separated by beautiful thin lips. Suddenly, Tom realized that he had stood up from the chair and they stood there entranced by each other. He began walking across the river, towards the girl.

He didn't know her, did not know what he was going to say to her, but he was going to say something, something stupid or useful, he did not yet know. Tom waded across the late summer river, soaking his jeans up to the knees. She kept smiling back at him.

The water flowed over the rocks. The dippers dipped and magpies cackled. The fish darted between his feet.

He came right up to her. They exchanged warm inviting glances as if they had done this before.

"Hi. I'm Tom," he said in a voice that crackled with nerves.

She twisted a strand of blonde hair around her forefinger. Continuing to smile at the boy before her, she said, "Hi Tom, I'm Sadie."

"That's a pretty name."

She smiled, still nervously wrapping her hair around her finger.

"Thanks. I was named after my grandma."

Love makes life's circle round. Like the seasons, the cycle of life and death continues over and over again. Snowflakes fall in winter, melt in spring and make rivers that give and take. The river is life and life is like a river.

About the Author

Allen Andrew Cooper lives to fish near Cody, Wyoming. He was a state trooper for many years. Now, he writes and performs music, is the author of short stories, books and screenplays. He has a son, a daughter and there's always a dog at his side. This is his first self-published novel. You can visit him at www.allencooperbooks.com.